Fool's Gold

Phillip Hardy

Dedication

There are so many who encouraged me along the way, but I want to dedicate this story to the man who is my hero, my father. We watched westerns together on the weekends, and he helped me develop a love of western literature through such legends as Louis L'Amour and Zane Grey.

My dad didn't brag, but I never doubted he could do anything he set his mind to. His calm confidence let us know that, even if he was unsure, he would tackle whatever came his way. I remember one night when a "lion" was sitting in our dining room. I guess I had watched a little too much Tarzan that day. I ran to my dad, who calmly walked out to face the "lion". He assured me I had nothing to fear. He turned on the light and the lion "fled". Dad was there. The lion was gone.

Dad taught us boys to stand on our own two feet and to take responsibility for our actions. To him, integrity was worth far more than money or prestige. We learned to stand up for the helpless by watching him do just that. We learned to work hard for what we wanted. My father is no longer with us, but I believe this story is something he would love. My dad is and always has been my hero and someone I can only aspire to emulate. Thank you, Dad. This book is for you.

Contents

Prologue

*F*ool's Gold picks up where ***Vengeance Is Mine*** leaves off. Returning to his family ranch after hunting down those who killed his family, James is faced with the growing problem of rustling and the question of what to do with the gold that triggered the slaughter of his family. His new friend and mentor, Preacher, stands by him as he treads the thin line between inaction and overreaction. Along the way, James intervenes on behalf of a young Lakota woman who steals the heart of one of his most loyal hands. As their romance blossoms, so does the turmoil on the *Lazy H.*

Claim jumpers, rustlers, and gold fever threaten to tear the ranch apart. Will his new faith in Christ help James tread the narrow path between mercy and justice? Can they extract the gold without destroying the range and starting a war? Will it be worth it in the end? Read ***Fool's Gold*** to find out.

CHAPTER I

"You're getting better, Jimmy Boy." Preacher laughed as his much younger opponent rose from the ground where Preacher had tossed him. Five foot six in height, he weighed about one hundred forty-five pounds. His once dark hair was seasoned with plenty of salt, which contrasted with his darkly bronzed face. "You almost throwed me that time. Someday, you'll learn to wrestle." Preacher's hazel eyes danced merrily as he taunted his opponent. He was stripped to the waist, and his sun-scorched body showed that his fifty years on this earth had not diminished his physical condition. If anything, his daily exercise routine gave him the strength and stamina of a man twenty years his junior.

That was a good thing because the one he laughingly called "Jimmy Boy" was not a boy at all. A couple of inches taller than the one addressing him, Jimmy outweighed the older man by fifteen pounds and carried no fat. He, too, was stripped to the waist. His younger body was covered with a layer of sweat and dust from where he had been tossed to the ground more than once. His body was also crisscrossed with livid scars that marred his strongly muscled torso. At twenty-two, James Harding was a man grown.

"Almost threw you? Almost only counts in horseshoes, you old goat." He laughed. "The day I manage to throw you, it will because you have two broken legs and one hand tied behind your back. Even then, I'll probably have to sneak up on you in the dark. Come on. Let's wash up at the creek. I'd hate to be late for one of Dinah's dinners because you were busy gloating," Jim continued.

"Gloating? I said you almost throwed me. Why, I'd say that was downright humble. If you was to ask me, which you didn't." The older man laughed again.

"Doesn't the Bible say 'Pride goeth before a fall?'"

"Nope. It surely don't. It says 'Pride goeth before destruction'. It's a haughty spirit before a fall. I'd say you had a few haughty spirits sneak up on you today because you sure fell enough." Preacher roared with laughter.

Jim just looked at his mentor and friend and shook his head. Both washed the dust and sweat from their bodies and donned their shirts. As they saddled up, Jim turned his blue eyes to Preacher. The man had turned him from the destructive path he was following not so long ago. His own pride and hatred had almost destroyed him. Had it not been for Preacher's not so subtle intervention, he hated to think where he would be now.

The two men mounted and headed back to the ranch by a different route than the one they had taken getting to the creek. "I think we've panned enough out this time around to get those bulls Tom has been talking about. If there's some extra, I'd like to get some good horse flesh too. Not that what we have is bad, but those M/M horses are really something. Besides, there is always a market for good saddle stock," Jim mused.

They had spent the last several days in a hidden corner of the Lazy H panning for gold in the stream where Jim's father had discovered the shiny metal several years before. It was the lust for gold which had brought evil men to the Lazy H, bringing death and destruction with them and changing James Harding's life forever. Only God's grace and meeting Preacher had saved Jim from himself.

"What's your partner think about horse ranching?"

"I haven't talked to him about it yet," Jim admitted. "But I think it would be a good sideline. Like I said, folks are always looking for good horseflesh. C'mon. I told Dinah we'd be there for dinner tonight, and I hate to miss her cooking." Jim urged his horse to a ground-covering trot.

On the way back to the ranch, Preacher and Jim met Curly, who was pushing some cattle out of rough country toward better grazing. "Hey boss," he said dejectedly. There was a cloud covering his normally happy face. He scowled and spat in the dust.

"Hey Curly, why such a long face?" Jim queried.

"There ain't enough" was the response, as if that would answer the question.

"Enough? Enough what?"

"Cow critters boss. There ain't enough cows. There should be a lot more and a lot more younger stock. A lot of what I been finding is older or really skittish." The bald puncher waved at the small herd he was pushing.

Jim had been absent from the ranch much of the time over the past couple of years and was still getting reacquainted with what was going on. He took a closer look at the herd before him and noted the decided lack of younger stock. Rustling had not been a big problem in this part of Montana, but with the vast range and more buyers becoming less careful about brands, it was a growing concern. There were also several new rawhide outfits moving into the area, and some of them were believed to cast a wide loop. From the look of things, the rumors might be right.

Jim's blue eyes grew as cold as lake ice as he asked, "Any sign of what might have happened?"

"No boss, but I got an idea. If I ever know for sure I'll let you know."

"You thinking that maybe some of those folks over toward Rosebud's been helping themselves?" Preacher asked. "It might be possible, but you can't go making that kind of accusation without some kind of proof."

"There are some over that away that might just do such a thing. Like I said, when I know something for sure, I'll let you know," Curly responded.

"There's nothing more we can do here tonight, Curly. Why don't we head on in before we're late for supper?" Jim was thoughtful as he spoke.

"That sounds good to me," Curly replied. His smile returned to his face.

"As long as I don't have to eat Jim's cooking tonight, I'll be happy," quipped Preacher.

The three rode off at a trot toward the ranch house. The rustlers were temporarily forgotten as the anticipation of a good meal filled their thoughts.

***

As Dinah was cleaning up after the evening meal, Jim caught her husband Tom's attention. The men moved outside to talk. It was a warm fall evening, so they retired to the porch to stay out of her way.

"Tom, I haven't been around as much as I should have been. Curly tells me we've been losing cattle. At least he thinks so. Have you noticed it?" Jim asked.

"I figure he's right. We've been losing some here and there, but the losses are growing. I talked to Colburn, and he's losing some too. It seems to have picked up since that Rosebud crowd moved in. There's no proof of anything, though.

"Jack Colburn's all for riding over there and burning them out, but there is nothing for sure, and there may be a few solid folks over that way. I'm not even sure that's the direction the stock is going. I'll have no part of a witch hunt nor of running families from their homes," Tom said.

"Why don't Jim and me ride over and take a look see? Could be we'll learn something. If not, it don't hurt to know your neighbors. What do you say Jim? You up to visiting your new neighbors?" Preacher asked.

So far, everything people thought they knew about Rosebud was speculation. Few, if any, had actually visited the town. "Sure Preacher. You won't miss us for a day or two will you, Tom?" Jim asked.

"I don't figure it'll hurt any. Besides, with all the work you two *don't* do around here, you won't be missed much except at the dinner table," Tom quipped. "Just keep Jim out of trouble, Preacher. We just got him back." All three men laughed.

CHAPTER 2

The next morning, Jim and Preacher saddled up and headed for Rosebud. The horses they chose wore brands other than the Lazy H. They figured they would hear more if they weren't recognized as being from one of the local ranches.

Arriving in the early afternoon, they rode down the rutted dirt path running north and south between several canvass and hide-covered structures. A few more buildings were found off the main street. The most substantial building was the saloon, located in the center of the cluster of shacks and tents. It was solidly built of logs and had a sod roof. A sign over the batwing doors advertised liquor. The entire town looked like a strong wind might blow it down. A few of the dwellings even looked like a slight breeze would be enough to flatten them.

"Notice anything peculiar, Jim?" Preacher asked. His eyes never stopped moving as they rode toward a large structure sporting a sign that read "Livery".

"You mean, besides the whole place looking like it's ready to fall down? It sure doesn't look permanent," Jim responded.

"Naw. Something else. Something that ought to tell you something. Something so obvious most folks would miss it."

"Obvious? You mean like the saloon looking prosperous while the rest of the town looks like a dump?" Jim asked.

"You're close. Don't be obvious, but how many horses do you see at the hitching rail of the saloon? Just a quick glance. No need for exact numbers," Preacher whispered.

"Quite a few. Probably more than a dozen. More than there should be this time of day during a work week." Jim's eyes grew wide. "There's too many horses," he exclaimed quietly.

"It took you a couple minutes to figure it out, but you're right as rain. Let's watch our step and keep our ears open."

Jim and Preacher stabled their horses. After some thought, they paid a few bits extra to sleep in the loft rather than the tent hotel. The stable looked cleaner and was probably a lot safer.

While they strode down the street, they scanned the town without making it obvious. They noted the brands on the horses before noticing the local mercantile. Jim inclined his head in the establishment's direction. "What do you say we stop in and see what they have to offer? I'm betting Sarah would like some sugar candy. It will give us a feel for the town, too."

"I reckon that's safer than the saloon. And seeing as I don't see a barber in town to pick up the local gossip at, it makes sense to me to see what we can find out while making a few purchases. Hope their supplies is better than their spelling." Preacher continued.

The two angled toward the combination canvas and wood structure bearing the moniker "Genral Stoor". A pair of racing horses caused both men to jump out of the street to avoid being run down. Jim started to turn, but Preacher touched his arm, stopping him. "Let it pass boy. No harm done. They're just not used to being around folks."

Jim took a deep breath and let it out slowly. Only a few months back, the lack of courtesy would have drawn Jim into a violent confrontation with the two riders. Such carelessness in town was dangerous, but like Preacher said, there was no harm done.

Entering the dim interior of the store, the men's noses were assailed by the smell of leather, dry goods, and a dozen other smells. The warm, inviting smells greeted their noses, but their ears were assaulted by a gruff voice raised in anger.

"Where are you, you ignorant half-breed? Why ain't this floor scrubbed yet? You're just like all breeds: dumb and lazy. You ain't worth two copper pennies. I oughta sell you to Riley at the saloon. He might get some use out of you upstairs."

Jim and Preacher exchanged angry looks. The speaker was a large, bearded man wearing bib overalls and a red plaid shirt that was partially open. Matted hair on his chest showed through the V of his filthy shirt. He spat on the floor that he complained needed scrubbing and glowered at a blanket-covered doorway leading to the backroom. From several feet away, the stench of human sweat overpowered the more pleasant smells of the mercantile.

Hearing Jim and Preacher approach, the man turned to greet them. "Welcome gents. You hunting for anything particular? Sorry about the noise. You know how breeds is, dumb, lazy and filthy." Noting the two men were strangers, his piglike eyes glistened with greed.

As if on cue, a young woman stepped from the back room carrying a large bundle tied with twine. She stood straight and walked with a quiet grace and dignity to the pine slab that served as a counter, where she deposited the package. Her large, brown eyes were clear, and her soft skin held a coppery glow. Willowy and not quite as tall as Jim, she moved confidently.

She wore her black hair tied back from her face which revealed strong yet delicate features. Her soft, cream-colored doeskin dress was neat and clean. A slight scent of wildflowers drifted from her to those nearby.

"Mister Claiborne, Mister Taylor's order is ready for him to pick up. This floor was scrubbed down long before you began your morning tasks. If you were to use the spittoon rather than the floor, it would remain clean most of the day," the young woman said.

"Why you smart-mouthed half-breed. Don't you talk to me so uppity. You ain't fit to wipe my boots, and if you don't start respecting your betters, I'll take a strap to you and then I'll give you to Riley." He stepped toward her menacingly. "You know your no-account pappy owed me when he died. So now you owe his debt."

The young woman did not retreat. Her eyes flashed in defiance at Claiborne. "I am paying my father's debt as you well know. As for being a half-breed, I am Raven Wing, the daughter of Tahatan and his white wife. She chose to stay with him when given the chance to leave and return to the whites. She was as much a Sioux as any woman and was proud of her husband."

Claiborne's anger flared. He caught Raven Wing by the hair and drew back his hand to strike her as she glared boldly at him. Her dignity was unruffled and she showed no fear.

Before the hand could descend, Jim vaulted the counter and planted both of his moccasined feet in the foul-smelling man's hairy chest. Stumbling backward, Claiborne lost his grip on Raven Wing's hair. He sat down unceremoniously in a pile of woolen shirts. Jim's blue eyes turned to flame. His face glowed red beneath his tan and his lips were drawn up into a snarl.

Claiborne began to rise. "Nobody jumps Saul Claiborne in his own store. You bought yourself a pack of trouble, mister, butting in where you shouldn't oughta. I'm gonna pound you to stuffings." He turned to Raven Wing. "And when I'm finished with him, I'll start on you," he growled

Preacher laughed out loud.

"What you laughing at old man? You want some when I get through with them?"

Preacher snickered all the more and held his hands out before him in mock surrender. "No sir, Mister Claiborne. I reckon by the time that boy gets done with you, you won't want to bother with little old me." His eyes twinkled in anticipation of Mister Claiborne's lesson in how to treat a woman. "The Good Book is clear about what happens to those who imagine evil. 'His own iniquities will take the wicked himself.' Proverbs 5:22. I reckon your iniquities are fixing to take you." Preacher laughed again.

Jim spoke through clenched teeth. "Mister Claiborne, I'm going to give you an option. You can take your beating right here in your store and probably wreck the place in the process, or we can go outside." Jim still saw red, but he was in control of himself enough to speak and to think of what he was about to do.

Claiborne lunged at Jim in response. His ponderous hands reached out in an attempt to catch Jim in his grip.

Jim's reaction was smooth and swift. His left hand swept across and back up, throwing both of his opponents' hands and arms to the left of his body. Using his own momentum, he continued to spin and drove his right fist into the bigger man's left ear.

Claiborne staggered past and crashed into the pine counter. Blood poured from his battered ear, his eyes were slightly out of focus, and he heard a loud ringing in both ears.

Jim stepped back ready to continue. His eyes never left the stumbling brute.

Claiborne shook his head to try to clear the fog. Flecks of blood flew from his injured ear. His eyes refused to focus on the smaller, young man before him. He moved forward laboriously and began wind-milling punches at Jim. A few made their way through, and Jim's own ears rang slightly. Backed against a shelf, Jim ducked his head against his opponent's chest and began battering his overstuffed paunch with sledgehammer-like blows. Exercise, hard work, and practiced efficiency made every blow count.

Driven backward, Claiborne tripped over some of the shirts that had softened his earlier fall. He fell against a shelf of canned goods, sending them crashing to the floor. The noise of the goods crashing to the floor could be heard from the street.

Claiborne scrambled to his feet and dove at Jim only to have Jim's hard knee meet his face pulping his nose and lips. He was driven upright by the force, and Jim swung both hands together into his opponent's chin. Claiborne stumbled headlong into another shelf sending it and dry goods tumbling to the floor. Sacks of beans, flour, and other items mixed with the goods that were already strewn across the floor.

Lumbering back to his feet, Claiborne drew his knife. The eleven-inch blade gleamed dully in the dim light of the shambles that had once been a store. "I'm gonna gut you like a fish," he snarled.

"I wouldn't do that if'n I was you," Preacher cautioned. "That would be downright foolish, was you to ask me. Which you didn't, but I'm telling you anyway."

"In this town? After he jumped me in my own place? Nobody'd question it. And maybe when I'm done with him I'll gut the two of you, too." He jabbed his knife menacingly at Preacher and Raven Wing.

"That weren't what I meant," Preacher responded. He shrugged. "It's your funeral."

Claiborne lurched toward Jim who drew his own knife. The seven-and one-half inch blade of the Cheyenne scalping knife was not as impressive as that of his opponent, but it was razor sharp.

"I don't want to cut you up, Claiborne. Why don't you put the knife away and let your beating be a lesson to you?"

"You're yella!" Claiborne sneered and lunged at Jim. Jim side-stepped and deflected the blade with his own. The slight clank of steel on steel echoed in the store.

Noise from the initial assault had attracted some spectators. Preacher kept a wary eye on them. He motioned with his rifle to one of those who had gathered in the store. "The shop keep asked for it. He drew steel first. The youngster advised him to leave it. As you can see, Mister Claiborne didn't listen to good advice. Let's leave him learn his lesson the hard way." Seeing the hammer drawn back on Preacher's old Springfield, the man shrugged. Most of the locals were happy just to spectate anyway.

Claiborne attacked again with the same result. "Put it away Claiborne, or you're going to force me to cut you." Jim's voice was hard and his blue eyes stormed like a deep sea. "Don't force my hand."

"Why you! I'll cut you open and use your guts for garters." Claiborne was fuming. A couple of the locals laughed, which added fuel to his raging anger.

"You ain't doing so good so far. If you reckon to gut him like a fish, maybe you got to catch him like a fish first." More laughter followed the comment.

"Yeah. Put a worm on a hook. Maybe you'll catch him that way." More hoots of derision followed.

Claiborne attacked Jim in a blind rage. The viciousness of his attack drove Jim backward. This time, Jim felt a thin line of pain across his chest. While barely a scratch, it was clear that now was the time to bring things to a close. If Claiborne could not be stopped with reason, then he would have to be stopped with force.

Claiborne took a wicked slash at Jim's stomach. Jim parried the attack which drove his opponent's blade down and away from his body. He quickly reversed his own blade raking a deep furrow in Claiborne's forearm. Changing the direction of his blade's movement once again, he brought the keen edge down across Claiborne's unprotected torso. Blood immediately welled from both wounds. Claiborne's knife clattered to the floor. While not deep, both wounds were painful and bled profusely. The shopkeeper clutched at them, trying to staunch the flow of blood, and sat heavily on the floor.

A year earlier, Jim would not have been satisfied at simply letting blood flow. Claiborne had no idea how fortunate he was that Jim had met Preacher. If not for his influence, Claiborne would be trying to hold his intestines inside rather than trying to stop some bleeding.

"You cut me squaw man! Over that no account half-breed squaw! I ought to..."

Jim stepped toward him and touched his knife to the other man's throat. "You tried. I could just as easily have split you wide open so you could see your own heart beating as you died. As for the lady, no man strikes a woman in my presence. No man! Now you shut your mouth before I do it for you."

Raven Wing spoke. "Mister Claiborne, you continue to belittle my ancestry and my intelligence. As for cleanliness, I believe a rutting bull buffalo smells better than you. Perhaps it is your own stench you cannot tolerate."

Several of those present laughed raucously. While Raven Wing kept herself and her clothing neat and clean, Claiborne was known to bathe at very irregular intervals.

"When it comes to education, Mister Claiborne, my formal education at the mission school was quite extensive. It included history, science, philosophy, mathematics, and the proper use of the English language. If it were not for Mister Peter's insistence that I work for you to repay a debt you told him my father owed before he died, I would not lower myself to work for the likes of you." She stood with her head held high. Her soft voice betrayed a hint of pity mixed with loathing for the man she addressed.

"One other thing. You cannot sell me to another man. Indentured servitude, that is slavery, is not legal. Now the rest of you clear out while I attend to Mister Claiborne's injuries.

"You may stay, Mister..." She looked at Jim.

"Jim, just Jim ma'am."

"Very well, Mister Just Jim." She smiled. "You and your companion may stay. You, too, have an injury that needs treatment." She eyed the thin cut in his shirt and chest.

Jim looked down at his chest self-consciously.

"Aw ma'am, that's nothing to fret about. I've hurt myself worse falling off a stump."

She looked at him sternly as she gathered bandages. "Maybe so, but without that wound being cleaned and cared for, it could become septic, and that is far worse than the scratch itself. Besides, you will need a new shirt. And you do not want to bleed all over it now do you? Now take off your shirt while I tend to Mister Claiborne."

Without waiting for a reply, Raven Wing ordered Claiborne to remove what was left of his tattered shirt. He meekly complied. She took a clean towel from one of the few shelves left standing and asked Preacher to fill a wash basin from the pump behind the store.

Preacher looked at Jim. "That's one gal what knows what she's about. Probably good for the shop keep it was you that did the cutting instead of her doing it. You best do what she says if you know what's good for ya."

Jim slipped out of his shirt. He would sew it himself after washing it. The coagulated blood had stuck to his shirt and pulled the slim cut across his chest open, causing it to bleed again. He grimaced slightly and used his shirt to keep the blood from dripping onto the floor.

He turned to face Raven Wing and Claiborne. Both of them stared with open mouths. Raven Wing discretely averted her eyes and continued to minister to Claiborne's cuts, having noticed the unmistakable scars on his back.

"This is not your first battle is it Mister Just Jim?" It came out as more of a statement than a question.

"No ma'am. I reckon I've been in a few scrapes here and there. And please call me Jim. Not Mister, Just Jim."

"Very well, Jim. And you should call me Raven Wing not ma'am nor Miss Raven Wing, please. I am almost finished with Mister Claiborne. If your friend would be so kind as to draw me some fresh water, I will take care of your injuries now."

CHAPTER 3

Preacher left to draw more water for Raven Wing. When he returned, she began to bathe Jim's minor cut with strong, sure, gentle movements. Avoiding his eyes as she worked, she bathed the blood from Jim's chest, gently touching the burn scar and bullet scars on his torso. Her eyes drifted deep in thought. She shook herself to bring her thoughts back to the task at hand.

Stepping back after bandaging the wound, she inspected her work and retrieved a fresh shirt from a shelf. She handed it to Jim. "Thank you," she whispered. "That was kind of you to stop him."

Jim slipped into the fresh shirt as Raven Wing began to pick up and straighten the merchandise that had been toppled during the fight. "You made quite a mess in here. Because of his injuries, Mister Claiborne is unable to help with the cleaning. Since you helped to make the mess, you may help to clean it up. There is a broom in the corner, but you can pick up the goods you knocked from the shelves first. I can see no reason why I should have to pick up after two grown men who behaved like little children."

Jim looked questioningly toward Preacher. His friend lifted his shoulders and smiled. "Don't look at me. You're the one who made the mess. I told you, she's a gal who knows what she's about.

Right now, I'd say she's about getting you to clean up your mess. I wouldn't argue none."

Preacher chuckled, turned to the pickle barrel which had somehow managed to stay upright, and drew out a large pickle. He tossed a nickel onto the counter and began to crunch. "I'll be back in a bit to see how you're getting along. I'm just gonna take a stroll 'round town." He canted his rifle over his shoulder and meandered out the door.

Dressed in a fresh shirt, Jim began lifting the heavier items back into place. He and Claiborne had managed to topple several shelves and their contents onto the floor. It looked as though a twister had made its way through the shop.

Claiborne glowered helplessly from his seat on the floor as Jim and Raven Wing put the store back into order. Hatred for Jim for humiliating him and hatred for that squaw who thought she was better than him boiled impotently in his bowels. He chose to ignore the fact that he was alive only because Jim had shown mercy. For some, mercy given is just another opportunity for them to do you harm.

"Don't forget. You owe me for that shirt, squaw man," Claiborne spat out. "As for you, you redskin whore, you won't get away with this. I'll take a whip to ya when your man ain't here to protect you. You'll wish..."

His words stopped abruptly, and his eyes bugged out as Jim's knife gleamed in the dull light as it touched his throat. He licked his lips. "You will apologize to the lady," Jim hissed. "And if you speak of her in such a manner again, I will shut your mouth permanently by giving you another one under your chin." He prodded Claiborne's throat gently with the tip of his blade. "Or, if I am feeling kind, I will just remove your offensive tongue. Am I clear Mister Claiborne?"

"You can't..." he began to stammer.

Jim's eyes turned to blue flames. "I can and I will," Jim purred. Claiborne read no mercy in his eyes this time.

"Fine. I apologize Raven Wing. You ain't a whore." He looked at Jim. "But you still owe me for the shirt." His voice cracked, and it sounded more like a whimper than a growl.

"As long as Miss Raven Wing is willing to accept your halfhearted apology, I am willing to pay for the shirt even though you are the one that cut my original one."

"I am satisfied," Raven Wing stated. She smiled at Jim, and he sheathed his blade. "A woman could grow fond of a man defending her honor. Such a display of chivalry is rare in Rosebud. For a woman of the Sioux Nation among whites, it is even more rare." The two resumed their tasks without more being said.

CHAPTER 4

Preacher wandered down the dirt walkway in front of the businesses on the east side of the street. His eyes never rested on one spot for more than a second or two as he munched on his pickle. During the stroll, he noticed that the horses carried a wide variety of brands, and there seemed to be few duplicates except for one that resembled a nest of snakes in a wrestling match. "A rustler's brand if ever I saw one," he murmured to himself. The multitude of lines and twists would cover almost any brand known in the area.

Another brand that was worn by two or three horses was the *B slash B*. The horses looked to be solid cow ponies but were not large enough for the harsh Montana winters. They were probably ridden by someone from New Mexico or southern Colorado. Crossing the street at the edge of town, he began to stroll in the opposite direction.

Absent in town was a marshal's office, but many small towns had no jail so that was not an anomaly. Men took care of justice for themselves. If something more formal was needed, they could always send for the county sheriff who was a couple days' ride away.

Stopping for a moment in front of the saloon, Preacher leaned against a post. He finished his pickle and licked the juice from his fingers while he examined the horses at the hitching rail. Finishing his perusal of the horses, he straightened from the post and continued his leisurely stroll through the rest of the town.

He struck up a conversation with the hostler at the livery barn. "Sure is a lot of nice horseflesh in town today. There's a big blood bay and an appaloosa that are a couple of the finest critters I've seen in a spell. Sure wouldn't mind throwing a saddle on one of those."

The hostler chuckled. His shaggy hair hung to his shoulders and his toothless grin showed from inside his bushy mustache and beard. "You shore can pick 'em stranger," he chortled. "Course, I'd be careful throwing my saddle on either of them two horses. Their riders wouldn't take too kindly to being left afoot. Not that they would be above doing the same thing to you if the notion struck, but you never heard that from me. No sir, you sure never."

Preacher smiled. "I'll remember that part about them not taking kindly to being left afoot. That sounds like good advice all around. Besides, I'm kind of fond of that ugly cayuse of mine. He might not be much to look at, but he's got it where it counts."

Changing the subject, he continued, "You must see and hear a lot that goes on around here. Where might a feller that was looking to stake himself a place and was looking for some cattle and horses get started? Anyone particular he should talk to?"

"Well now, that depends. You just asking, or you looking to start up?" the hostler responded.

"I ain't asking just to flap my gums old timer. I'm at a point where settling down sounds right nice. Getting a little long in the tooth to keep running around the countryside looking at the backside of another man's cows."

"He-he! I can sure enough understand that. I surely can. If'n you ain't looking too close at the brands I'd say them fellas what own them horses we was talking about earlier'd be a good source. McCabe and Simmons is their handles. Like I said though…"

"I never heard it from you," finished Preacher. "I already remembered to forget. We'll be back later to get some shut eye. Maybe I'll look them fellers up. What do they look like?"

"They's hard to miss. McCabe - he's got him a beak alright. Looks like it's been busted a few times. Got sandy brown hair and hazel eyes and a walrus mustache. Maybe 'bout the same height as you. Looks strong as a bull."

"Now Simmons," he continued, "he's 'bout the opposite. Tall galoot. At least a half foot taller than your young friend. His hair's almost white but best not make no mistake and call him Whitey. He don't cotton to that moniker. Got green eyes and he keeps hisself clean shaved. Not a whisker on his face. Like I said, can't miss 'em."

Preacher took his new knowledge with him and retraced his steps to the mercantile. It hadn't been more than thirty minutes since he left, but the town wasn't all that imposing. He found his young companion lifting a set of shelves he had toppled back into place. Raven Wing stood to the side, giving advice while Claiborne watched sullenly.

"Just set it… Careful please… Don't…" Raven Wing grimaced. The shelves teetered as if about to fall again and Raven Wing jumped to lend her strength to Jim's. Their shoulders almost touching, they shoved the toppled shelf back into place.

"Ahem!" All three of the store's occupants were so absorbed with what was happening with the shelf that none of them noticed

Preacher's quiet return. "Some fellers'll do anything to get close to a pretty gal," Preacher chuckled.

Raven Wing stepped back now that the shelf was safely in place. She blushed deep enough for it to show through her coppery complexion. "He would have been crushed if that shelf had fallen on him. I could not let that happen."

"Course not. That's what I was sayin'. He dang near got hisself squashed like a beetle bug just to be close to a pretty gal. Now me, I'd rather ask her to a barn dance and hold her close whilst twirling her round the floor. But these young bucks…" Preacher shrugged his shoulders. "Of course, I'm a bit older and oughta have more sense than a pup like him, but I'd hoped he'd learned something from me by now."

"Is that all you came back for was to embarrass Miss Raven Wing? If so, why not take another stroll around town?" Jim growled.

"Hold on now. I do my best not to embarrass such a lovely maiden. I thought I'd come back and cause you some consternation though. It 'pears I was successful." Preacher laughed at Jim's discomfort. "Now that all the heavy lifting's done, would you two like some help with the rest of it?"

"That's very kind of you Mister…" She paused. "I am afraid I do not know your name."

"That's quite alright ma'am. It's been so long, I near on forgot it my own self. Most folks just call me Preacher." He proffered his calloused hand which she took.

Claiborne's eyes narrowed. An evil grin crossed his face and then disappeared as he thought of how this information might prove profitable. Conscious of his injuries, he busied himself putting smaller items onto the shelves. He directed Jim and Raven Wing where to put the disarrayed inventory.

By the time they were finished, Claiborne had hatched a plan. McCabe and Simmons would want to know about these two being in town. They might even pay for the information. Some of the stock he had seen moving through the hills at night carried the Lazy H brand. These men had to be doing more than visiting.

CHAPTER 5

When the store was finally back in order, Preacher turned to Claiborne. "You said this gal's pa owed you money. What for? From when? Where at's the IOU? And how much exactly?" There was gravel in his voice.

"Well, um. It was for a saddle and... um some cloth and..."

"Shut your yap," Preacher snarled. "I don't know who the agent was that let you get away with it, but them are lies!"

Claiborne started to protest. "You can't talk to me that way old man! Nobody calls me a liar in my own store." His face was bright crimson.

Preacher's hand dipped to his belt and flashed forward. His Green River knife flashed by Claiborne's face sinking the tip an inch into the beam beside his head. The flash of steel and the kachunk of the blade striking the pine post cut his words short.

"I can and I just did," purred Preacher "In case you're wondering, I don't much cotton to liars and those who'd take advantage of a young gal's integrity. I put them in the same category as back shooters and cowards. That's slightly lower than a horny toad's belly."

He turned his attention to Raven Wing. "Your pa never had no saddle did he ma'am?"

"How did you know that?" She responded timidly.

"No Lakota warrior'd be caught dead riding in a white man's saddle. They hate 'em. Didn't know your pa, but I know horse warriors. Heavy saddle'd slow their horse. They say they can't feel their warrior brother with a saddle between them."

She looked at Claiborne. Her eyes blazed. "Is that true? My father never owed you that money?"

"Well, I thought it was his bill what was owed," he replied lamely.

"You thief!"

"Way I see it, Claiborne, you can pay the lady for the time she's worked for you, or the thrashing the boy gave you will be nothing compared to what I'll do."

He glanced at Raven Wing. "How long you been working here ma'am?"

"Forty-two days."

Jim walked over and pried Preacher's knife from the post. He tossed it hilt first to his mentor. "Let's call it a dollar a day. Now pay the lady and we'll be out of here with our goods. We will pay you for them. Unlike some," Jim stared hard at the shop keeper, "we pay our bills."

Claiborne reluctantly paid the amount Jim had demanded.

"If'n she stays working for you, you'll pay her the wages Jim just negotiated. If you don't, we'll come calling again," Preacher warned.

"She ain't welcome here no more. You take that..." Claiborne stopped before hurling the intended insult. Jim's face had turned hard. His eyes blazed and Claiborne took the warning. "She can take her stuff and get out. Good riddance."

Raven Wing quickly gathered her belongings and walked out with Jim. Preacher remained behind to settle the bill. He opened his poke and removed two gold nuggets of more than sufficient weight to pay for their purchases. Claiborne's eyes gleamed with greed as he watched Preacher return the rest of the gold to his pocket. A plan began to form in his mind for revenge and possible reward.

CHAPTER 6

"D o you have anywhere to go?" Jim asked Raven Wing. "This town doesn't seem too friendly for a lady with no place to stay."

She gave some thought to the question. "No, I suppose I do not have any place in town to stay. The hotel would not be safe and the few good women in town would not like an Indian in their home." She looked defeated as she looked at Jim. "What do I do now?"

Preacher caught up to the two of them and spoke up. "The barn'd be warm and secure. In the morning, Jim and me're heading back home. The lady of the house'd be glad of some woman company. Indian or white don't make her no never mind. You can ride out with us in the morning. We'll get you there safe and sound. Then you can decide what you want to do."

Jim looked at Preacher. Having anticipated being in town a few days to investigate the movement of stock through the area, he raised his eyebrows questioningly. He was used to Preacher's propensity for taking charge, but this was presumptuous even for him. There must be some reason for the quick departure.

"Preacher's right. Dinah and Tom would enjoy the company. Someone to talk to about things other than cows and horses. Their little ones would love a visitor too. I suppose Preacher and I can sleep outside so you can have some privacy tonight. It won't be the first time we did, and knowing Preacher, it won't be the last." Jim smiled.

"As long as you are sure it will not be an imposition, that will be all right. I do not have a horse; how will I travel?"

"Don't worry about that. We can find a mount for you easy enough," Jim responded. He took Raven Wing's bag from her hand and the three of them started toward the barn.

"I'd say let's shake the dust from this town tonight, but we'd be just as vulnerable on the trail and Miss Raven Wing would be less comfortable. That shopkeeper practically drooled when he saw my poke. I'm thinking we might have some company tonight," Preacher said to Jim.

Raven Wing gasped. "I did not mean to bring you trouble!"

"You did no such thing. Preacher and I can do that well enough all by ourselves. At least this way, we have a good cause." Jim smiled and winked at the young woman. "The trick is to be ready when it comes."

"Don't you worry none. Jim and me will be ready," Preacher assured the young woman.

"In the store you said, 'No *Lakota* warrior would use a white man's saddle.' How did you know my father was Lakota?" Raven Wing asked.

Preacher stopped for a second. "Well now, I suppose it's because you're Lakota. You've got the look, although prettier than most. You carry yourself like a warrior's daughter. Kinda regal-like." He resumed walking. "I been around a bit and can usually tell one tribe from another. Of course, dressed like you are, I was hoping I was right."

"You were," she responded.

***

The trio reached the stable, and Preacher entered first. The hostler came out of his office. "You two come to town and found the prettiest filly around," he chuckled. He had watched them approach from his office window. "Yes sirree, redskin or not, she sure is somethin'. Not that it's any of my affair. No sir." He smiled. "No extra charge for her to stay neither. No sir."

"That's good," replied Preacher in a neutral tone. "See that she is not disturbed and nobody goes into that loft but her. She's a lady, and I'll hear no more talk about her. Am I clear?"

The hostler gulped. "No offense intended mister. It's just, she is the prettiest gal in town. I'll see she ain't disturbed none."

Preacher smiled. "I didn't figure she would be. You run a nice place. You said so yourself. I'll leave her bag here with ours. I'm sure it will be safe under your care." Preacher's smile failed to hide the steel in his voice.

The hostler nodded. His grin never left his face. "Yes sirree, I surely did say so, and that you did hear that from me." He laughed. "Just put her stuff with your'n and it'll be safe as a babe in its mamma's arms."

"I don't know about you, Preacher, but I'm about ready to see if there's some place decent to eat in this burg. What about you Miss Raven Wing?" Jim asked. "Is there a decent place to get something to eat in this town?"

"Missus Appleton's serves good food. Nothing fancy but very good. And it is just Raven Wing not Miss Raven Wing," she replied.

Preacher chuckled. "We'd best get to this Missus Appleton's. My belly is starting to think my throat's been cut."

After a simple meal, the trio began a leisurely walk back through the tiny town. "Why don't you two youngsters go enjoy the evening? I think I'll stop by the saloon and see if I can catch up on the local gossip."

Jim looked quizzically at Preacher. The puzzled look only drew a smile from his mentor. The older man did not frequent saloons. Jim finally nodded. "Sure old timer. Just make sure you stay out of trouble."

CHAPTER 7

They parted company. Jim and Raven Wing walked to the edge of the dusty ramshackle town and Preacher slipped quietly into the saloon. He took a seat at a table in the shadows and asked for a pot of coffee. "Just leave it on the table with a mug. I can pour my own." He smiled at the bartender. That suited the bartender just fine. Serving those drinking alcohol would keep him busy enough without the coffee drinker. Booze was profitable; coffee was not.

It wasn't long before Claiborne found his way into the bar. The store owner quickly scanned the dim interior. Preacher was easily missed in the gloomy recess where he was seated. Besides, Claiborne's interest was in two other occupants of the saloon. Simmons and McCabe were seated at the bar.

"Give me a whiskey," Claiborne hollered at the saloon keeper. He slid up to the bar near the two men with whom he sought an audience. When his drink arrived, he tossed it back with a grimace.

"Mister Simmons, Mister McCabe. I've got some information you might like to know," he whispered conspiratorially.

Claiborne waited and McCabe turned toward him. An annoyed look crossed his square face. "What do you have that we could possibly want?" he growled.

Claiborne knew that McCabe didn't like him. In fact, McCabe disliked just about everybody. Claiborne thought the information he had was worth risking the short, powerful man's wrath. He glanced around and leaned toward Simmons. "Them two what busted up my store. They ain't just here buying supplies and starting fights."

McCabe burst out laughing. "No, they sure aren't. From what I heard, they run off with your help too." Simmons joined the laughter.

"Tell us something we don't know or haul your sorry carcass out of here," Simmons snarled.

Claiborne licked his lips. "The younger feller is called Jim." He was quickly cut off by McCabe.

"So what? I know a dozen Jims and twice that number of Bobs and Johns." His dark countenance grew more brooding.

Claiborne's eyes widened in fear, but he continued. "But there's not so many Jims that partner with a man called Preacher. That's who them two are. Jim Harding from the Lazy H." He had their attention now. "And that ain't all. Preacher's carrying a pouch full of raw gold."

McCabe and Simmons exchanged a quick glance. "You don't say," responded Simmons in a more congenial tone. "Now that is something we might not have noticed."

"Barkeep, another round here," Simmons ordered. His smile did not dim the calculating look in his eyes. "Why don't you fill us in a bit after you wrap yourself around that drink. Maybe we can help each other."

Claiborne smiled and downed his drink in a few gulps. The loss of blood caused the alcohol to have a much faster and stronger effect than normal. He leaned toward the pair and began his narrative. His words weren't slurred much, yet.

"After that Jim busted up my place, they made me pay that no good squaw. They bust up my place and then make me pay her!" he raved.

McCabe glared at him as he raised his voice. Taking the hint, Claiborne lowered his voice. "Then they hustles that redskin out of there saying I was robbing her when she was the one what owed me."

"The gold," reminded Simmons. "Your help quitting on you is none of our concern."

"Oh, yeah. Well, that Preacher fella says, 'unlike some, we pay our debts.' Then he pulls out a poke stuffed full of dust and nuggets. He plunks down two the size of sparrow's eggs and says, 'that ought to cover it'. It sure enough was, but that there pouch was still full. The other one is probably carrying a poke the same size. It was raw gold, but there was plenty of it.

"Knowing who they are, I figure they might be hunting lost stock," he continued quietly. "I figure anybody moving stock might want to know. Them two could be trouble if there was ever a question of ownership. Just thought I'd let you two know, seeing how ya'll know pretty much everyone around here and handle a bit of stock yourselves. Legitimately, of course," he quickly added. "But them two could be a burr under any cattleman's blanket."

"I reckon they could at that," growled McCabe. "Now, just what was you figuring was in it for us?"

Simmons had poured a third drink for the merchant as McCabe posed the question. Claiborne quaffed it and wiped his lips with the back of his uninjured hand before continuing. "Well, I figure you'd maybe want to make sure they never seen nothing. Maybe they'd close their eyes permanent-like and wouldn't need all that gold. Course, with me being injured like I was by that sneak attack, I can't do nothing myself, but ya'll might know someone who'd handle things for you."

Both outlaws stifled a laugh at the mention of the "sneak attack". They had both heard enough of the account to draw their own conclusions, none of which were complimentary to the man before them. However, knowing who these strangers were was worth the small amount they were spending gathering the information from Claiborne. They had no desire for the Lazy H owner and his companion to take a look at their Double Six Domino cattle. Even a cursory exam would not bode well for them.

"Tell you what Claiborne," drawled McCabe. "You just enjoy yourself on us tonight. Me'n Simmons will figure this out." He slapped a Double Eagle into Claiborne's hand. "Keep the bottle too, on us."

Claiborne smiled through his battered lips. "Glad I could be of help." He poured another liberal quantity of raw whiskey into his glass and proceeded to get drunk.

CHAPTER 8

Preacher had heard enough. His keen ears had picked up enough of the conversation to know that McCabe and Simmons would make an attempt or send someone to make an attempt, on his and Jim's lives. He slipped out of the shadows and out the back door of the bar unnoticed. Claiborne was too deep into his cups to notice, and the other two did not know who he was.

Reaching the livery, he slipped inside and waited for Jim and Raven Wing. "I reckon we'll have to read them from the Book when they come tonight," he whispered into the quiet air. "Just keep them two young 'uns safe until we can get ready," he said with concern in his voice.

He pulled his revolver from his holster and checked the loads. He stripped the caps from the nipples and replaced them with fresh ones from a pouch on his belt. "Thou shalt not steal. Thou shalt not bear false witness. Thou shalt not covet. Thou shalt not kill. I'm thinking them four are pretty high on their priority list to break right now. It may be time someone preached them a sermon. Just don't want all of them to be with a six...." He spun with amazing speed and eared back the hammer on his 1858 Army revolver. "...gun," he finished.

"Hold on! It's just me," squawked the hostler. He held out his hands open palmed. "I heard you talking and slipped in to see if'n you needed anything else." He looked around, confused. "I know I heard you talking but I don't see nobody else. Who was you talking to?"

"Well, God of course," Preacher replied. "He's the only one here besides us and the horses and whatever other critters are in this here establishment. While I do talk to old Molly here from time to time, I don't expect her to keep anyone safe. Least wise, not unless they're riding her. Don't you never talk to Him?"

"I... I reckon I ain't done so in a long time. And I don't think I ever just talked to Him like you was. It was like you know Him and He knows you. Like He was right here and not way off in the clouds or what not. Like you knowed He was listening."

"That's because He is." Preacher smiled. "You see, He ain't just up in the clouds. He's with those that ask Him to keep them from Hell and mean it. You can't just say. 'God save me' or 'God help me' or 'God do this for me' and keep living for the Devil. It don't work that way. It don't mean you won't go astray, like some ornery cow critter sometimes, but He don't go astray ever."

The two men spent the next few minutes in conversation as Preacher explained about sin as well as Christ's death, burial and resurrection. "He paid a debt no man could pay hisself. So ya see, it's pretty simple, but you have to accept His salvation. Not gonna say it's always easy, but it is simple."

The old hostler rubbed his hand across his chin. Then he ran his fingers through his hair. "I gotta give this some thought. I ain't never heard it put quite like that before. Most God fellers are all hellfire and brimstone." He paused and turned slowly. He looked back over his shoulder. "Yes sir. You sure give me something to contemplate." He then disappeared into his office that doubled as his sleeping quarters.

A second or two later, the hostler made himself known as he popped his head back out the door. "But if Jesus was God, why'd He let them fellers kill Him like they did. He could have squashed them like a gnat."

"If He'd have done that, then our debt wouldn't have been paid, and we'd all be on our way to Hell," Preacher replied.

"Oh. That makes sense, I guess." He turned back into his office again and closed the door.

Ten minutes later, Jim and Raven Wing returned. She had her arm through his and the two were talking as if they hadn't a care in the world. Laughter bubbled from their lips as they strolled into the barn.

"That must have been quite the sight. That old mule knocking his antagonists to the ground like a mighty charger of old. And you hired both of them after what they had done to that poor beast?" Raven Wing smiled at Jim.

Jim exploded in laughter. "Wally? That 'poor beast', as you call him, had them both corralled pretty much by the time I got there. If memory serves me correct, they, not he, needed rescuing. Besides, they were just having fun. No harm intended. They're both top hands too." He looked at Preacher. "Better than some I could name."

"They gotta be good hands to make up for the no account that hired them," Preacher replied with a smile. He winked at Raven Wing.

"Miss Raven Wing, it's gettin' late, and we need to get an early start tomorrow. Why don't you climb up in that loft and settle in for the night? Me'n Jim need to palaver about some things before we turn in. Don't fret none if you wake up during the night and you don't see us. We'll be around. Go on now and get some rest."

"Yes, father." She giggled and gave him a peck on the cheek before scrambling up the ladder into the loft.

Preacher blushed. His sun-darkened face turned even more red. "Dag-nabbed gal's gonna be more trouble than you can shake a stick at if she keeps that up," he muttered. "See if she ain't." His mouth curved up into a grin.

Raven Wing must have heard his mumbling. She giggled even more and tossed a double handful of hay from the loft which landed squarely on Preacher's head. "Is that better?" She laughed. They could hear her rustling down into the hay for the night.

Jim laughed at Preacher's lopsided grin. Preacher brushed the hay from his hair and clothing. "So, what did you need to talk to me about?" Jim asked his mentor.

Preacher gestured to the open barn door. He ushered Jim quietly back out into the night. Once outside where no listening ears could overhear what he had to say, he filled Jim in on what he had heard and what he surmised. "It appears Claiborne couldn't leave well enough alone. I figure we'll have us some visitors tonight. I didn't want to alarm Miss Raven Wing but, we'll have callers for sure."

"So do we wait for them here or go hunt them down?" Jim asked the older man.

"We don't know for sure who nor how many are coming so going huntin' would be a waste of time. Besides, we ought to be able to set up a nice welcome for them when they arrive. We should give them a right proper greeting and learn them some proper manners about when someone should come calling. Help them to mend their ways." Preacher smiled. "We wouldn't want 'em to feel unwelcome now, would we?"

Jim smiled knowingly. Preacher's methods of helping someone "mend their ways" were far from delicate at times, but most got the hint. Jim recalled a day when he had been the recipient of such a lesson. He almost grimaced at the memory of repeatedly finding himself on the ground looking up at what he mistook for a helpless old man. "So, we wait here for whoever comes? You've had a bit longer to think on this than I have, but I figure we keep whoever it is outside the livery."

"Them's my thoughts too. If we string up some cans, they'll wake us, but it'll let them know we're onto them. Why don't we both slip on our moccasins and scout around where they're likely to be coming from. Then, with some preparation, we can get some rest before the festivities begin."

Jim replied, "That sounds like a good idea to me."

The two men slipped back into the barn and donned their moccasins. They then dabbed some soot from the lamp chimney onto their faces and turned the last of the lamps down low before gliding silently back into the night. They listened long enough to make sure Raven Wing was sleeping. Her soft, even breathing gave testimony of her repose.

They equipped themselves with some rope, pigging strings, and their knives. Only Jim carried his Colt pistols. They planned to handle things quietly, but if gunplay was needed, Jim was capable of handling it until Preacher could retrieve his artillery and join the fireworks. It was doubtful that gunfire would be needed that night. Their preparations would hopefully see to that.

CHAPTER 9

While Preacher and Jim prepared for their "guests" to arrive, McCabe and Simmons were busy recruiting said "guests". They would remain safely ensconced in the tavern and collect their "finder's fee" without taking any risk themselves.

"So, what do we do if the hostler butts in?" a bearded man growled. He bore a livid scar that ran through his left eyebrow that puckered into an ugly white mass when he scowled. He was scowling now.

"I doubt he will," said McCabe, "But that's up to you to take care of. You get nothing extra for his scalp."

"Talkin' of scalps, what about that squaw they're sneaking off with?" another of the recruits asked. Lust was written plainly on his face.

Simmons chuckled evilly. "She ain't nothing but a squaw. Nobody will care what happens to her. Nobody'd believe a dirty redskin anyway." He glared at the six hirelings. "Just make sure you bring the gold here to be split. The gal you can have. Bring the gold, not her."

"I ain't gonna molest no woman, injun, white or otherwise," said one of the six. "I've done plenty of things in my time, but that ain't one. Count me out." He rose to leave. "I reckon it's time for me to see some fresh country anyway. I hear Colorado's nice this time of year." He turned his back on them and started for the door, ignoring the glares aimed his way. There are some lines even he would not cross.

The collaborators stilled their nerves with liquid "brave maker" while biding their time until they were sure their intended victims would be asleep. The other patrons intentionally avoided them, knowing something was afoot. As long as it didn't involve them directly, they would turn a blind eye. The less they knew, the better. Being too curious about McCabe's and Simmons's business dealings was not a healthy pastime.

Well after midnight, the thieves, doubling as assassins, slipped out of the bar one at a time. They were all slightly inebriated, but none were completely drunk. The plan was to meet behind Claiborne's and then advance from there along the back of the buildings to the livery barn. When they arrived, they would slip quietly into the darkened barn and commit their vile acts.

Jim's eyes popped open. Preacher was on watch and squatted nearby. It wasn't Preacher that had awakened him, but some noise where it should not have been. The soft crunch of boots on hard packed earth was easily heard. Jim rose silently from the shadow of the wagon where he had been sleeping. The horses had also heard it and were milling about restlessly.

A shadow glided to Jim's side. He showed no alarm and continued to concentrate on the approaching boots. Boots meant men, and at this time of night, men approaching meant someone was up to no good. "How many do you count?" whispered the shadow.

"Four. No, five," replied Jim in an almost imperceptible whisper. He was not startled to hear Preacher so close. "They make more noise than half a Cheyenne camp doing a war dance."

"I got five too. You ready?" Preacher asked.

Jim smiled. "Born that way," was his softly breathed response. Silent as smoke, both men faded into the night in the direction of their not so silent adversaries. They had no intention of being pinned down while their enemies had freedom of movement. Against a foe with superior numbers, they preferred to take the dispute to their antagonist. Tonight was to be a warning. Nobody would be hurt.... too much.

Like wraiths, Jim and Preacher crept around the approaching party and slipped behind them. That was the easy part. The gang was far too noisy to notice the approach of their intended victims. The problem was, as bunched up as they were, it would be difficult to cut any of them silently from the pack. That dilemma was solved when their leader decided to scout the approach before bringing the entire gang up.

"You two stay here," he ordered a pair of the men. "Us three'll sneak up and get a better look at things. Then we'll all move in together and take 'em by surprise." His whisper was far louder than need be. If they had been trying to sneak up on a Cheyenne, Blackfoot, or Crow village, their hair would already be decorating some brave's scalp pole.

Without waiting to make sure his orders were understood or followed, the leader led the other two forward. Almost before they disappeared, two apparitions materialized out of the dark. The struggles were brief and silent. The touch of cold steel and a soft warning breathed into the ears of the two left behind ended their resistance before it began. They were quickly disarmed, bound, and gagged.

Preacher grinned in Jim's direction. His smile was invisible in the night. The two dragged their hapless captives into the darker shadows and drifted after the remaining would be assassins, as silent as the shadows themselves.

They had hardly traveled twenty yards when a crash and a startled yelp reached their ears. Both men stifled a chuckle. "Think he'll take the lead next time?" Preacher whispered.

"Not likely," was Jim's almost inaudible reply as the two moved swiftly and silently forward.

The scene that greeted them, seventy-five yards from the livery, was almost exactly what Preacher and Jim had expected. Even so, they both chuckled to themselves. Dangling by one foot three feet off the ground was the bearded man who had asked what to do with the hostler. His gun had fallen from his hand and lay in the dust just out of reach of his fingertips. He spun in lazy circles as his two compatriots gawked, unsure of exactly what to do. His scarred eyebrow puckered in pain and frustration.

The human-sized snare had not been that difficult to set up. Some rope, a wagon on a downhill slope, a stout tree limb, and a trip wire was all that was needed. Not only was it simple, but it was also effective.

The two remaining gun bunnies tried to pull their leader back to the ground against his protests. Jim and Preacher had little trouble slipping up on them and clubbing them into unconsciousness. Once they had bound them, they searched them both, removed all of their weapons, and placed them into a burlap sack with those they had taken from the early captives. The leaders' weapons were also quickly added to the collection.

"You just hang around here and we'll be back... eventually," Preacher said. "We need to let some folks know they can go back to sleep. You got nowhere else to go tonight, and there ain't no need to disturb their rest on your account."

They left the whiskered man dangling upside down. "Jim, you scoot on back to the barn and reassure Miss Raven Wing, and I'll dismantle the rest of our contraptions. Then we'll have ourselves a confab with these fellers. Not that there's any doubt who sent them, but maybe they can tell us something we don't know."

"Sounds good Preacher. I'll be back lickety split."

CHAPTER 10

When Jim got back to the barn, the door was slightly ajar. He almost panicked, wondering if they somehow missed one of the attackers. He was sure no one had gotten by them, but he and Preacher had closed the doors tight behind them when they left. He drew his revolver and inched forward on catlike feet.

Thirty feet of open space stood between him and the door. The door was the only way into the dark barn. Pausing at the edge of the shadows, he listened. Hearing no sound, he took a deep breath and moved forward into the intervening space.

"Halt where you are, or I shall be forced to shoot you." Raven Wing's voice was clear in the night air. Unlike many who would stick the barrel of the weapon out of the crack where it could be seen, she had kept it and herself hidden in the inky interior where she remained unseen. She was invisible, but intruders would show up clearly in the slightly open doorway. For added emphasis, she eared back the hammer on whatever weapon she had. The double click of the hammer being brought to full cock was ominous in the still night.

"Miss Raven Wing. It's Jim. Are you okay?" He had wisely halted at her command. At this range, nobody could miss, and he had no desire to be shot by mistake.

"James!" Relief was evident in her voice. "I almost shot you. I heard a crash and then yelling. I did not know what was happening. You and Preacher were gone and…" She lowered the hammer on the rifle she was holding and hurried to him. A tear formed in the corner of her eye as she realized what she had almost done.

Jim looked at her as she stood trembling. He smiled and put his arms around her to reassure her. He had already returned his pistol to its holster. "Everything's alright. We had some callers, but they decided to wait outside. I guess they reconsidered their late hour for visiting." She put her forehead against his chest.

"As for shooting me, I guess if a man has to get shot, it might as well be by the prettiest girl in town. It sure beats who shot me last time." Her dignity gave way and she wept at the enormity of what she had almost done and his casual acceptance like it was an everyday occurrence to him. "Besides, you didn't shoot me, so all is well."

He held her for a few more minutes while she composed herself. "How can you make light of almost being shot? I could have killed you by accident, and you behave as though it happens to you every day." She stepped back and looked at him from arms length.

"But you didn't," he replied. "You were brave and kept your head. If it had been one of our callers, you would have been justified in stopping him. Go back into the barn and try to rest. Preacher and I will be in soon. You're safe now. Just bar the door until one of us comes back."

She turned dutifully and re-entered the barn. He heard her strike a match to relight the lantern before he turned back to where Preacher awaited him. His mind was more on what happened near the livery than what awaited him. The smell of her hair and the feel of her in his arms was only part of it. It was more the sense of being a protector. Strong and sure and yet unsure. The God-given instinct of a man to protect and defend the fairer sex, to comfort and reassure in times of stress and fear. It is part of what raises man above the beasts. It made men risk their own lives for the sake of others.

"Ya took long enough," Preacher said in way of greeting. "I was beginning to think you took a nap and was going to leave me to do all the work."

Jim grinned. "I reckon I came closer to getting shot tonight than you did, so I figured to take my time."

"Shot?" Preacher was incredulous. "I thought we had them all."

"We do, but Raven Wing didn't know that. She was all set to stop any that got by us. That being said, she thought for a second I might have been one." Jim quickly recounted what took place at the livery, leaving out Raven Wing's tears and their embrace. Some things Preacher did not need to know. While Jim relayed the story, the two men dragged all the bound culprits to where "Whiskers" still dangled upside down.

With that accomplished, Jim lowered their final captive unceremoniously to the ground. Finding himself back on the ground, their captive tried to gain his feet, but the leg from which he had been dangling collapsed beneath him. He flopped back to the dirt with a whimper. "My leg's busted," He groaned.

"Let that be a lesson to you to not go sneaking around dark alleys at night," Preacher said in his best school master's voice. "'And this is the condemnation, that 'the light is come into the world, and men loved darkness rather than light, because their deeds were evil.'

John 3:19. Now it seems, you boys like the dark. So, what evil deeds were you up to?"

"We wasn't up to nothin'," growled Whiskers. "We was just strolling along mindin' our own business when you bushwhacked us. Maybe you was the ones up to no good taking that injun gal into the barn and all."

Before anyone could react, Jim's Colt was in his hand with the muzzle resting against Whisker's right eye. "Don't you ever talk about a lady like that," he snarled. Everyone present knew what would have happened had these men not been stopped.

The bearded man swallowed. He had not seen Jim's hand move before he felt the cold ring of steel press against his eye. Preacher was even caught off guard by his young friend's action. "Put the gun away Jim," he said firmly. "This feller is in no shape to do any harm. Besides, I think he really wants to tell us the truth and make amends. He can't do that with his eye shot out the back of his head now, can he? Too many holes in his head that away."

"We can get angry as long as we don't sin in doin' so. That's what the Bible says. 'Be angry and sin not'. I think it'd be a sin to blast this feller to Perdition without giving him a chance to turn from his evil ways. I don't figure it'd be a sin to convince him to confess them sins though." A twinkle showed in Preacher's eyes, and a smile played on his lips.

Jim got the message and holstered his pistol as quickly as he had drawn it.

All five of the assailants were awake by now. Four were bound and still gagged as Jim dragged Whiskers into the darkness. His hands were bound and his broken leg forced Jim to drag him along the ground like a sack of grain, while he complained about his broken leg the entire time. Jim's grim visage had the desired effect on the four who remained under Preacher's watchful eye.

"That boy's plumb upset." Preacher spoke quietly and shook his head slowly. "I sure hope he don't shoot that fool." Preacher shook his head again as if having given his comment some thought. "Naw, he wouldn't do that. Too noisy. Of course, he does have that there knife Standing Bear give him. There's always that." Preacher spoke as if he were talking to himself but loud enough for his captives to overhear.

Shortly, they heard a brief scuffle followed by the terrified voice of Whiskers. "No! No! You can't do that. You're a white man! NO!" This was followed by a blood-curling scream and then silence.

"Maybe shootin' him would have been quieter after all." Preacher shook his head again.

Jim returned a few minutes later. He materialized with no more sound than the shadows from which he appeared. Tucked into his belt was a hank of hair the same color as the bearded man's. It looked as though there was blood dripping from it. Jim casually wiped the blade of his knife on his pant leg before returning it to the sheath. It was too dark to see what he wiped from the blade.

Jim squatted beside Preacher. "Well," inquired the oldster.

"He wasn't much for repenting," Jim replied. "Maybe one of these other fellers would like to go next. A grave's a lonely place, and I'm sure what's his name wouldn't mind company." Jim rose and moved toward the man who looked most defiant. "He looks likely."

"Now wait a minute, Jim. You can't just haul them off one at a time without givin' 'em a chance to make their peace."

"You're too soft on them, Preacher, but go ahead and pull his gag and see what he has to say."

Preacher removed the gag and when the outlaw began cursing he quickly replaced it. "I guess he's got nothing worth hearing after all." Preacher waved Jim toward the bound man. "Maybe you can get him to repent."

The outlaws eyes grew wide with terror and then hardened in defiance. Jim dragged the most defiant one into the night by the collar. When they stopped, he could see his companion's body lying motionless on the ground. The dirt around his neck and groin was stained dark with some sort of liquid just visible in the faint moonlight.

Jim turned his new captive away from the sight. "He said some mean things about Miss Raven Wing. He sure squalled more than a bull calf when he's cut or a horse when he's gelded. I sure hope you ain't as noisy. Like to have bust my eardrums with his screaming."

Jim flipped his captive onto his back and drew his knife. "Well, it's your turn now." The man's eye grew big as saucers as comprehension sank in. "Did you have something to say?" Jim asked. "Maybe I should take that gag out of your yap so you can talk." Jim removed the gag.

"You wouldn't," the man whispered hoarsely. "You couldn't."

"You saw and heard your friend. What do you think?"

The man tried to twist his head. When he did, he saw the lock of hair in Jim's belt.

Jim's gaze followed the man's eyes. Then he looked at him and smiled. "I lived with the Cheyenne for two plus years. You learn some things."

"I don't believe you," the man said at last.

"Calling me a liar? Most men I'd shoot for that, but for you, I'll just cut your tongue out." Jim drew his knife and reached for the man's face.

Screams similar to those heard earlier reached the ears of those with Preacher. Jim returned with a second lock of hair matching the second man's tucked into his belt. "He wouldn't believe," Jim said quietly. "Do you think any of them has the sense God gave a goose?"

"I hope so, but Jim, you can't just go around scalping folks like you were back with those heathen Cheyenne."

"Why not? There ain't no law on the books against it that I know of," Jim retorted.

"Maybe not. But it ain't decent," responded Preacher.

"I'll think about it. So, who's next?" Jim eyed the captives expectantly.

"That one looks smarter than the rest." Preacher indicated the one who appeared the most frightened.

Jim quickly grabbed his collar and dragged him into the night in the direction from which the earlier screams arose. Two still forms now lay motionless in the faint light of the moon. The ground near both looked to be soaked with blood.

Jim drew his knife and jabbed it at the first form. "That one made such a ruckus he might have woke the dead. I guess he didn't like the thought of being gelded. That one," he pointed his knife at the second form. "Well, let's just say his tongue won't ever get him into trouble again. He called me a liar. Can you imagine that?"

The man gawked in their direction. His face grew pale even in the limited light. Jim squatted between him and the still forms on the ground. "What about you? You got something to tell me?" Jim stared at him and the outlaw nodded vigorously. "That's right smart of you. Those two wouldn't be in the condition they are now if they had just showed the sense you are."

Jim slipped the gag from the man's mouth, and he worked his jaws vigorously to loosen the muscles. "Okay," began Jim, "what was this all about?"

"McCabe and Simmons told us 'bout the gold ya'll have on ya. We was to make it so's you couldn't talk and got the gold. 'Bout what you was to talk about, I ain't for sure. Honest! That's all I know."

"What was to happen to the gal and the hostler?"

"Oh mister, please!"

"Tell me!" Jim's voice was as harsh as a Montana blizzard.

His eyes were hard as cold blue steel.

"It wasn't me. It was Rory and him." He indicated the bearded man with his chin. "He asked about the hostler and was told to take care of him. Rory wanted the gal."

Jim's fury came to the surface. "Why you dirty, filthy cowards!" He drew his foot back to deliver a kick but stopped. The man before him was sobbing.

"It was Rory not me! Please don't geld me. I swear I wouldn't hurt her. Just please," he spluttered.

Jim dragged his still whimpering captive back to Preacher. "I'll be right back," he grunted to Preacher. His anger had not subsided. "It looks like I threatened to make a steer of the wrong one."

He returned a few minutes later with both of the captives he had taken earlier. Aside from both missing a fist full of hair, neither seemed too much worse for the wear. Jim had frightened them into hollering and screaming before clamping his hand over their mouths and giving vent to his own death rattle. He then clubbed them unconscious and replaced their gags. Drenching the ground near both victims gave the appearance of them both lying in pools of their own blood. It was a neat trick, unless you were the one it was being played on. Then, it was most terrifying and usually produced the desired effect.

CHAPTER II

"So, now we know for sure the who, but not so much the why. We can make a pretty educated guess, though. Now the question is, what do we do about it?" Jim asked Preacher.

"That, and what do we do with these snakes," replied Preacher. "It's a cinch. We'd be dead if the tables was turned."

"Turn the other cheek?" Jim asked. "Of course, if they try to smite that one too, the instructions are a little vague, so I think they'd be fair game."

Preacher cocked his head to one side and rested his chin in his hand. "I reckon everybody's entitled to one attack of ignorance. But, now these boys know better."

Jim nodded solemnly. "I didn't see a jail in town."

The outlaws looked on helplessly as their captors discussed their fate. One with fear and pleading in his eyes, another with open defiance, and the others with a mixture of uncertainty and curiosity.

Jim and Preacher spoke in hushed tones for a few more minutes before reaching their decision. "That should work," said Jim. "They'll either learn, or they won't. One of the two, guaranteed."

"Let's pray that they learn. If not, their blood will be on their own heads next time."

"If we're not too careful with the barbering, there might be blood on their heads this time." Jim laughed. Then he grew serious.

"You planned to rob and murder us in our sleep tonight. You planned much worse for Miss Raven Wing. For that, we have the right, and some would say the obligation, to hang you." He stopped and looked at each man in turn for emphasis. "Nobody would blame us, and some would even thank us, but that's not what we're going to do." Jim smiled. Surprise registered on all of their faces. They knew for a fact that what Jim had said was true.

"Oh, you will be punished, somewhat, but because nobody was hurt, besides Whiskers there, we're going to go easy on you.

"First, you will all receive a haircut of sorts. I suggest you be very still for that. My knife is sharp as a razor. In fact, I shave with it sometimes, but I am not much of a barber." He drew his knife and tested it against his thumb.

"Next, come morning, the livery where you intended to make a huge mess, can stand a thorough cleaning. You will be there to make sure it is cleaned. And last, you will ride out of the country never to return or live here under my rules. Of course, it will be under our conditions that you ride out of the country too, if that is your choice."

Jim didn't raise his voice while delivering the ultimatum, but left no doubt that compliance was required, not requested.

"Since Whiskers there has a busted leg and won't be able to help clean the barn, why don't we start with him? He'll look real nice in his new haircut." Knife in hand, Jim approached the injured man.

Whiskers's eyes grew big as saucers when Jim grabbed a handful of his long, unkempt hair. He tried to struggle unsuccessfully.

"Relax," Jim said. "If I was going to scalp you, I'd have done it already. Besides, the only thing you can do by struggling is maybe lose an ear. We don't want that."

Preacher grabbed the man's head in an iron grip to help hold him still. Jim casually hacked off hands full of the greasy hair from one side of their captive's head. It was a crude, uneven job, but half of the man's hair had been cut close to his scalp. The other side was left full length. "You'll keep this hairstyle for a bit.

At least until you ride out of the country, or we're satisfied you can grow it back without it interfering with your decision to stay on the straight and narrow. We'll leave your beard be though. We don't want you to feel too lopsided," Jim said when the job was finished.

Each of the other four was forced to submit to the inept barbering. The last one was defiant and had to be held down.

"Just hold still Rory," Whiskers yelled. "Keep fightin' and you'll likely lose more'n half your hair."

Half of Rory's curly black locks were removed despite his struggles. Because he refused to be still during the process, he also received several small cuts to his scalp. A trickle of blood dribbled down his face as he glared at Preacher and Jim. When they removed his gag, he spat invectives at them. "I'll kill both of you for this!"

Jim leaned in close to the raging man. "You already tried once. Don't be a fool. Come for us again, and I'll assume you refused correction. Then, my ways won't be so gentle." By now, predawn light was creeping into the sky. Jim's blue eyes turned glacial. "God forgive me, but I'll enjoy it if you do."

Rory stared defiantly at Jim for a moment but was unable to hold Jim's gaze. He lowered his eyes while still muttering threats. Jim backhanded him across the face, spinning him into the dust.

Rory looked up. "Take these ropes off me and I'll…"

"You'll clean the barn," interjected Preacher. He still had much to learn about and teach his young protege. Perhaps not the least of which was to keep his emotions in check. He still did not know the whole story behind Jim's sometimes explosive methods of dealing with those who perpetrated evil, especially against women. He knew it had a lot to do with what had happened at the Lazy H years before. Of that, he knew much but not all. [1]

Rory turned his bloodshot eyes on Preacher but found he could not hold the older man's gaze either. Preacher continued. "When that's done, you'll have a choice. You can stay or go. But not before the barn is cleaned."

Jim nodded towards Whiskers. "I should get a doctor to set this man's leg right so it heals proper," he said. "If he's going to walk the straight and narrow, it wouldn't hurt to have two good legs." He looked at the man's pale face. "Is there a doctor in this burg?"

"The sawbones has a place next to the saloon, but he's probably drunk or hungover." Whiskers managed to say between clenched teeth. The pain was increasing from his broken leg, and it continued to swell. "Don't know as I'd trust him to set my leg, but he's all there is."

---

1. *(To learn more about Jim's past, read **Vengeance Is Mine**.)

"He'll have to do then," Jim replied. "Can you keep an eye on these fellers while I go get the doc?" Jim asked Preacher.

"Go on boy. I can handle these hogtied hooligans just fine. Just see you don't get lost along the way."

CHAPTER 12

J im set off quickly toward the doctor's residence. He found it just where Whiskers said it would be. At first, he knocked gently. After no answer, he knocked more firmly. Finally, after no answer, he pounded on the door, rattling it in its frame until he heard a slurred voice and shuffling steps approaching.

"Go 'way," someone growled form inside. "It's too early for office hours." The steps began to retreat, and Jim pounded again. "Go away!" shouted the voice again.

"You a doctor or a drunk?" Jim shouted back. "You've got five seconds to open this door, or I'll open if for you and drag you out. Somebody is hurt and needs a doctor now, not when you sober up!"

"You wouldn't dare!" The doctor responded.

"Five, four, three." Jim counted loud enough for the doctor to hear clearly.

"Okay! Okay! Just give me a minute to put on some pants!" There was more muttering from inside, but the sounds made it obvious that the doctor was gathering himself and his tools of the trade. Five minutes later, the beefy physician opened the door. His face was lined with veins, and he had the red, bulbous nose of one who consumed alcohol in large quantities. His face was unshaven, and his breath smelled of stale whiskey. He stared in bewilderment at Jim through bloodshot eyes.

"So where's the patient?" the doctor asked. "You look healthy enough to me." He turned as if to retreat into his office.

Jim clamped hold of his arm. "Oh no, you don't. The one who's hurting is down by the wagon yard. He's got a broken leg that needs set. For reasons that will be obvious, I wasn't about to bring him to you myself."

The doctor brushed Jim's hand from his arm. "Fine then. Lead on, but we will need to get him to my office to set the leg right."

Jim led the way to the stricken man and his cohorts.

When they came into view, Preacher looked up and grinned.

The doctor stopped short and stared at the five men with half their hair cut close to the scalp and the other half left full length. He blinked and rubbed his face as if expecting the scene before him to change. He opened his eyes again and was greeted by the same sight. He shook his head ponderously like an old bull buffalo.

"No Doc," Preacher began. "You ain't still soaked. They all come calling last night, and we give 'em a fresh haircut. That feller there's your patient." He indicated Whiskers with his thumb.

The doctor took a closer look. "Dubois! What in tarnation happened to you? I always figured I'd have to doctor you or bury you some day, but this beats the band."

"Dubois? I guess that's better than calling him Whiskers," Jim said. "Anything you need help with, Doc?"

"Get these ropes off'n him, and I figure I can get him to my office. Other than that, I just need to know how he expects to pay."

Dubois looked forlorn. "I'm 'bout as busted as my leg," he muttered.

Jim interceded. "I'll cover the cost. I reckon we're slightly to blame for breaking it. Just make sure it's set straight. I'll be by the office after these four get finished cleaning the livery."

Jim cut the pigging strings binding Dubois's wrists. Together, the doctor and Jim lifted the injured man to his feet.

Leaning heavily on the doctor, Dubois hobbled off in the direction of the physician's office.

"Time for you boys to get to work," Preacher announced.

He covered the men while Jim removed their bonds.

They rose gingerly to their feet. The tingling of circulation returning to numbed extremities made rapid movement, therefore any resistance or retaliation, unthinkable. When they had recovered sufficiently, they were paraded at gunpoint to the livery barn. Jim rapped on the door. "Raven Wing, it's us," he announced.

He could hear movement from within as the heavy bar blocking the door was removed. The portal swung open, and the weary young woman stepped into the early morning light. Her tousled hair had wisps of straw tangled in it.

"James," she began. "I heard some screams after you left and then you did not return. I did not know what happened, and I was afraid for you." She noticed the four captives covered by Preacher's appropriated pistol. She smiled and asked, "Are these our would be late night quests?"

Preacher laughed. The four prisoners stared daggers. "Not sure if I'd call them guests, since I don't generally ask my guests to clean the barn, but yep, that's most of 'em. One with a busted leg is at the Doc's. These four *volunteered* to clean some stalls this morning." His eyes danced with merriment.

Under the watchful eyes of Jim and Preacher, the four would be assassins shoveled, scraped and cleaned every stall in the barn, much to the delight of the hostler. When the cleaning was complete, fresh straw was strewn in each of the stalls and the four fell, exhausted, into the corner to rest.

"You done a good job," Preacher proclaimed at the end of their labors. "Don't that feel better'n thieving and killin'?"

The youngest of the group grinned. "Yep, it do. And there ain't nobody likely to string ya up for cleaning their barn."

"Shut up Calloway!" Rory grumbled. "There ain't nothin' good about the blister end of a shovel."

"There is nothing wrong with feeling good about a job well done." Raven Wing piped in kindly.

"You shut your face you stinkin'…"

Jim stepped quickly toward Rory. "Don't say it," he growled.

"Yeah, squaw man. You're pretty hard when you're wearing a gun and I ain't. You'll get your'n. You and that Preacher man!" Rory snarled.

Jim started to unbuckle his gun-belt, but Preacher stopped him. "Now ain't the time. Give him a chance to think. He's alive and he could be dead. His punishment was cleaning the barn rather than hanging. They done a right good job cleaning it too. If he thinks on that for a bit and still wants a row, then you can give it to him. But right now, they got a choice to make. Remember?"

Jim re-buckled his gun-belt and began to speak. "Here's the rules for staying. They're pretty simple. You wear your hair like it is for the next week. When folks ask you why, you tell them it's a reminder not to do evil like stealing or killing the innocent. And you don't ever, and I mean ever, steal from the Lazy H, any of our neighbors, or any of our hands. You keep away from those who do such things. We will know if you break our rules. If you do, you pay the price."

"Now the rules for leaving. You leave on the mounts we provide for you, since it's our guess the ones you rode in used to belong to someone else. And you never return. Break the rules and you pay the price. We figure none of you have family here so no ties to hold you back."

"When do we leave?" One of the men asked dejectedly.

"Right after you get fed." Preacher answered. "We won't send any of you off on an empty stomach."

"And if I don't like either choice?" queried Rory. "You just gonna shoot me?"

"No," Jim replied. "In that case, I'll tie you belly down over your saddle and send you out of town that way. Once you work your way loose, you can get up in the saddle and just keep going." Jim smiled at the truculent malefactor. "And, in that instance, I will tie you across the most spavined nag I can get my hands on, maybe even a mule or a jackass. Going willingly is a much better option."

"Them rules about staying. You never said if we can keep what horses we got if we stay. I got a couple of nice mustangs I caught myself." This came from young Calloway.

"As long as they're legitimate, you can keep them." Jim responded.

"I'll stay then."

"Anybody else staying?" Jim asked.

"What about our horses?" asked another outlaw.

"Consider them traded for the horses you ride out on when you leave."

"Count yourself lucky, Slim. You'd be lucky if your old nag could carry you out of town. Mine ain't much better. If the ones he gives us are walking, we're trading up."

The men were then trooped into the nearest cafe and fed a hearty meal.

Jim purchased the three who chose to leave sound but not prime horses from the hostler. The outlaws were permitted to retrieve their saddles and personal affects under Preacher's and Jim's watchful eyes. Then, their weapons were stripped of ammunition and returned. They were sent out of town down the middle of the street with instructions to never return. Two heeded the warning.

As soon as they were out of sight of the town, Rory reloaded his pistol and turned his mount around.

"Whatcha doin' Rory?" Slim asked as he reloaded his own pistol.

"Nobody makes a fool of me and gets away with it!" Rory sneered. "I've got two scalps to collect. You comin'?"

"Nope," replied Slim.

"Not me neither. We come out of it with a whole hide. I say, let sleeping dogs lie. Somethin' about that pair gives me the willies. You're heading back to your own funeral, I think. But that's up to you."

"C'mon Slim. We're burning daylight." "Cowards!" Rory shouted.

The third man halted his horse and turned toward Rory. "No," he replied steadily. "We just know to leave well enough alone. You're no match for me, and there's something I seem to recollect about that kid from the Lazy H. You're sure fire no match for him. Let it be." He then turned his back on Rory and rode off with

Slim. Neither of them looked back. They could start over again somewhere else.

CHAPTER 13

Jim, Preacher, and Raven Wing were just leaving the diner when Rory returned. He slid his mount to a halt, swirling dust around the three of them. Jim slipped the hammer thong from his right-hand Colt revolver.

"You and Raven Wing mount up. I'll be along directly," Jim said to Preacher.

"Jim, don't hunt trouble," Preacher responded.

"I'm not, but it found me. No use in all of us being delayed. I'll try to talk sense into him, but it appears he wants that row now." Jim looked resigned.

Preacher helped Raven Wing into the saddle and mounted his own horse. The sleek appaloosa filly that they purchased for her fidgeted nervously. Raven Wing expertly handled the reins of the spirited animal.

"I'll see if I can scare up some fresh meat on the way to camp," Jim said. "Now you two best be moving along."

Jim walked toward Rory as he dismounted. "I thought we had an agreement," Jim said quietly. "You leave town and all is forgiven."

"Not so easy. You can't make a fool out of me and get away with it. After I'm done with you, I'll hunt down that old man and the gal too." His face became contorted as he spoke.

Jim smiled. "It's tempting to let you try that, but Preacher would be mad as a wet hen if I was to give in to temptation. After he buried you, he'd sure enough brain me but good. Best I don't do that. Besides, I couldn't make a fool out of a fool because a fool is already a fool." Jim looked at Rory and shook his head. "Get on your horse and ride. I've no desire to kill you nor even give you a good thrashing. Don't force an issue where one doesn't exist. It's too nice a day to die Rory. Ride out and live."

Jim turned his back on the outlaw and started for his horse. A shot rang out and dirt geysered near his feet. Then another shot and more dirt flew into the air. Jim continued to walk. When a third shot rang out, Jim turned reluctantly toward his antagonist.

"So, the table's turned, and now I've got the drop on you." Rory grinned, clearly enjoying himself.

Jim gritted his teeth. "Put the gun away. I told you I don't want to kill you. Don't make me do it."

Rory laughed. A crowd had begun to gather, carefully out of the line of fire. "You all heard him say he was going to kill me. That makes this self-defense." Rory casually leveled his pistol. As he began to ear back the hammer, he saw a blur of movement and a flower of flame as something struck him solidly in the chest. Taking two steps backward, he sat heavily in the dirt. His pistol fired into the ground near his own feet, and he toppled sideways into the dusty street. The sky was so blue. Why had he never noticed it before?

"I tried to tell you Rory," Jim said softly. "But as Proverbs 26:11 says, 'Like a dog returneth to his vomit, so a fool returneth to his folly'. This was folly. I'm really sorry. It didn't have to be this way, but you gave me no choice."

Those were the last words Rory heard before he was greeted by darkness, unbearable heat, and wails of anguish. Those wails were soon joined by his own as he began his eternal reward in Hell.

Jim looked at the crowd. "Give his horse and tack to Calloway. Bury him with his boots on. Who's the undertaker?"

A distinguished looking man stepped to the fore. "That would be me."

"What's the cost to bury him proper? You don't keep nor sell any of his gear."

While the cost was negotiated, which Jim paid in gold, Calloway was summoned to collect the horse and tack. The undertaker arranged to have the body taken to his parlor to be prepared for burial. When Jim rode from town, the tiny hamlet was abuzz with talk of the shooting. Two men in particular, McCabe and Simmons, showed a special interest.

"What do you mean, Rory had his gun out and pointed at him, and he still never got off a shot?" McCabe demanded. "Nobody is that fast. Nobody!"

"Not meaning to disagree with you, Mr. McCabe, but them's the facts. That ain't second hand neither. I saw it myself. One minute, Rory's starting to ear back the hammer and the next, he's on his butt dyin'," said a mousy little man. He licked his lips nervously. His eyes darted back and forth between McCabe and Simmons. "I never saw the like. Not even a snake is that fast. I never saw his hand move. Just a blur, and Rory was done for."

Simmons spoke. "Then he paid in gold to plant him? Was it raw gold? Dust? Nuggets? Could you tell that?"

"It wasn't coin. It was raw gold."

"Okay. Have a drink on us and then get out of here," Simmons ordered him.

The little man scuttled out, forgetting his drink. He wasn't much of a drinker anyway, and it was well before noon.

"So, our boys not only failed, but Rory got himself killed, Dubois is at the doc's with a busted leg, and Calloway quit us and has half his head dang near shaved. We've been made to look the fool in all this," Simmons mused.

"We underestimated them this time, but that won't happen again. That raw gold came from somewhere," McCabe replied. "Maybe we can come out of this even better if we can get us a tracker to follow 'em to their claim. We'll be more careful next time."

Simmons stared blankly ahead for a moment. "He paid to bury Rory. I heard he paid Dubois's doctor bill too. What an odd duck." He shook himself from his daze. "No matter. That odd duck will be our plump pigeon soon. Who can we get that could follow them without detection and keep it quiet?"

The two fell into deep conversation, waving off any who dared to approach. The thought of gold displaced their current plans of rustling. Who could they use? Who could handle the takeover of the claim with them? They dare not trust that to underlings. They would need to be there themselves. They needed to plan and to find a tracker.

CHAPTER 14

J im followed the trail at a slow walk, oblivious to the schemes being hatched behind him. His eyes scoured the hills for anything that seemed out of place. Without conscious effort, his eyes and ears noted any unusual movement. A squirrel scampering up a tree, the shadow of a hawk overhead, and the tiny titmouse flitting through the forest were not hidden from his keen senses.

He carried his rifle across the pommel as he watched the trail for danger and the surroundings for game. He and Preacher had seen plenty of signs of both mule deer and pronghorn on their earlier trip. Either would provide plenty of meat for the trail and some for the home ranch too. While beef was readily available, a change of diet was always welcome.

Movement to his left drew his gaze. A mule deer doe stepped into a small clearing a hundred yards away. His rifle rose fluidly to his shoulder, and he drew a bead on her vitals. He waited a few heartbeats and then lowered it. Two small fawns stepped daintily to her side. Jim wasn't averse to killing a doe to eat, but he would not leave the fawns orphaned to die of starvation nor would he shoot a fawn. There would be other game.

Another mile down the trail, Jim's patience was rewarded by the gobble of a tom turkey not too far away. He dismounted and tied his horse. The gobble was answered by a second tom. Jim slid silently toward the first gobbler. He found him, strutting and gobbling, daring any other tom to come close while displaying himself to the hens that were gathering.

Jim hunkered down to wait. The second tom was answering the challenge and was on his way. If Jim played things right, he might just collect both. It was worth the try.

Ten minutes later, a dozen hens had gathered, and the second tom arrived. The two dominant birds strutted and postured. Their tails were fanned out and their wingtips dragged the ground as they putt-purred threats to each other. If neither one relented, there would be a battle. The toms would try to spur each other with the one-inch spikes that grew on the backs of their legs. Such fights were in earnest and more than one combatant had been killed in such a contest. Of course, during such a battle, the combatants were oblivious to anything but their enemy.

The two circled one another, each confident in his own strength. With an eruption of feathers, the two joined in combat. Jim watched the fury of the two birds for a few seconds before taking advantage of the situation. As the huge birds collided in a flurry of wings and kicks intended to injure or kill each other, Jim took careful aim and fired.

A puff of feathers exploded from one of the birds. As the stricken turkey flopped about, his adversary spiked him a few more times ensuring his demise. The hens scattered at the gunshot but the combatant, in his fervor, never heard the shot. He puffed himself back up and began strutting around again, calling to the hens. Jim's next shot removed his head and ended his proud displays forever. "'Pride goeth before destruction,'" he whispered.

Jim caught up to Preacher and Raven Wing just as they were stopping for camp. It was still early, but all were tired after their previous sleepless night. As he approached them, Jim held aloft nearly forty pounds of wild poultry. "I brought dinner," he announced.

"Hmph!" Raven Wing snorted. "Typical man. Goes off to play mighty hunter and brings back raw meat for supper. No herbs, no breads, no berries. Nothing but raw meat. And then he says, 'I brought dinner'." She slid from her saddle and stalked off into the forest. Whether to gather wood for a fire or for those things she thought were needed to accompany the "raw meat" for their evening repast. Neither man was quite sure.

Jim looked questioningly at Preacher as they both dismounted. "I don't think I've ever seen a woman get mad before because you brought fresh meat for the pot."

"She's been a bit edgy since we left you behind in Rosebud. Still, it is a bit peculiar at that." Preacher spoke as they removed the saddles and bridles from their mounts.

Raven Wing noisily reentered the camp with an arm load of dry wood. She promptly dumped it on the ground before storming off in the direction of a small creek a short distance away.

"She don't seem happy about something." Preacher stated the obvious. "We best get set up before she gets back. I ain't sure if it's you or me she's mad at, so I ain't taking chances."

The two men went about setting up camp with practiced ease. Preacher laid out the bedrolls while Jim picketed the horses. Taking extra time with Raven Wing's bed, Preacher gathered soft leaves and grasses for her comfort. He found a mouse nest in the hollow of a log which he used to start a fire.

Raven Wing returned as Preacher was kindling the fire. She had a fistful of wild onions and sage when she returned to camp. Seeing the fire started, she took both turkeys with her as she turned back toward the creek.

When Raven Wing returned to camp the second time, Jim was just returning himself. He had traveled down their back trail scouting for anyone following. Seeing no evidence of that, he returned to camp.

Raven Wing carried one of the turkeys, plucked and ready for roasting. The body cavity was filled with tuberous roots which she intended to serve with the dinner feast. The other bird was nowhere to be seen.

"James, would you be kind enough to bring something from the creek for me?" she asked formally. Whatever had been bothering her apparently still was. "It looks like a large ball of mud. You should be able to find it easy enough."

"Umm, sure. A ball of mud?" Jim followed her tracks toward the creek, somewhat confused.

Raven Wing skewered the turkey she had returned with. After putting pieces of wild onion into some slits she had cut into the skin and rubbing the skin with sage, she hung it over the fire to roast. "Preacher, do you, perchance, have a Dutch oven in your kit? It would make baking biscuits so much simpler," she inquired.

"Sorry, we don't have one, but we got a skillet and some corn meal if that'll help."

"That will be just fine. I can make cornbread with that, some water, and a pinch of salt. You do have salt?"

"We always got salt," Preacher replied.

The skewered turkey was roasting merrily above the flames when Jim returned with a huge ball of mud. Encased in it was the second turkey. "I don't believe I've ever seen someone pack a turkey in mud before. It IS the other turkey, isn't it?" Jim asked.

"Yes, it is. Now put it down near the fire and go wash. You are filthy," Raven Wings snipped.

"Now just wait a minute," Jim responded. "I don't know who put a burr under your blanket, but I only just got here, and I brought some fresh game to boot. I don't know what your problem is gal, but I wish you'd just spit it out!"

"Oh, you don't know? You don't know?" Her voice rose as the cornmeal batter took a beating. "Of course, you do not know! Go wash!"

Jim opened his mouth to respond but was unsure what to say. Instead, he gritted his teeth and stalked off to wash the mud from his hands and arms. "Preacher's right," he muttered to himself. "She is trouble."

He returned and sat sullenly near the fire. He stared into the darkening night, and they sat in silence while their dinner roasted over the fire.

Preacher broke the silence. "Miss Raven Wing, you figure to put that second bird in the coals tonight to cook?"

"Yes. In the morning, we can crack the mud off, or we can carry it still in the clay. If we leave it encased, it will still be warm for supper tomorrow night. It is very good baked that way."

"Well, we'll be to the ranch house tomorrow in time for supper. That might be a treat, and it'd save Tom's bride some cooking. The one over the fire smells right good," Preacher said.

She smiled at Preacher. "Thank you. It will only be a little bit before it is done. That will give the cornbread a chance to cook as well."

Jim turned his attention back to the camp. He had to agree with Preacher. The turkey did smell good. His stomach growled in assent. "It does smell good," he said neutrally.

Raven Wing made no response other than to check the cornbread and to turn the turkey on the spit.

"Look, I don't know what you're upset about, but it's a stone-cold cinch, I did whatever it was," Jim began. "Don't you think it's only right to let a man know what it is he did wrong?"

"You really don't know do you? Last night, you were almost killed, BY ME! I almost shot you, James, and you behaved as though that is an everyday event. Then, you and Preacher set five men, who were sent to murder you, free. Not only that, but you paid the doctor's bill for one of them and bought the horses on which to send the others away.

"One of them then returns to exact his vengeance on you, and you do not even consider Preacher's assistance. Instead, you send us both away. You promise to catch up quickly but go hunting instead. We do not see you. We do not hear from you. I begin to wonder if that evil man, or others like him, may have killed you. All day, I worry that you are dead. Then, you ride into camp as though nothing is amiss. It was inconsiderate of you." She turned to add wood to the fire and to rotate the turkey.

Some fat from the turkey dripped into the fire causing the flames to flare up illuminating her face. In the firelight, Jim could see her lips tremble slightly. Her dusky face showed lines of worry that he had not seen earlier. No, he really did not understand what she was upset about, but it bothered him that she was. He was here. He was safe and sound. What was there to be upset about?

"Well, I'm here now with a whole hide," he said lamely.

"Yes, and that makes everything just peachy," she retorted. "Get your plates. The turkey is done enough, as is the rest of the meal."

Preacher asked the blessing, and Raven Wing carved slabs of turkey onto plates for all of them. She added cornbread and the tuberous roots she had fried with some wild onions and bacon. Jim could not remember a better tasting camp meal.

After cleaning up, the mud ball was covered with coals to cook through the night. Then, Raven Wing curled up in her bed and was soon fast asleep. The two men stayed up a little longer talking. They were both tired after the previous night but would take turns keeping watch.

The night passed without incident other than a curious raccoon looking for scraps. The camp bandit stole close to the fire only to scamper away when he realized he was being watched by the camp's sentry.

In the predawn mist, they broke camp and ate cold turkey and cornbread for breakfast. Jim donned some heavy gloves and pulled the now hard clay ball containing the second turkey from the coals. He secured it in his bedroll for the trip back to the Lazy H.

The purples and pinks of sunrise were dissipating from the sky as they began their southern trek. For a long time, they rode in silence, simply enjoying the morning. The sound of their horses' hooves and the creak of saddle leather were the only sounds to disturb the morning stillness.

By the time they stopped for the noon meal, Raven Wing had begun to show the effects of the strain she had been under. Her face was weary, and she fidgeted in the saddle due to the discomfort from the long ride.

Jim hopped quickly from his horse and helped her gently from her saddle. She walked gingerly to a small seep to get some fresh water and wash the dust from her face. She dipped a small cloth in the cool water and held it to her neck to cool herself. Never once did she utter a complaint about the ride.

"I don't reckon she's done much ridin' lately," Preacher said sympathetically.

Jim watched as she carefully knelt to wash her face. "She's beat but never complained." He snickered. "I'm thinking she'd like to cool the other end for a while too."

When mounting back up, Jim assisted Raven Wind tenderly into the saddle. As she settled back onto the seat, she grimaced but refused to cry out.

"We'll try to take it easy, but if you need to stop, you just let us know," Jim said. "It's only a couple more hours. After that, you can rest."

"And cool the other end?" she asked with a grin, which became a grimace when her horse shifted positions.

"I, uh…" Jim stammered. His face turned red with embarrassment.

Raven Wing laughed despite her discomfort. "I have very good ears, Mister Harding. And yes, you are correct. I would like to 'cool the other end', as you put it, but for now I will endure. Let us not dawdle."

CHAPTER 15

"Daddy! Mommy! Jim and Preacher are back!" young Sarah shouted as they rode into the yard. "And they brought someone with them!"

Tom came from the barn where he and Curly had been cleaning stalls. Dinah stepped from the house onto the porch. Both waved a welcome to the trio as they rode into the yard.

"Turn the horses into the corral," Tom hollered. "There's hay and water. We can grain them after they cool down."

Sarah hurried after the arrivals and watched with wide eyes as Jim helped the young Lakota woman from her horse. Sarah's dog scampered about under the horse's feet nearly earning itself a good kick or stomp.

"Mommy, Jim brought a girl home," Sarah informed her mother. "She's pretty! She looks like an Indian though. Are you an Indian? What's your name? Are you staying for supper? Did you marry Jim?" She fired off the questions so quickly that nobody could possibly answer any of them. Then she saw the appaloosa and went silent. Her mouth dropped open, and she stepped cautiously forward. "Wow, she's beautiful," she breathed softly. "Can I pet her?" All other questions were forgotten.

"Raven Wing, this exuberant youngster with all of the questions is Sarah, Tom and Dinah's oldest. Little Tom is probably in the house. We'll make proper introductions shortly," Jim said.

"Sarah, yes, you may pet her. She really is quite gentle," Raven Wing replied to Sarah. "Have you ever seen an appaloosa before?"

Sarah inched forward, shaking her head. She tentatively stroked the young filly. "Does she have a name?" she asked quietly.

"I have not had time to name her yet. Perhaps, you have a name that would fit her?"

Sarah continued to stare at the markings across the horse's rump. She stroked the velvety muzzle and then rubbed the horse's cheek. "She's so beautiful," she repeated as she looked the filly over. She scrunched up her face in thought. "Splash," she cried out. "For what looks like paint splashed across her rump."

"Then Splash it shall be." Raven Wing smiled.

Sarah smiled too. She turned her attention back to the young woman. Splash was forgotten for the time being. "So?" asked Sarah.

"So what?" replied Raven Wing.

"You know. So my questions. Are you an Indian? What's your name? Are you staying for supper? Did you marry Jim? Well, I know your name now, but, you know, that stuff." She repeated the questions as though they should be obvious.

Jim and Preacher had stripped the gear from the horses and were proceeding to rub them down before turning them into the corral.

"Sarah, why don't you take Miss Raven Wing into the house and introduce her to your ma," Preacher said. He pointed to the bag containing the turkey. "Do you think the two of you can carry this into the house?"

Raven Wing smiled at Preacher. "I am sure that, with Sarah's assistance, we can manage. Come Sarah, and I shall try to answer your questions, if you pause long enough between them. To answer your first one, yes, I am Lakota, of the Sioux Nation..." Their voices faded as they proceeded to the house.

Curly poked his head out of the barn door and watched as Sarah led Raven Wing to the house. Even though she was in pain from her long ride, her steps were graceful. Her glossy black hair hung to the middle of her back in a single, long braid.

"Who's that?" Curly asked Jim and Preacher as they carried their tack into the barn.

"That's Miss Raven Wing," Preacher replied. "She's a guest for now. She was in a bad fix, and Jim, being Jim, jumped in with both feet." Preacher laughed as he remembered how Jim had, quite literally, jumped in with both feet.

"Huh?" Curly responded as he leaned on the pitchfork he had been using to clean the stalls. Tom stopped to listen too, as Preacher recounted the episode with a few minor embellishments to the captivated audience.

When he finished, Curly jammed the tines of the pitchfork into the last pile of manure and hitched up his pants. "Why that low down, thievin', no account skunk! I'll go straighten him out but good. Takin' advantage of a lady that away. He oughta be horsewhipped. Maybe I'll do just that." He started for the barn door.

Preacher gripped his arm and smiled. "Hold fast there Curly. There ain't no need for that. Someone done took the kinks outta his tail. Just simmer down."

Curly reluctantly complied. "It ain't right," he muttered. It shocked Tom and Jim to see the usually jovial puncher get so riled so quickly over someone he had yet to formally meet. It simply amused the older and wiser Preacher.

"No, it ain't right," agreed Preacher. "But he's already had his comeuppance. Besides, if you go racing off tonight, you'll miss quite a meal. No beef and beans tonight, but something special prepared by our guest."

"Is that what was in that bag that Sarah and her carried to the house?" Tom asked.

"Yes sir. And, if it's as good as last night's fixin's, you're in for a rare treat," Preacher replied.

When all the hands returned from their chores, they gathered for a meal different from what they were used to.

"That were right good Miss Dinah," a new hand named Boise said.

Dinah smiled. "I can take credit for the blackberry cobbler, but Miss Raven Wing made the turkey. I must admit, I've never seen one cooked in a ball of mud before, but it was delicious."

Boise glared at Raven Wing. "The cobbler was great Miss Dinah."

The other hands mumbled their compliments for the meal. All but Curly. He didn't mumble.

"That there turkey was delicious!" he exclaimed. "I ain't never had none better. No ma'am. Miss Raven Wing, I surely ain't. Miss Dinah that there cobbler was the toppin's fit for such a meal. That turkey though... you think I might could get another slice?"

"Mud turkey, and Curly wants more," Boise muttered contemptuously.

"Shut your yap Boise," Curly responded. "You wouldn't know good cookin' if'n it smacked you in the mouth. Which, by the way, this good cookin' did. Now, if you don't want more, I'll be happy to take your share too.

"You go right ahead. I'm finished, unless there's a bit more cobbler?" he asked hopefully.

"There is," said Tom. "But Miss Raven Wing is a guest in this house, and you will speak respectfully to and about her."

"Yeah. Okay. Now about that cobbler?"

"Help yourself. There's plenty for seconds," Dinah said.

Discussion ceased as the serious business of eating resumed. Finally, when belts were loosened and bellies were full, the men headed back outside to smoke or to the bunkhouse to play cards or read the well-worn newspaper and dime novels. All but Curly, that is. He tried to help with clearing the table or anything else until Dinah shooed him out of the kitchen and house.

"I'm sorry about Curly," Dinah said to Raven Wing as they washed the dishes. "He doesn't mind helping out, but tonight, he sure got under foot. I don't know what got into him."

Raven Wing smiled. "I think it was very sweet of him to offer to help. Most men would never stoop to do 'woman's work'." She grinned. "Not even James nor your Tom made such an offer."

"That's because they both know I'd run them out of the kitchen. If you ever saw either of them wash dishes, you would too." Both women laughed.

"Mommy, can I go outside?" Sarah asked. "Tommy is sleeping and Raven Wing is doing dishes like I usually do after dinner. I won't get into any trouble. I promise." She looked pleadingly at her mother.

"Okay, but don't wander off. It's almost bedtime for you, young lady," Dinah replied.

"I won't! Thank you Mommy." She dashed out the door.

Curly had stopped near the corral and was talking to Tom and Preacher. Jim had walked to his family's graves. He wanted to be alone during these visits. It was best to leave him to his quiet time of healing.

Sarah skipped up to the men. "Daddy, can I go look at the horses?"

"Sure, chipmunk. Just don't get them all riled up," her father responded.

"I won't. Curly, do you want to see Splash?" Curly was her favorite hand. He was always telling her stories and jokes. He was even teaching her to ride, with her father's permission of course.

"Splash? I ain't sure who that is, but sure, little cowgirl. Excuse me fellers. It appears I have important business looking over some horse or other." Curly quickly accepted Sarah's invitation.

She took his hand and half dragged him to the corral where the horses were milling around. She pointed to the appaloosa. "See. She's Splash. She's got paint splashed on her." Sarah laughed as she spoke. "Isn't she pretty? She's Miss Raven Wing's horse, or at least she rode her here."

"She sure is a right pretty filly," Curly confirmed. He pulled a carrot from his pocket and held it out to the appaloosa. Other horses, far more familiar with the gentle puncher, pushed forward first. He gave each a bit of the carrot. Finally, the appaloosa filly stretched her nose tentatively toward the proffered treat. Her velvety muzzle tickled Curly's calloused palm as she gently accepted the last bit of carrot from his hand.

"I ain't seen many appaloosas, but this one is, for sure, good stock. I'd love to have me a herd of 'em like her." The object of his attention nuzzled his hand looking for another treat. He pulled an apple he had picked earlier out of his pocket and held it out for her. Splash accepted it less tentatively than she did the carrot. "Sorry gal. That's all there is," Curly told the horse as she snuffled his pocket. He stroked her sleek neck.

"Well little cowgirl, this old cowpoke needs to turn in and get his beauty sleep. Not that it helps much, but when you're as old as me you need all the help you can get." Curly winked at Sarah as he spoke.

She giggled. "You're not old Curly. You gotta have gray hair for that, and you don't even have any hair yet."

"Well now, I like your way of thinkin' on that. If'n that's the case, I won't never grow old." Curly grinned.

"Sarah! Time for bed," her mother called.

"Coming Mommy. See, I need my beauty sleep too!" She laughed as she ran toward the house.

***

The next few weeks passed in a flurry of activity. Ranch work was never finished. Curly, who, unlike most cowhands, never seemed to mind doing work that required more than riding and roping, found more and more tasks near the ranch headquarters. A harness that needed mending became an emergency needing his immediate attention. The barn had also never been cleaner and the corral posts were straightened to perfection. He even volunteered to haul stones and build a flower garden near the house.

He always seemed to find some excuse to ask Raven Wing some inane question or to talk to her about what he was doing. One morning while on the range, Curly found a field of wildflowers and picked a handful. He found Raven Wing near the kitchen door and held the colorful bouquet out for her. "I saw these and kinda thought, you know, you might like them for the table or something." He blushed slightly.

"Curly, they are lovely. Thank you. They will definitely make the dinner table brighter. She smelled the flowers and smiled at Curly. "You do know though, Curly, that my father would expect ponies, not flowers. Of course, he was a Lakota warrior so that is to be expected. I think the flowers are lovely though. Much prettier than a horse." The smile never left Raven Wing's face as she turned to go back into the house.

Dinah hollered out the kitchen window. "Why Curly, you never brought me flowers for the table." She feigned indignation.

"Well, Miss Dinah, I, uh, well, ain't that Tom's job?" Curly stammered.

"Yes it is, and he does quite good at it, usually. But it has been a while since we've had flowers on the the table," Dinah replied. Curly could hear Raven Wing humming in the background.

Dinah came out onto the porch and spoke in a more serious tone. "Curly, you're a good hand and a hard worker, but what do you have to offer that girl? I know how much, or rather, how little you make. I'm not trying to embarrass you, but have you thought this through? Besides, she is Lakota. That could make things difficult for both of you."

A dark cloud of hurt and anger marred Curly's normally jovial face. "Miss Dinah, I been saving my money since I started working here. It ain't much, but I got a couple hunnert dollars, and two good saddle horses. Like you said, I ain't scared to work. I might not have much, but what I got is honest git. Her being Lakota don't bother me none at all. At least she knows where she come from, which is more than I can say for myself. My ma died when I was a sprout, and my pa left me with some folks when I was about nine or so. They were good Christian folks who taught me to be honest, work hard, and treat others kind and respectful.

They never taught me to hate no one nor to look down on others regardless of who or what they was. They were good folks. No, I ain't thunk it all through, but I know this. What I have to offer any woman is an honest man. Me! Nothing more, nothing less."

Curly turned away. "I better get back to work," he growled. Dust puffed up around his boots as he stomped to the barn. Trace chains could be heard rattling around. "C'mon Wally, you old lop eared no account. We got work to do, you and me. I reckon that's all a puncher and a mule is good for. Work! Not fit company for decent folks, I guess."

Wally brayed his response. Whether it was in agreement or not, Curly had no idea. Wally plodded along behind Curly's horse, content to follow this man and do whatever work was asked of him. Since their first encounter, the two had become almost friends. Curly was won over by the mule's intelligence, and Wally by the puncher's gentle but firm ways.

Dinah intercepted them as they started for the woods a half mile from the house. "Curly. I'm sorry," she said. "I never meant to hurt you. You're a good man. I just don't think you're…" she hesitated.

"Go on and say it! I ain't good enough! A cowpoke ain't good enough to hope and dream. I got work to do. Me and Wally will be out cutting wood. If I ain't back before dark, don't fret. I ain't worth the worry." He gigged his horse forward. "I never dreamed

I'd hear such from anyone on this ranch, Miss Dinah." He lifted his horse into a trot with Wally tagging along behind him. He wouldn't let her see the tears coursing down his weathered face.

CHAPTER 16

Curly threw himself into his work. Huge chips flew from the downed timber as he cut it to length. Wally hauled the logs doggedly to where Curly stacked them in piles to be loaded onto a wagon. From there, they would be taken to the ranch yard to be cut and stacked against the winter cold. Dusk came and he still worked until it was too dark to see.

Wearily, Curly tightened the cinch on his saddle horse and slowly led Wally back to the barn. The lantern still burned in the bunkhouse as he rubbed down the mule. He got a curry comb and began combing him. "You deserve a good rub down and some oats. You sure do. Why, you worked like two mules today."

"You look as though you did as well, Curly." Raven Wing's voice startled Curly and he dropped the comb.

"Aw, Miss Raven Wing, you sure surprised me," he said as he retrieved the curry comb. "All I did was chop a little wood. Poor ole' Wally here had to drag it out of the woods to be stacked. He sure enough earned his oats today." The sweat stains on his shirt belied his humble response.

"I do not think that even Wally believes that Curly. You are indeed a hard worker. I saved you some dinner," she said. "You must be hungry."

"Yes ma'am, I reckon I could eat a bite," Curly replied. He set the curry comb aside and patted Wally's hip. The mule contentedly munched some hay. "You go on with your meal, you old goat, whilst I eat mine. I'll finish combing you down once I build my strength back up." Wally stomped his foot, oblivious to the fact that he was only half curried.

Raven Wing produced a checkered napkin wrapped around two thick sandwiches and a large slice of apple pie. "I had to hide this," she said, indicating the pie. "Otherwise, someone else would have surely eaten it."

Curly smiled around a mouthful of sandwich. "Thank you kindly," he muttered.

"You should not talk with your mouth full, but you are very welcome. The others all had at least one slice of pie. I thought you should enjoy some as well," Raven Wing replied.

Curly swallowed. "I surely will."

Raven Wing sat quietly watching him eat. After a moment, she rose, walked to Wally, and rubbed his long ears. He twitched them and looked at her. Deciding that she posed no threat to him or his food, he resumed eating.

"May I say something?' she asked when Curly finished eating.

Curly resumed Wally's care. "Of course you can."

"I hope you will not be angry with me, but I overheard part of what Dinah said to you and part of what you said to her. I am terribly sorry, Curly. She is wrong."

"Miss Raven Wing, I'm right sorry you heard that stuff. I surely am. I shouldn't oughta talk to Miss Dinah that way, but well, I was downright mad clean through."

"Curly, I need to ask you something. It truly does not bother you that I am Indian? Men will call you *squaw man*. Will that not bother you?"

"Miss Raven Wing, I been called a whole lot worse things than that. Besides, you are every bit a lady. You know who you are. Plenty of fellers out here have no idea."

"You would not worry that I, being a savage, might someday decide to scalp you?" She giggled as she asked the question.

Curly laughed out loud. "Shucks no. I ain't got no hair for you to lift off'n my head, so I reckon I'm safe enough." Then he turned more serious. "Besides, you ain't no savage. You're a lady. A mix of gentleness and strength and beauty, the likes of which I ain't never seen before." His words startled them both. He because, except for being so tired, he would never have spoken them out loud. She, because she knew he meant them. She picked up another comb and began to brush the mule too.

They worked in silence until Wally was completely groomed. "Miss Raven Wing," Curly started to speak, but she put a finger to his lips.

"My name is Raven Wing. I think you may call me that rather than 'Miss Raven Wing' if you would like. I know I would like that. I do not call you 'Mister Curly,' do I?"

"Why, I do think I'd like that, as long it is not too forward of me, Raven Wing." He smiled at her.

"No, it would not be," she replied at last. Their eyes locked, saying things that words could not express. She watched quietly as he put away harness and tack. Then he extinguished the lantern and walked her back to the house.

"G'night Miss, I mean, Raven Wing."

"You have a good night as well, Mister Curly," she replied, and they both snickered.

Curly's feet barely touched the ground as he made his way to the bunkhouse. His body cried for sleep, but his mind was racing. Finally, sleep took him. In his dreams was a woman with raven black hair and laughter that sounded like angels singing to him.

He awoke to voices the next morning as dawn began to break. "I'm telling you boys, that's what I saw." It was Boise's voice. "Him and that squaw was sneaking outta the barn real late."

Curly had taken some good-natured ribbing for his clumsy courtship of the young Indian woman from his bunk mates, but Boise's was not good-natured. His comments were suggestive, and Curly did not appreciate them. His peaceful temperament had kept him from growing too angry. The others were just having fun, but Boise was demeaning.

"Maybe them flowers paid off," Boise continued. "I mean, squaws don't think nothing of....". That's when Curly hit him.

"You can shut your filthy mouth now, or I'll shut it for you!" Curly snarled. "You don't talk about a lady that way!"

Boise hoisted himself from the floor where he sprawled. Blood flowed from his mouth. "Hit a man when he ain't lookin'. That's what I'd expect from a squaw-man. Must be I was close to the mark." Curly's next punch blackened Boise's left eye, but this time, Boise responded with a blow of his own.

Shouts erupted as the two men grappled. Boise had twenty pounds on Curly, but Curly's fury would not be abated. For every blow he received, he delivered two of his own. The men crashed through the bunkhouse door and spilled into the dirt outside. The ranch hands followed, hollering encouragement and advice. Dust rose around the combatants as fists struck flesh.

The door to the house flew open. Jim and Tom burst onto the scene. Each grabbed one of the adversaries and pulled them apart.

"What's the meaning of this?" Tom snarled. "You know we don't allow fighting amongst our own hands. Especially in view of the house. Somebody best speak up fast."

Boise glared at Curly through puffy eyes. Curly glared back, ready to resume hostilities. "Curly hauled off and slugged me for no reason whatsoever," Boise mumbled.

"Curly? I find that hard to believe. Somebody better start talking sense," Jim said.

Bob, one of the older punchers, spoke up. "Curly threw the first punch, but I don't reckon he thought it was for no good reason."

Tom looked at Curly, who was still seething. "I'll not repeat what he said," stated the bald puncher. "But he said some insulting things about Miss Raven Wing."

"And you took exception to them?" Tom asked.

"Yessir, I reckon I did," Curly responded defiantly. He was battered, but Boise looked like he had been dragged through the Badlands behind a wild horse.

"Well Boise, what do you have to say?" Jim asked.

"I was just talking about that squaw sneaking around was all." Tom caught Curly just before blows began again.

"By 'squaw', I take it you mean our guest, Miss Raven Wing?" continued Jim.

"She's the only one on this ranch I know of," replied Boise hotly. "I don't know what all of the hullabaloo is about. She's just a squaw."

"Well. Let me tell you then." Jim spun Boise so he could look him in the eye. "First of all, she's a guest, and ALL guests are treated with respect here. You have made insulting comments more than once. Second, she may be the only Indian woman on this ranch today, but later this year, a band of Cheyenne will stop by for a visit. A few years back they saved my life and are welcome here. They would take great exception to their women being insulted. Generally, they kill a man for that. And third, I despise gossip."

"The way I see it, you have two choices. Make peace with Curly and keep your mouth shut about Miss Raven Wing or draw your time. You can decide after breakfast. I'll send no man away hungry."

"Curly, I see you have a door to rehang," Jim said, looking at the broken bunkhouse door. "If Boise decides to make peace, this is over now. Understand?"

"Yeah Jim. I hear you clear as a bell," Curly responded.

"Good! Now everybody get cleaned up and ready to start the day. There's plenty to do so save your strength for working."

Boise drew his pay after packing away a healthy breakfast. "The grub and pay is good, but I don't figure to work for no Injun lover," he said before mounting and riding north. The rest of the crew fanned out to start the day's work while Curly started to rehang the bunkhouse door. Boise was a good enough hand, but he could be querulous. He wouldn't be missed.

"Curly," said Tom. "After you fix that door, I want you to catch up with Bob up to the northwest. You'll find him up by Bell's Creek where it forks. He's got some stock up there he could use some help with.

"I'll get there as soon's I can," replied Curly.

CHAPTER 17

Jim rode out alone to an area of the ranch with few cattle. The area wasn't ideal for them, but it wasn't cows he was looking for anyway. Today, he was heading to the gold claim nestled back in the rugged hills on the back of the range. Although few of the hands knew he occasionally rode this range, none knew why. There was too much work for them to do to worry about the boss's comings and goings. Only Tom and Preacher knew of the rich gold deposit and where it might be.

It was a cloudless day as Jim rode his favorite mount, Buck, towards his destination. The horse's coloring blended into the background and his smooth gate made riding him a pleasure. Not only that, but Buck was wild bred and was well aware of his surroundings. He had warned Jim of hidden dangers more than once. Today, there were none.

As the day wore on, Jim worked farther upstream than normal, eventually losing all trace of color. Then, he worked back downstream until he found the densest concentration of gold. At that point, he looked around for the possible source.

About two hundred yards to one side of the stream he was panning, a sheer rock face rose a hundred feet or more. Its craggy surface was worn from years of heat, ice, snow, and rain. Only a small trickle flowed from it now, but in the early spring, the runoff from melting snow would bring torrents of water from the rock face to the stream carrying mineral deposits along with the mud.

After collecting enough gold for their immediate needs, he decided to do some exploration. Following one of the dry washes, he worked his way toward the stone tower. He watched for signs of gold as he worked his way uphill toward the cliff. He stared at the cracks and fissures, looking for any indicator of the source of the gold.

When he reached the face of the cliff, he noticed one of the fissures had a vein of quartz in it, ribboned with gold. In another crack, some twenty feet higher, he could see another deposit of quartz filled with ribbons of the yellow metal. It didn't require an assayer to know this was a rich strike.

Jim whistled softly. "Pa, you never knew how rich you were," he said quietly. He thought for a moment. "Then again, maybe you did and wanted to keep things quiet. I sure never expected this. The question now is what do we do about it?"

Jim hiked back down to the creek, hiding his trail as best as he could. It would be impossible to hide it completely, but it would take an expert tracker plenty of time to follow it, and for what purpose? He figured his trail was hidden well enough for now. He wasn't worried about his hands. They were all honest cowhands and had no reason to be up this way. There were others, though.

He stopped by the stream and stowed his tools. Then, he sat to contemplate. He legally owned all the land where he found the gold. His father had purchased or filed on all of it plus much more. Buck shoved his nose against Jim's shoulder interrupting his thoughts.

"What do you think?" Jim asked the horse. "Maybe my dad did know how rich he was. Maybe he just didn't quite know what to do with it either. What do you think, Buck? Maybe that's why he brought it out a little at a time. Bring out too much at once and folks get curious." Jim rose and stroked the horse's neck. "We'd best get back now. We've got a lot to contemplate."

He rode into the ranch yard just as the hands were preparing for the evening meal. He had taken extra time today to hide his trail. Something was nagging him. On the return trip, he felt watching eyes on him. Maybe it was the discovery of the source of the gold that had him feeling jumpy, but he couldn't shake the feeling.

CHAPTER 18

That night, Jim confided in Tom and Preacher. Tom was his partner, and Preacher's wisdom would be welcome. They sat around the table after the hands had retired.

"I'm not an expert, but that rock face is where the gold comes from. That quartz was literally full of ribbons of the stuff," Jim said soberly.

"You mean, we're rich?" Tom exclaimed.

"Slow down a mite there," Preacher said. "I reckon Jim's got some things in his craw about this that are troubling him."

"To answer your question Tom, we could be. But, as my dad used to say, 'Finding gold and keeping it are two different things.' If we aren't careful, we'll have people crawling all over the range, digging it all up looking for gold, and ruining the range. They'd foul the water and trample the grass hunting for gold. The ranch owns the land where the gold is, but that wouldn't stop them if they have the fever."

Tom responded. "Yeah, I figure you're right at that."

"If we decide to go after the gold, there's some things we need to get straight from the git go. I'm quite confident my father knew about the gold. That's why he bought or filed on all the land where the gold is. The thing is, we need to be able to develop it without destroying the range or starting a range war to protect it."

Tom's initial exuberance had settled some, but the thought of being rich had an allure even for him. "So, how do we do that? Can we do both? I mean the ranch and the gold? I say, we go get the gold now and worry about the cows later." The fever had bitten.

"No Tom," Jim replied quietly. "I'll not destroy all my father built over years for some shiny metal." He held up his hand as Tom began to protest. "Hear me out. I want Preacher's thoughts too. The gold will still be there in a few days while we think this through."

"He's right Tom, and you know it," Preacher interjected. "God said, 'The love of money is the root of all evil.' I've seen many a good man destroy themselves and lose all they had chasing after gold. Don't let it get its claws into you."

Tom sat quietly at Preacher's mild rebuke. "Yeah, I guess you're right. It just seemed so easy. The gold's there so let's go get it. I reckon it can blind you to what's really important."

Right then, Dinah walked into the room with Little Tom to give his daddy a hug and kiss goodnight. Sarah followed suit. "I'll heat you men up some coffee," Dinah said. "As soon as I get these two tucked into bed." She took the children into their bedroom to tuck them in. Tom watched them with a dreamy look in his eyes.

"Now you've been reminded what's important. What do you say we find out what Jim's got in mind?" Preacher asked Tom.

Tom returned his attention to the conversation at hand. "So, what do you have in mind?" he asked.

Jim was silent for a moment. When he finally spoke, it was in a quiet tone. "I'm thinking we need an expert. A mining engineer or someone who knows how to extract the gold without fouling the land or the water. We'll need some samples. I don't know where to find someone like that without drawing a lot of attention, but that's something I don't want."

"Someplace close by would draw attention like cow pies draw flies," observed Preacher. "Somewhere, like maybe Denver, would be better. A longer trail, for sure, but not so likely to raise eyebrows there. Maybe a better chance to find a mining engineer there too."

"That's a long trip," said Tom. "What do we do in the meantime? And, who would go?"

Jim replied. "I'm thinking, I couldn't ask you to go, Tom. You've got Dinah and the kids. I couldn't take you away from them. That wouldn't be fair to you or to them. Besides, you know far better than I do what needs done around this ranch, and we do have the ranch to keep running. Preacher and I going off like we do would also be much less likely to raise questions than you going. Until we get back, I guess just keep running the ranch as usual."

Tom sat in thought. "That sounds reasonable to me. The gold's been there a long time. I don't reckon a few more weeks will make any difference. Besides, Dinah would have my hide tacked to the barn door if I took off for that long."

The men laughed and began making more specific plans. Dinah came from the kitchen with a pot of steaming coffee and some sandwiches. "So, what are you boys conspiring about now? Cows can't be that interesting, can they?" She smiled as she spoke and settled in close to Tom after pouring coffee for all.

"I'm glad you joined us Sweetheart," he said, putting an arm around her shoulder and pulling her closer. He took a deep breath. "Mmm, you smell good."

"You're just saying that to get on my good side," she replied.

"I haven't found a bad side yet." Then, Tom grew more serious. "Jim and Preacher are going to be gone for a few weeks. They're taking a trip to Denver on business."

She looked at them askance. They were alone in the house. Raven Wing had gone out to talk to Curly, and the other hands had headed for the bunkhouse.

"You know that I bring in some gold from the hills from time to time when we need it," Jim began. "Well, it turns out, at least from what I could see, there's a lot more than what we've been thinking. I found some quartz up in the hills full of ribbons of high grade, unless I miss my guess."

"That's good news, isn't it?" she asked.

"Potentially very good news," Jim responded. "The problem is, how do we get it out without wrecking the ranch in the process? My father worked hard to build this place, and I won't see it destroyed for the sake of some shiny yellow rocks. We need some expert advice and the best place to find a mining engineer is in Denver. It's a long trip, but we can ride the rails and save some time."

"When will you be leaving?" Dinah asked.

"Soon's possible," Preacher interjected. "I figure the boy wants some samples to take with us, so we'll head up in the morning and gather a few. Then we'll head off to Helena to catch the rail cars. We oughten to be gone too long."

CHAPTER 19

While the owners were discussing Jim's and Preacher's trip, Curly and Raven Wing were also in earnest conversation.

"Curly, you should not have fought Boise. Look at yourself. You are sore and battered, and for what purpose?" She gently touched his bruised cheekbone. A dark purple blotch marked one side of his face. His body carried many other bruises from the morning's fight, but he ignored them.

"Raven Wing," he said firmly. "No man talks 'bout a lady like that in my presence. 'Specially the gal I care about. What kinda man would I be if I let such talk go unanswered?"

"But you are hurt," she responded.

Curly's lips twisted into a grin. "So's he." Then he winked at her. "Besides. I been hurt worse falling off a log. Fact being, I busted my arm once doing just that."

They stood close together in silence listening to the whippoor-will. Curly shyly took her hand in his own calloused hand. She looked down, slightly surprised. Then she entwined her fingers in his. Unsure of what to say, she gently leaned against his shoulder.

"I been thinking," he said quietly. He stared at the half-moon slowly rising on the horizon. "You said your pa would want horses not flowers."

She looked at him questioningly. "But my father is dead."

"True, but he'd want a man that could provide for you before he'd let you marry, wouldn't he? I figure he'd be right about that too. Miss Dinah was right too."

She stepped back and looked questioningly at him. "Curly, what are you saying? You are a good and honest man. That is enough." He could read the hurt and uncertainty in her eyes. He held tight to her hand as she started to pull away.

"Please, hear me out. I'm serious about this. I been thinking all day. That's a heap of thinking for me." He grinned as she started to relax.

"Yes Curly. What have you been thinking about all day?" She asked.

"Well now, your pa. How many horses would a Sioux warrior want for his daughter? And what would it take to start a small place of our own?" He looked deep into her eyes. "I don't know the answer to the first question."

She interrupted him. "I do. He would want five horses. All good stock, of course."

"Five!" he blurted out. "Why that ain't nearly enough for a gal like you." He took her other hand in his free hand. "I figured twenty and all good stock. No scrubs. I know where I can get 'em too. They're wild but sturdy stuff."

She looked confused. "As I said though, my father is dead. You do not need to bring horses."

"I know that, but for the sake of his daughter, I figure I can collect them horses to give us a start. It'll take some doin' but anything worthwhile takes some work." His voice grew excited, and she could see a sparkle in his eyes. "Maybe a month or two to trap enough. Maybe I can get Tom and Jim to let me break some here in exchange for a few head." He looked deep into her eyes. "Maybe five horses." He laughed. "If'n you'll have me, I need to talk to the boss."

"Curly, I shall be here when you return." Then she laughed. "You would give my father twenty horses for me? Never in my clan has anyone given such a gift."

"I'd give that, and my best saddle," he said, the grin still on his face. "So, I reckon I got some work to do for myself, or us, now." He walked her back to the house where she gently kissed his bruised cheek.

"I shall see you at breakfast." She went into the house, leaving Curly to contemplate all that had just happened.

"Well, you old cue ball," he said to himself. "You done lassoed yourself quite a gal. Now, you need to do things right and do more than dream. You got work aplenty to do." He made his way back to the bunkhouse for the night.

During breakfast, the extra attention given to Curly by Raven Wing was lost on no one.

"Well daggone. If I knowed all it took to get extra flapjacks was to get drug through the brush by a horse, I'da done that ages ago," quipped Toby. Toby was as thin as a rail, but he could put away more chow than any other two men on the ranch.

"Toby, you'd kiss a skunk if'n you thought you'd get more grub." Bob laughed. "Now me, I reckon it was them table decorations he brought a couple of days ago."

Reno, a red-faced puncher barely old enough to shave, and who had never been to Nevada, chimed in. "Yep. Bring flowers and get kicked by a mule. That usually works for me every time I tried it."

"Whad'ya mean Reno?" You wouldn't know flowers from poison oak," Toby responded. Only two weeks earlier, Reno had found himself in a patch of poison oak. The itching had only recently subsided.

"Well, I never said I tried it much." Reno laughed.

"I must say," Dinah remarked. "This is the most lively I've seen this bunch before noon in a long time. I must learn the secret of giving you this much energy so some work gets done." The whole table laughed. None of them ever shirked their duties.

When the crew began to disperse for their daily tasks, Curly stayed behind. "I need to talk to you boss," he said to Tom. "Jim too if he's got a minute." Tom and Jim stopped on their way from the house and Preacher continued to the corral to saddle up for the day.

"You look pretty serious Curly," Tom said.

Curly looked down at his boots. Raven Wing came from the house and stood beside him. He took her hand and looked up at Tom and Jim. "What I got to say is serious Tom. Ya'll have been good to me. Better'n I deserve after how we met that first day Jim." He smiled slightly, remembering their first encounter with him sprawled on his back and Wally, the mule, standing on his coat, pinning him to the ground and staring down at him.

"You're a good hand Curly. None better or harder working," Jim replied. "What's this all about?"

"Thanks Jim. That don't make this no easier. You see, I got me a dream. Right now, that's all I got." Raven Wing gave his hand a gentle squeeze. "Well, I reckon a bit more'n a dream." He blushed. "But for that dream, I need to kinda make my own way.

I'd appreciate it considerable if you'd let me take some time away and watch over Miss Raven Wing while I'm gone."

"She said her pa wouldn't be all that impressed with flowers. He'd want horses. I reckon he's gone on to his reward, but he'd be right. I gotta be able to take care of her and provide if," he looked down at his boots once again. "Well, if'n I'm gonna marry her," he blurted out.

Dinah had come out onto the porch after finishing the breakfast dishes and heard the last part. "Curly! Raven Wing!" she exclaimed. "Are you serious? When did this all happen?" All of her doubts about Curly disappeared in the excitement.

"Miss Dinah, I reckon it's been coming on for a while now. I reckon I owe you a bit of thanks for making me see that I need to do more than dream. I need to be more than a cownurse if'n I want a family." Curly looked from her to Tom.

"So, what are you saying Curly?" broke in Tom.

"I know where I can get some horses. Good stock, especially for mustangs. I plan to gather some and start a small spread of my own somewhere." He looked at Raven Wing standing by his side. "Well, our own."

"I got some wages comin' and I got some money saved up. I'd like to buy a few head of cattle from you too, if'n you can spare some breeding stock. I figure that would give us a start. For now though, I'd just want you to watch over Raven Wing whilst I'm gone."

"You don't even need to ask, Curly. Of course we'll look out for her. She's our guest and our friend. You look out for yourself. That, and I am truly sorry for what I said the other day. I was wrong.

Can you forgive me?" Dinah said before either of the men could respond.

"Thank you kindly, Miss Dinah. And don't you think nothin' about what was said. It made me ponder," replied the smooth pated puncher.

"We'll miss you, but we'll get by. With Boise gone, you gone and Jim and Preacher gone, we'll be a little shorthanded, but with the calving done, we'll manage just fine." Tom extended his hand to Curly who took it in a firm grip. "You bring in some good saddle stock and maybe we could work out a trade for some cow critters. We can always use good remounts."

"Sure thing Tom," Curly replied. "I reckon I best get started." He headed to the corral and dabbed a loop on each of his personal mounts. He tossed his rig onto the back of a steeldust gelding and led it and his second mount, a long-legged roan stud, from the enclosure.

Raven Wing stood nearby watching him. "You be careful my Curly. I shall miss you."

He winked at her. "I'll be back before you know I'm gone. And I'll be bringing back at least twenty of the prettiest ponies you ever did see. Shucks, you won't even have time to miss me." He turned as if to mount and then spun and swept her into an embrace.

"I already do," she whispered to him. The tears began to run down her face.

Curly swung aboard and rode southwest from the ranch. He turned at the crest of a hill and waved. Raven Wing waved in return and watched until Curly could no longer be seen.

"Come with me," Sarah said, tugging on Raven Wing's hand. "I want to show you something." She too had watched Curly ride out of sight.

Raven Wing wiped the tears from her eyes. She smiled at Sarah. "Very well, let us see the sight you want me to see."

Sarah led the way to the chicken coop where peeps and cheeps could be heard. "See," Sarah said. "That hen sat on her eggs and now the chicks are hatching. Look, I'll show you one." She reached beneath the hen, who pecked at her arm, to draw out a fuzzy yellow chick. "Aren't they pretty?" She placed the tiny ball of fuzz into Raven Wing's hand.

Raven Wing touched the tiny chick to her face. "They are so soft, but soon they will be out in the yard where I can see them every day. Why did you want to show them to me now?"

"Because you seemed sad about Curly and I thought they would make you smile. Don't you worry. Curly'll be back before you know it. Just watch and see!" Sarah carefully took the chick from Raven Wing and returned it to the nest. The mother hen watched suspiciously.

"I'll tell you a secret, but you have to promise not to tell," Sarah whispered, as they left the hen house.

Raven Wing looked at her questioningly. "Promise," Sarah said sternly.

"Of course, I shall keep your secret. I promise."

"I've always wanted a big sister. I mean, being a big sister to Tommy is great, but he isn't old enough for some things and he's a boy so, you know, he can't do girl things. And Mommy, well, she's Mommy. You know what I mean?" Sarah pressed on without giving Raven Wing a chance to reply. "I mean, you can share your secrets with a big sister, and she can share her secrets with you, and you can talk to her about anything."

"Can you not do that with your mother?" Raven Wing asked.

"Well, yeah. Most times, but it's more fun with a sister, I think. I mean, I've never had a sister, but I'm pretty sure it's more fun with a sister." Sarah took a breath.

"What could you not talk to your mother about that you could talk to a sister about?" Raven Wing asked.

"Well, like if a boy tried to kiss me or something like that. I could tell my sister, but mommies don't know about that kind of stuff." She wrinkled her nose.

Raven Wing laughed. "I am not so sure mommies do not know about that kind of stuff. So, tell me, did some boy try to kiss you last time you were in town?"

"Naw. But Davy Peterson tried to catch me. I'm too fast for him."

"That is good. You are too young for boys to try to kiss."

"That's what Curly said too. I was gonna marry him but he's too old. Besides, he acts like a big brother, and who wants to marry their big brother? But he's funny and really nice. Are you going to marry him?" Sarah asked innocently.

Raven Wing paused. "Yes. As soon as he returns, we shall make plans."

"That's good. He needs someone to take care of him. He does all right, but he's a boy, and you know how boys are." Sarah gazed intently at Raven Wing. "Will you be my big sister?"

The young woman smiled at Sarah. "Only if you will be my little sister, so I can tell someone if a boy tries to kiss me."

Sarah giggled. "I think Curly would punch them in the nose if they tried. Unless it was Tommy. He kisses everybody." She rolled her eyes.

"Why did Curly go away this morning with two horses? He usually just rides one."

"I am afraid it was something I said," was Raven Wing's quiet reply.

"He's not mad at you?" Sarah asked apprehensively.

Raven Wing laughed. "No, he is not angry with me. He is just doing what a man will do. He will come back just as he said." She stopped and looked soberly in the direction Curly had ridden.

"You're worried about him, I can tell. But you don't need to worry. Curly can ride anything with hair so he won't fall off his horse. And if he said he'll be back, he will. He don't lie. Not never!"

"You are a very wise young girl," said Raven Wing. "I am worried about him, but I know God can protect him."

"You know God?" Sarah asked the question with a touch of awe.

"Of course. I went to a school that was run by a missionary where I learned about God and how Jesus died on a cross. But, He did not stay dead. He rose again. The God who can do that can keep my Curly safe. Still, I shall worry."

"Why don't you ask God to help you not worry?"

"He already has," responded Raven Wing. "He has given me a little sister to tell my secrets to." They both laughed.

CHAPTER 20

Jim and Preacher rode to the gold claim by a circuitous route. They kept their course as hidden as possible and tried to make their trail tangled and confused. Now that they had found the source of the gold in the streams and decided to develop it, they wanted to keep the location secret until they were ready to proceed. They didn't want to start a gold rush and destroy the countryside.

"Twenty horses," mused Preacher. "That boy must've sunburned his brain."

Jim had been contemplating their path. "What are you muttering about?" He glanced at the older man.

"Curly," Preacher responded. The piebald mare he was riding shook her head disturbing the deer flies that had landed on her nose. "Twenty horses is a tall order. Of course, he is a determined feller." He smiled wistfully. "To be young and sure."

"I'm not sure about Curly, but we need to get a move on." Jim nudged the dun he was riding to a trot and the two men fell silent. The sound of their horse's hooves was muffled by the thick bed of pine needles. Trees hid their movements in shadows, and the pine needles left no sign of their passing.

When they reached the cusp of the valley, where the gold was, Jim halted. Preacher halted beside him in the shadows and the two surveyed the area. Nothing appeared out of place, but Jim felt like something was wrong. He had a feeling that something had been there that did not belong. He dismounted and switched his boots for the moccasins he kept in his saddle bags.

"You got your hackles up boy. What is it?" Preacher asked quietly.

"I don't know. It just feels wrong," was Jim's whispered reply. "I'm going to slip down and scout around. I don't see or hear anything out of place, but it feels wrong. I'll whistle you in if it's all clear."

"And I'll come a foggin' it if things get exciting for you," Preacher replied. "Let's pray they don't go that way."

Jim slipped silently from their vantage point into the surrounding forest. He was soon invisible among the lush vegetation. Several minutes later, Preacher spotted him moving forward cautiously along the valley floor. The only other movement he saw was a large porcupine waddling into the wood line.

Fifteen minutes after leaving Preacher's side, Jim let out a sharp whistle. Preacher urged his mount forward leading Jim's dun.

"So, it was just a feeling then?" Preacher asked when he joined Jim.

"I'm not sure. Everything looks like it was when I left it. Nothing seems to be missing." Jim shook it off. "Maybe I'm just getting jumpy. I'll feel a lot better once this trip is over and we get back with some answers."

"Well, let's get some rocks so we can get some answers then."

The two men got out the pick from where Jim had left it, and Preacher produced a hammer and chisel. These would be the best tools for collecting the samples they wanted.

As Jim gripped the handle of the pick, he felt several rough grooves in the hickory handle. "Well, what in Billie blue blazes?"

"Maybe that explains your feeling that something wasn't right. A porky pine got to gnawing on that. I saw one waddling away while you was working your way down here."

"Well, that ain't good. He'll be back and gnaw the handle clean in two! I reckon there's no help for it now. Let's get what we came for and deal with the porcupine situation when we have time."

"Lead on. Let's get this done and then have some coffee," Preacher replied.

Jim led the way to the rock face where he had discovered the gold deposits. Preacher took a close look and whistled. "That there sure does look like the mother lode," he exclaimed.

"And if you look up about twenty feet, you'll see another vein of quartz as rich as this one. I think a couple of samples from each should be plenty to let us know what we have. I'll climb up to the higher one if you don't mind prying a few chunks out down here," Jim said.

"Climb away youngster. Just be careful you don't drop no rocks nor that hammer onto my poor head."

"I'll be careful to toss the rocks out away from the cliff so they don't land on your noggin. Probably break them to pieces if they were to do that," Jim said with a grin.

Preacher retorted, "With that hard head of yourn, you could just butt the rocks up there and knock 'em loose. Course, you'd probably start an avalanche, so you best use the hammer instead. Now climb on up there and quit insulting your betters."

Jim scrambled up the stone face. Once safely out of Preacher's reach he hollered, "I don't know about anyone here being my betters, but you are definitely my elder and my pa taught me to respect my elders."

"Your elders is your betters! Now hush up and get to work," Preacher responded.

After only a short time, the two men had sufficient ore samples for their needs. Preacher then produced a coffee pot and began brewing some of the dark liquid while Jim took a piece of paper and drew a rough sketch of the stone wall where the gold was found. It was no work of art, but it would suffice for the purpose of showing a mining engineer what they were thinking. He was sure many had seen far more crude drawings.

The men finished their coffee and a lunch of cold meat and warm beans. They set about erasing all signs of their small fire and hid the tools they would not need in the cache where they had been stored earlier. Jim did his best to make it impregnable for a porcupine in hopes of his pick not needing a new handle on his return. When they packed up to depart, neither man knew that there was more than one "porcupine" nearby.

CHAPTER 21

Small Porcupine had remained hidden at the edge of the woods where he could observe without being seen. Earlier that morning, he had followed one of Jim's tangled trails into the valley. Jim had sensed his presence but never saw him nor any sign of him. Small Porcupine was indeed an excellent tracker and warrior. Even so, he had succumbed to the curse of the white man's brew. He figured to make enough from this foray to stay drunk a good, long time. He could almost taste the burn of the liquor, but for now he was working. He never drank when working. That was one of his absolutes.

When he arrived near the claim, he settled in to watch. His Blackfoot heritage had instilled in him a strong degree of patience. Watching the two white men collect their samples, he knew he had made the right decision.

He watched the two pack the samples of rock, confident he had found what his employers wanted. He waited until they had been gone for at least an hour before moving in for a closer examination. Something about the way the two moved about and remained alert at all times warned the diminutive warrior that attempting anything before they left would be counterproductive at best and quite possibly fatal. His own hunger and thirst would have to wait.

When he finally left his hiding place, he slid to the stream to slake his thirst before exploring closer. He examined the tool cache while his eyes continued roving for danger. The instinct of countless generations of hunters and warriors made him constantly vigilant. After finding nothing of interest in the cache, the watcher turned his attention to the escarpment a short distance up the slope.

He walked confidently to the rock face and searched for signs of work. The fresh tool marks and pieces of quartz lying on the ground were easy to see. He looked up and saw the area where Jim had chipped at the quartz formation. He scooped up several small pieces of the gold ribboned quartz to take with him. They were the proof he had found what his employers wanted.

The Blackfoot warrior turned and trotted from the valley. His horse was hobbled a few miles away. It felt good to stretch his legs. This was indeed a good day, he thought as he jogged along while chewing on a hunk of jerked venison. His thirst and hunger assuaged, he was content for now. He would spend this night like almost every other night of his life, sleeping on the ground under the stars. Tomorrow would be early enough to report his findings. The gold was going nowhere, and if it did, that was not his concern. He had been hired to find it, and that is what he had done.

Small Porcupine trotted his scraggly-looking pony into town well after dark. His employers had told him not to arrive during daylight hours. They had no desire for others to learn of their plans nor of their involvement with this renegade Indian. For his part, Small Porcupine was confident his information would make him welcome. He had no idea why the white men acted so foolishly about the yellow metal. It was far too soft to be of much use. He didn't care either, as long as he got the money he was promised.

McCabe opened the back door to the office when Small Porcupine lightly tapped on it. "What took you so long?" He growled. "We been waiting days for this information. It better be good!"

Nonplussed, the diminutive Indian stepped into the dimly lit room. His stoic expression never wavered. "I found what you seek," he said, and displayed the fragments of gold-bearing quartz. "You pay me now, and I will tell you where it is."

McCabe started forward as if to overpower the smaller man. "Why you lousy redskin. I should just beat it out of you."

"You may try," responded the smaller man as he slipped his knife from its sheath. "Some have tried. They are gone. I am not."

"Relax. We promised to pay for the information, and we shall do just that." The third occupant of the room had spoken with a calm authority. "No need to argue among friends."

He turned his attention to the spy. "Can you draw us a map? If you can do that you will be paid, just as we promised."

"I can draw a map," Small Porcupine stated. "You pay me and I draw it. You not pay, I not draw."

"We said we'd pay you and we will." Simmons pulled out a sheet of paper and a stub of pencil and handed them to the Indian. "Now if you would be so kind."

Small Porcupine accepted the pencil and paper and a crude map quickly took shape. "Yellow metal is here." Small Porcupine indicated with his middle finger. The map was not perfect, but it would suffice to get the white men to the gold. That was all their agreement required.

"You're sure?' asked the burlier of the two outlaws. "You wouldn't lead us astray now, would you?"

"Even you can follow a map white man," the Indian stated scornfully. "If you don't believe me, go and see, then pay, but it is true."

"I reckon your word is good enough for us," said Simmons. "Here's what we agreed to. Now get on out of here and forget all about this."

"Forget what?" Small Porcupine laughed, accepting the agreed on amount. "I forget already."

As he slipped out the back door, he looked down at his ill-gotten gains and grinned. Then he looked up and his grin faded. Realization set in. His face contorted and he clenched his teeth attempting to draw his knife. The cudgel fell on his skull, crushing it before he could raise a defense. His last thought before entering Hell was that he had been a fool. But then, Hell is full of fools.

The man wielding the club stepped from the shadows and retrieved the money pouch from the dead spy. He smiled down at his victim and calmly stepped over the body. He would dispose of that later, but for now he needed to return the funds to his employer. He had no desire to suffer the fate of the prostrate form in the alley. A fate he would surely suffer if he betrayed those who hired him. He calmly opened the back door to the office.

"Here you go. Not sure what this is all about, but then I don't need to know. I'll pick up my twenty dollars later. I need to get rid of that little heathen before he stinks up the alley." He smiled and stepped back out into the night air.

"You see McCabe, a bargain is a bargain, even if it is made with a savage. It's always a good thing to pay what is owed."

"And he kept his part of the bargain by forgetting, permanently." Both men laughed.

CHAPTER 22

Curly's travels took him through rough country and into Idaho. He traveled to a remote basin he had passed through some years before and had seen dozens of wild horses that looked better than most mustangs he had ever seen. Bigger than the usual broomtails farther south, these horses were sturdy and clean limbed. That was what he was after.

Riding slowly across the thick grass carpeting the floor of the basin, Curly saw abundant evidence of the wild horses he sought. The rich clover and blue stem grasses would provide better than average food for the hundreds of wild horses that roamed the area. His own horses cropped contentedly on the ample fodder as Curly scanned the lush meadows.

There were no horses to be seen, but that did not discourage Curly. Such rich graze was far too good for the herds to leave willingly for too long. Fresh water was something they would need, and the herd stallions would lead their mares, colts and fillies to the safe drinking water in the basin. With such a bountiful food supply and fresh water available, they would inevitably lead their herds back.

The sun began to sink in the west as Curly set up camp in the forest near the edge of the vast grassland. He found a tiny stream to meet the needs of himself and his horses. As darkness fell, a plan began to take shape.

Curly awoke to the sound of hooves in the meadow and his own horses fidgeting around. It was still dark, but at least one group of horses seemed to have returned to the lush forage. Curly rose quietly and moved toward his own horses to quiet them. His gentle touch and reassuring presence worked well for the gelding, but the stallion was not so easily calmed. The herd contained several mares and his instincts were still strong. He had not been that long out of the wilds himself.

It took several minutes before the big chestnut was calm enough for Curly to move to the edge of the clearing and attempt to see the mustangs. Because it was before dawn all that was visible to him were dim shapes and shadows. Curly's best guess was that this herd contained about forty horses, but he could not tell for sure. Forty was double what he had promised Raven Wing and that was only one herd. What if there were more and larger herds? He licked his lips in anticipation of the new day.

By the time the sun crested the eastern horizon, Curly was in the saddle slowly working his way along the edge of the trees.

He did not try to get close to the wild horses but walked his mount in the shadows cast by the wood line. Trying to get closer would spook the mustangs and maybe keep them away for a long time. Man was the one thing that all wild things feared. What he wanted now was simply an idea of how many there were and what kind of shape they were in. This morning, he rode the gelding, unsure of the stallion's dependability after his earlier fidgeting. Perhaps bringing an ungelded horse had not been the wisest of choices, but since he only owned two horses it left very few options.

The early morning sun revealed the herd through a light fog. Their sleek coats shined with the morning dew. A young charcoal gray stallion with white spots across his rump stood guard on a slight rise. Curly took out the binoculars he had brought with him and studied the animals from hundreds of yards away. His gelding quietly cropped the lush grass in the shadows, oblivious to his master's plans.

A soft whistle escaped Curly's lips. "Hey, horse," he whispered to his mount. "Those are some nice-looking nags out there." He looked again and noticed a few foals with similar markings to those on the leader of the herd. Every other color of horse also seemed to be present. "Looks to be about thirty or so out there," Curly continued softly.

Suddenly, the appaloosa stallion tossed his head and snorted a warning to his harem. He spun and started them away from where Curly sat. Once they were started, he swung behind the herd and urged those that were flagging to greater speed with nips from his powerful teeth.

Curly was sure he had not been close enough for the herd to have seen him, and the wind was still so he doubted his scent had gotten to them either. He pondered what would have set them off so quickly.

From behind him came the cry of his own stallion. He turned in the saddle to see a large, brown shape lumbering toward his camp from the meadow. A grizzly bear stood on its hind legs to gaze around and to try to catch a scent. The smell of horse was strong as was the aroma of other things that might be good to eat. There was also the smell of man the closer the bear got to the camp. The instinctive fear of man made the bear cautious. Still, the smell of food drew him nearer to Curly's picketed horse.

Curly now knew what had spooked the herd. He also knew that if he did nothing there was a very good chance that the bear would destroy his camp and quite possibly kill his other horse. He would not allow that to happen if he was able to stop it.

He spurred his nervous mount toward the bear, drawing his carbine from the scabbard and shouting at the top of his lungs. Seeing this mad man charging at him like a tempest, the bear thought better of his intentions and raced into the forest. He wasn't that hungry, and the noise was more than he was ready for. Humans.... you could never tell what they were up to.

Curly brought his uneasy horse to a halt alongside the stallion and tried to calm both animals. It took several minutes for his own racing heart to slow. Sweat poured down his face even though it was a chilly morning. He wiped his brow with the back of his hand. "Well horse, we know now what started them to running. Now we need to figure out how to keep that old bear away from them and us. I don't think any of us want him for a neighbor. Maybe that's why them wild ones don't stay close by."

Curly contemplated his options. He could move his camp, hunt the bear down, or keep his camp where it was and hope the bear did not return. He pondered this while preparing his breakfast. Moving his camp would not guarantee safety. Because he carried a lighter caliber carbine, hunting the bear down was not a particularly appealing option either. Staying where he was and making his camp as secure as possible, while not perfect, might just be his best choice.

He scoured the area around his camp for the spoor of any predator larger than a coyote. What he found was weeks old. Perhaps the larger predators did not come here often. At least, he hoped that was true.

Returning to his camp he began setting up fortifications around his base. He sharpened three-inch diameter poles and drove them into the ground with the points facing outward, hoping that the spikes would deter any hungry bears from trying to get too close. He also cut some brush back to give himself a better view. He would keep his horses in close at night to protect them and to give him warning of any approaching predator. That was the best he could do for the moment.

Late that afternoon, another, much larger herd wandered onto the grassland. The herd stallion was a large roan who carried many battle scars on his otherwise glossy hide. The appaloosa from the earlier herd was a much comelier animal, but there was little doubt which one was the sturdier.

The herd patriarch stood a short way off from the herd on the same knoll the earlier stallion had used. He surveyed the surroundings. His eyes were constantly moving and his ears twitched to and fro. Not even the slightest unfamiliar sound was missed. Bending his graceful neck, he took a mouthful of the luscious grass. Immediately he raised his head again and continued his examination of the vicinity. Nostrils flaring, he caught the scent of the bear from earlier that day. He stamped nervously and tossed his head. The bear was gone, but his was a smell that the master of the herd did not care for. He could smell the earlier herd too, but they did not trouble him. Leisurely, he began cropping grass again.

Curly watched from his hiding place. He dared not try to get any closer due to the vigilance of the roan. He let out a silent whistle. "That's sure one fine critter," he whispered to himself. "Must be a hundred head in that bunch," he thought. He watched silently through the afternoon, picking out the animals that would best meet his standards. In this herd alone, he could tally at least thirty mares and foals that he would be proud to slap his brand on. Now he chuckled softly. He had forgotten to think of a brand. "I reckon I better think of something before I start tossing a loop on them critters."

When the herd finally began to move off, another small herd came in to feed. They stayed far from the large herd and fed quietly hundreds of yards from where Curly stood to observe. Even from where he was, Curly could see the nervousness of the leader of the smaller band. The roan eyed the other herd as if calculating if the fight to take the herd was worth the effort or not. Apparently, he was satisfied with the mares in his harem and led them slowly from sight, whistling a challenge that was not answered. The leader of the smaller herd knew what the outcome of a battle would be and refused to be drawn into a losing encounter. Content with his small band of mares, he continued to graze.

Curly watched the last herd until the sun set, which forced him to return to his camp. While setting up his fortifications, he gathered plenty of wood for the fire. After seeing the bear earlier, he planned to keep the fire going through the night. It was the prudent thing to do. Why make his camp any more inviting than it already was? Besides, he wanted a hot meal.

***

For the next few weeks, Curly watched the herds come and go, analyzing their routes and time between visits to the meadow. The meadow was perhaps three-square miles, and it offered lush grass and a large clear stream on the western edge. Each time the horses came to feed, they also took time to drink at the quietest part of the stream. So far, the bear had not caused any problems, but it did return more than once. Each time, it was a little bolder.

As Curly was dreaming of his future, other events were taking place which would affect him and those he knew and cared about.

CHAPTER 23

Jim and Preacher rode into Helena as the sun kissed the mountain tops to the west. The pale gold changed to orange and then a brilliant crimson. Each change in hue was reflected on the snowy caps of the mountains as the sun sank behind their craggy shoulders. The scarlet of sunset gave the ragged peaks the appearance of the jagged teeth of some enormous carnivore drenched in blood. The purples of the early dusk drove the reds from the mountaintops, leaving the impression of a bruised land. It was a beautiful display of God's glory for those who had eyes to see, but was it a harbinger of things to come?

Neither man pondered these things as they rode wearily down the street searching for food and lodging. Both had seen numerous sunrises and sunsets over the years, and this sunset was fading behind them. It was food and shelter they sought, not sunsets.

"Let's get these horses taken care of. Then we can fill our own bellies," Jim said. "I figure they carried us more than we carried them." It was a rare western man who looked to his own needs before those of his horse. One never knew when his mount's ability to go just a bit farther or faster might spell the difference between life and death. Those who failed to care for their horse were poor stockmen and never lasted. It had cost some their lives.

"That sounds right good to me but let's hurry it up. My stomach is beginning to think my mouth's been sewed shut," Preacher replied. "You see a livery anywhere?"

"Nope, but there's got to be one somewhere nearby. As for your stomach thinking your mouth has been sewn shut, my ears tell me otherwise."

The two found a livery barn behind one of the local hotels. They rubbed the horses down and made sure they were fed and grained before returning to the main street. They quickly found Charlie's Cafe which the hostler had recommended.

The covered porch was well lit by kerosene lamps as was the interior. Red and white checkered curtains covered the windows and tablecloths of the same pattern covered the heavy wooden tables inside. The antlers of a huge bull elk adorned one wall, and the well-tanned skins of coyotes, beavers and otters decorated the other walls. The walls and ceiling were painted white and kept immaculate. That was not the normal state of affairs in Montana, or anywhere else at the time. The floors, too, were spotless. That was no easy task in such a country.

Both men scraped the mud from their boots and knocked the trail dust from their clothes with their hats before entering. Seeing the pristine condition of Charlie's, they both felt a twinge of guilt for not bathing and changing clothes before entering.

Their guilt quickly abated when they were greeted by a cheerful, smiling hostess. "Ya'll just grab you a seat any ole' where and me or Rosie'll fix you up. Don't fret none about a bit of mud or dirt on them boots, neither. A man who don't get a bit dirty from time to time ain't hardly working, and for sure ain't worth feeding the food we serve here. Besides, Charlie'd throw a plum pickle fit if he ain't got something to clean."

"Yes ma'am," Preacher replied. They walked to an empty table nearby. The hostess strolled around the cafe refilling coffee cups and exchanging friendly banter with all of the patrons.

"Evening gents," said a buxom, dark-haired woman in her forties. The lines around her eyes spoke of years of smiles and living life. She flipped over two heavy crockery mugs and filled them with scalding black coffee without asking. "We got some honey to sweeten it with if you like, but we're plumb out of cream this time of night." She grinned at Preacher. "I'll be back in a jiff to see what you want to eat. We got bear, moose, deer, beef, and buffalo. Plenty of spuds to go with them. We even got some fresh peas and bread baked fresh today. Give it some thought and I'll be right back." She bustled off, picking up empty plates and dishes from other tables on her way.

A man big enough to be a bear or moose himself came from the back with a broom in one hand and a dustpan in the other. He was as neat and clean as the establishment itself, wearing a starched blue shirt and a black bowtie. His black trousers had a crease you could cut yourself with and a bowler hat was perched jauntily on his head. He moved swiftly and efficiently sweeping the floor, never missing even the most minute particle of dirt. He followed the trail of dust and mud to Jim and Preacher. Instead of the look of disdain they expected, the bear of a man, tipped his bowler and continued to sweep. His smile never left his face.

The waitress returned, smiled at Preacher and winked. "I'm Rosie. So, what'll you fellers have?"

"Well now, Rosie, that buffler sounds good to me. Plenty of taters and peas to go with it, if you don't mind." Preacher returned the smile and wink. It was something that Jim did not miss.

"I'll have the moose and plenty of spuds. Gravy on the whole shebang if you've got some." Jim completed his order.

Rosie returned with platters piled high with food and the two ate quietly after Preacher asked the blessing. Rosie returned to check on them several times, and Preacher found something to say to her every time. Then they left the diner, leaving Rosie a generous tip.

Pasqual watched Jim and Preacher. They walked unconcernedly down the street toward the livery to check on their horses one last time before retiring for the evening. They didn't seem to be searching for anything or anyone, but that did not alleviate his fears. If it was him they were seeking, he wanted to be sure he picked the time and place where they found him.

"What do you think, Jim?" Preacher asked.

"About what?" Jim responded. "You making calf eyes at the waitress?"

"Calf eyes? What are you talking about? I meant about this trip. What do you think will come of it? Is it going to draw unwanted attention, or do you think we can keep it quiet? And I was not making calf eyes!"

"Oh, that," Jim said in mock surprise. "That is why we are going to Denver. It will be a lot less likely to draw attention there. There are a lot of mining interests there. I don't figure it will draw much attention at all. Maybe us looking for a mining engineer that can get the gold without destroying the land might, but I think most people will put that down as eccentricity. They'll probably figure we are off our rocker."

"Well, in your case, they'd be right." Preacher laughed.

"A crazy person is the most qualified to make that assessment. I think that makes you more than qualified," Jim quipped.

They reached the livery and dropped the subject. While such talk might not draw much attention in Denver, it was sure to tickle the curious ear in Helena.

The men took their time fussing over their mounts. Neither horse had ever ridden on a train before. The men thought that the extra attention might keep the horses calmer when it came time to load them into the stock car.

The hostler noticed. "Them's some fine critters you fellas got there. I can sure see why ya'll make such a fuss over 'em."

"They'll do," Jim replied. "They carried us a long way, so they deserve some extra attention. You mind if we bed down here for the night?"

"For a dollar, you can both sleep in the loft or in the stall with your mounts."

"Fair enough. When's the next train for Denver?" Preacher asked.

"She pulls out early tomorrow afternoon," was the response. "If'n you're taking your horses, you'll want to get there early to load them up."

"Thanks," Preacher replied.

The next morning, the two men rose early and strolled around town before taking their horses to the station. Preacher left Jim there with the mounts and strolled back through town to pick up a few last-minute items for their trip. Pasqual and another man stepped from an alley as Preacher approached, blocking his progress. Both men held drawn weapons. Preacher stopped, and they motioned him into the alley from which they had just emerged. His gaze shifted from one to the other, and he glanced at their leveled guns.

"I don't reckon arguing'll do any good will it?" They motioned with their guns, and he allowed himself to be directed into the shadows of the cluttered alley.

"That's far enough old man," Pasqual growled.

Preacher turned toward his assailants, and a smile of recognition tugged at his lips. "I'm surprised to see you here, Pasqual. I see you got your hair all trimmed back up proper. I never figured to see you again. 'specially here in an alley and over a gun." He continued to smile.

"I figured the same. You told us to ride out and we done that. Now you and that kid show up on my trail. I aim to put a stop to that here and now," Pasqual replied.

Pasqual's companion spoke up. "Let's get this over with. I ain't fond of doing this in the daylight. Somebody might've seen us."

Preacher winked at the second man. "So, you're not too fond of doing your deeds in the light of day? A feller named John wrote something about that a long while back. He said, 'And this is the condemnation, that the light is come into the world, and men loved darkness rather than light, because their deeds were evil. For everyone that doeth evil hateth the light, neither cometh to the light, lest his deeds be reproved.' I reckon ya'll are figuring to perpetrate some evil act on poor little ole' me." Preacher had moved casually toward a pile of junk while speaking. Before his assailants realized it, he had moved so only one could get a clear shot at him without endangering the other.

Pasqual realized what was happening just as Preacher placed his companion between the two of them. "Ernst! Move over! You're blocking me," he shouted.

Ernst looked back over his shoulder, which was all the break Preacher could hope for. Before Ernst could turn back toward him, he scooped up a piece of a broken crate and hurled it at the unsuspecting man's head. Seeing the scrap of wood careening toward his skull, he threw up his arms to protect his face. The broken crate struck his arms, knocking the gun from his hand. Preacher drew his old Army revolver and put a well-aimed shot into Pasqual's right foot. He howled in pain and tried to bring his gun to bear.

"Don't do it!" Preacher shouted. His old Army .44 was held in a rock steady grip. The muzzle was now aimed at the center of the other man's chest. "I could have just as easily made you dead."

By now, Ernst had recovered from his shock enough to realize he was unarmed and faced with a man who looked far more fierce than the compliant "victim" they had led down the alley just moments before.

Blinded by pain and rage, Pasqual continued to bring his gun into alignment. Preacher mouthed a quick, "forgive me Lord," changed his aim ever so slightly, and fired.

Struck in the shoulder by the soft, round lead ball, Pasqual spun to his right and fell dropping his cocked Colt to the ground. It discharged harmlessly into the hard stone wall of one of the buildings lining the alley.

"Thank you, Jesus. Nobody had to die," Preacher whispered.

Ernst was still in shock over the change of events. He raised his hands slowly.

"Take your partner to the sawbones and get him patched up as best he can. You can leave them newfangled Colts right where they are. I reckon they'll bring enough cash to cover the doctor's bill. After he's patched up," Preacher indicated Pasqual, "you'd both best consider why you're still alive. God might not be done with you, but I am. Next time either of you try to draw iron on me, there'll be a burying. I aint' hunting nobody, so next time we meet, you just tip your hat and say 'howdy'".

The town marshal pushed through the small crowd that had gathered at the mouth of the alley. "What's all the ruckus about?" he demanded.

The two outlaws froze in their tracks. If their acts were revealed, they may well be hung or face a long stint in the territorial prison at best.

Preacher spoke up. "Twern't nothing marshal. These two fellers brought me down the alley to show me their fancy shooting irons, and this young feller's went off accidental like. I think they done give up playing with guns for a while. I sure was disappointed though. I never got to see nobody shoot no rats."

Relief washed over the faces of both outlaws, and the marshal looked dubiously at all three men. Technically, everything Preacher said was true. He simply omitted a few key details.

"Ernst, you'd best get Pasqual to the doc. He's gonna need some tending. He's leaking pretty good. I'll see your guns bring a fair price so's you can cover the bill." Preacher turned to the marshal and continued. "You know anyone who could use a couple of decent side arms? I figure they're worth about twelve dollars each."

Ernst led Pasqual through the crowd in search of a physician.

The marshal shook his head as if trying to clear it. "Sure. I'll take care of that." He turned to the crowd. "Ya'll git out of here. There's nothing more to see."

He turned his gaze back to Preacher. "There's more'n an accident that happened down that alley. I'd put my last dollar on that, but you ain't gonna tell me about it, so's I won't bother to ask." He gathered the discarded pistols.

"Why marshal, everything I said was true," Preacher responded in a wounded voice.

"I ain't doubting *what* you said. It's what you ain't saying that has me wondering, but like I said, it's your business unless you want it to be mine. Try not to have no more accidents in the alleys, would you?"

"That sounds like a right smart idea to me marshal."

The two parted, and Preacher finished his errands before returning to the railroad depot. Jim had purchased their tickets during Preacher's absence, but they still needed to load their horses.

"If they never rid the rails before, you might want to ride in the stock car with them when the train moves out until they get settled in. Most horses get mighty fidgety when the train starts jerking and pitching as it pulls out of the station. They'll settle in once you're moving along," the ticket agent suggested.

"Truth be told, I don't much care for it either," said Preacher flatly. "These iron horses make me a might fidgety myself, but if I got my eyes closed, it ain't too bad."

"Eyes closed? Why, you'll miss seeing all that country rolling by. Never did know something could go so fast as these new rail cars. They say some can go forty miles in an hour in some places, and the scenery plumb flies by." The ticket agent's face was flushed, and he was almost breathless as he spoke.

"That there's what I'm talking about," Preacher replied. "I prefer to see the countryside at a bit slower pace."

The railroad man seemed baffled that anyone wouldn't share his enthusiasm for his railroad. He pointed to the stock car where the horses would ride, and the two passengers led their mounts to the car and up the ramp. They stayed with their horses while they waited for the train to pull out.

"Thought I heard some shooting a little after you left. What was that all about?" Jim asked.

"According to the marshal's report, a couple of fellers accidental like dropped their guns in an alley and they went off all by their lonesome."

Jim looked skeptically at his friend. "Accidental like?"

"That's what's written in the report. Least-wise, that's how it was reported."

Jim just shook his head and laughed. He knew there was more to it than that, and that his friend was probably involved. A grin spread across his face.

CHAPTER 24

Shortly after noon, the train whistle blasted, and the horses snorted and tried to break free. Their eyes rolled back in terror as they plunged against their lead ropes. Things got even more harrowing when the train jerked into motion. Jim and Preacher held tight to the animal's halters and spoke soothingly to them as the horses pitched and nearly toppled to the hard floor of the stock car. After struggling for about five minutes, the horses began to calm, just as the ticket agent had predicted.

The train stopped to take on water and wood several times during their travel. Each time, Jim and Preacher had to spend several minutes calming their horses before they could return to their own seats. Finally, the train pulled into Denver.

"Denver Station!" came the cry from the conductor. "Everyone off for Denver!"

"I suppose that means us. Let's get them horses unloaded and let them stretch their legs. They've been stuck in that car for too long," Jim said.

"I couldn't agree more," Preacher replied. "Them critters ain't meant to ride the rails all boxed up like that."

The horses bounded down the ramp, happy to be out of that loud, vibrating crate. They stamped their hooves on the street as if making sure the ground underfoot would no longer move. Jim and Preacher stretched to get the kinks out from their ride as well.

"Glad to get off that noisy rattletrap," Preacher said. You can't hardly hear yourself think. Kinda feel cooped up in there too, when you're used to an open sky overhead."

"True," Jim said as he twisted his body from side to side. "It did cut our travel time by several days, though."

"Speaking of that, let's get these horses saddled and away from this here depot before they decide to blast that whistle again, and these critters decide to run all the way back to Montana without us."

Jim nodded in agreement and the two were quickly mounted and on their way away from the depot.

"Where do you suppose we'll find someone who knows about mining?" Jim asked. The street was lined with saloons bearing names like Gold Dust, Lucky Strike and Mother Lode. Other businesses appeared to be an afterthought.

"Why you asking me? I sure ain't sure, but I figure someone around here does judging by how prosperous the town and saloons are." Preacher replied.

As they rode past the Lucky Strike, two men burst out the bat-wings and sprawled into the street. A crowd followed them shouting advice as the two combatants regained their feet and continued their brawl. They stumbled into Jim's horse, which reared, nearly toppling Jim from his saddle.

In anger, Jim kicked the nearest man between the shoulder blades, sending him face down into the dust.

Seeing his opponent supine before him, the second fighter turned his attention to Jim. "This was a private fight you poked your nose into," he growled. "You got no cause to kick Clem like that." Clem began to stir.

"Agitate my horse again, like you did, and I'll for sure have cause," Jim's face was red beneath his tan, and his eyes were like blue flames.

Clem turned on Jim as well. "What's the big idea, kicking me when I ain't looking?"

"Do the same thing again, and next time I'll kick you in the head," Jim responded.

"We ain't got time for such nonsense, Jim. Let them fellers have their fun." Preacher spoke up as the three younger men began to square off. "No need for you to get down in the dust with them. Besides, if your horse was too upset, he'd of done some kicking of his own."

Jim glowered at the brawlers and then at Preacher. "Fine. I'll let things go. Let's get on with why we came to town to begin with." The men kicked their mounts into motion.

"Hey, you can't just ride away like that," Clem shouted at their retreating backs. Getting no response, he turned back toward his earlier antagonist. Together, they walked back into the Lucky Strike.

CHAPTER 25

While Jim and Preacher were heading to Denver, Curly began building his horse trap. He knew water was the one thing the wild horses could not do without. The lush meadows made food easy for the herds to find, but there was only so much surface water. He added a little more to his makeshift corral each day, reducing access to the water hole with each addition. When he was finished, all he would have to do, when they came to drink, was pull some poles into place to trap the mustangs. Then the hard work would begin.

The roan stallion was alert to the slight changes but continued to lead his mares to the waterhole. The other stallions were less cautious, perhaps trusting the instincts of the older, larger stud. The time would come when Curly would have to decide how to cull the herds for just the horses he wanted, but for now, catching them was the first step.

The horses came and went day after day, each time finding a narrower path for their daily drink. Each day the stallions were the last to drink and the first to leave. When there was no more than a narrow gate left, Curly stayed away to let the horses feel safe until he was ready to spring his trap. During this time, he built a holding pen near his own camp.

Brush and limbs were dragged into place. When the pen was "horse high, bull strong, and hog tight," Curly began spending the days getting closer to the trap so the mustangs would be less likely to see him as a threat. The roan stud was still cautious. He distrusted the man-thing, but he allowed his mares and foals to drink while he kept a careful watch. Because he was the most cautious, Curly decided to try to capture his harem first. Once the trap was sprung the first time, Curly doubted the roan would return for a long time.

The morning started like any other, with the wild horses coming to the watering hole for a drink before heading to the meadows for forage. Curly had made a cold camp near the entrance to his trap, leaving his own mounts back in his original camp. His plan would require him to work with more stealth than speed, and having his own mounts close by would betray his presence.

He quietly watched the roan lead his harem in. He selected several mares and foals along with some mares that were with foal for his purposes. "That stud sure is fidgety. I hope he don't bolt with my picks before I get that gate up," Curly said under his breath. Almost as if he wanted to reward Curly's patience, the stallion brought his mares in with very little delay.

Curly quickly slid the top pole into place then slid the remaining poles into place blocking any exit. The trap was sprung and the horses raced around the enclosure seeking an escape. The gate was the only way out, and it was now closed.

Curly smiled as he looked over the trapped animals. "I wasn't too sure you'd bring 'em in today," he said as the herd leader snorted his disgust at the man-thing. Flaring his nostrils, he charged at

Curly with bared teeth. The gate stood between them, stopping the stallion's charge.

"You got some spirit," Curly quipped. "I'll take a few of your mares and foals, then let you out to run free." The stallion backed away from the unfamiliar sound of Curly's voice. "You ain't quite fearless, are you horse?" Curly chuckled.

Now came the hard part. Picking the horses he wanted and separating them from the rest of the herd. He watched closely as the herd milled around and selected more than two dozen mares and foals for his own herd. He decided to wait until they settled down some before trying to dab a loop on any he wanted. He wasn't sure what the roan's reaction would be when he roped those he wanted.

The next morning, Curly rode his gelding to the enclosure and opened the gate just enough to allow them to slip in. The wild horses moved fearfully to the back of the trap while the man-thing dismounted and put the gate back in place.

Mounting and moving slowly around the pen, Curly tried to cut out the mares he wanted. The stallion kept between the herd and this strange creature snorting and pawing the air. Each time Curly swung one way, the big roan moved quickly to intercept him. Curly's horse fiddle-footed anxiously. He was gelded, but he still had the instincts he was born with.

After several tense minutes playing cat and mouse with the big herd stallion, one of the mares Curly wanted broke from the herd. He quickly spun his mount in her direction and dropped a loop over her sleek neck, barely having time to dally the rope around his saddle horn before Strawberry, as Curly had dubbed the leader of the herd, charged him with teeth bared and ears laid back. Barely turning his own horse in time to miss being bowled over, Curly shouted and waved his free arm in the air. This unexpected noise and movement drove the roan far enough off for Curly to haul the struggling mare to the gate.

He worked all day long hauling one after the other to his holding pen near his camp. He turned them into the smaller enclosure and closed the gate carefully behind him. Three were in foal and another four had foals follow behind them. When night finally fell, Curly had more than twenty mares plus one colt and three fillies in his pen. He rode wearily back to his trap.

"Well big feller, I reckon I got the pick of the herd this time around. Time for you to take the rest of your ladies back out." He removed the bars blocking the wild horses' exit and rode quietly into the enclosure, hazing the horses back to freedom. The stallion flared his nostrils and drove what was left of his herd out of the small opening at full speed.

The process repeated itself a couple of days later when the appaloosa stallion brought his herd in to drink. They had seen the commotion from the larger herd so had been cautious, but thirst prevailed. Curly was prepared for that and remained patient. While waiting, he took time to get the wild horses he had captured to become accustomed to his smell and movements. He would sing and talk quietly to them from both outside and inside the makeshift corral. He even put his gelding into the pen with them so they would get used to him coming into and moving around the pen.

When the day came that the appaloosa brought his mares in to drink, Curly was rested and ready. The bars to the gate went quickly into place, and he again entered the trap and dragged the mares he wanted to his holding pen. The only difference this time was that Curly decided he wanted to keep the stallion as well as several of the mares. There were several other young studs who would be only too willing to take the leadership spot, and Curly knew that this stallion would make a perfect mate for Splash.

The mares and foals were enough of a task, but when the loop fell around the neck of the sleek stallion, war broke out. The wild stallion reared and fought the rope. When that didn't work, he charged Curly, nearly knocking his horse to the ground. Both horses stumbled, and Curly almost lost his seat. He spun around and snapped a loop around the animal's front legs, causing it to falter. Taking advantage of the stallion's off-balance moment, Curly shortened the lead rope and quickly drew him toward the gate and the holding pen. The stallion raced around the new enclosure but found no escape.

Having collected a total of forty-two horses, Curly was ready to begin calming them for the drive back to the ranch. He didn't waste time worrying about the drive but let his gelding into the pen and spent time walking around the pen, feeding the herd and talking to them in soothing tones. He also made sure to dismantle his trap so the wild herds could once again have easy access to the watering hole whose denial had been their downfall.

The horses became accustomed to Curly moving near them and soon allowed him to approach and even lay his hands on them. Quivering, the appaloosa stallion finally allowed Curly to touch him gently. The last conquest to be won by the gentle hand of this bald puncher, or so he thought.

Squeals of terror drove all sleep from Curly as the sun was rising. From near the waterhole, the sounds of a lone horse could be heard. The sound was one of fright. Curly scooped up his rifle, jumped aboard his uncut horse bareback, and raced toward the sound. As he approached, he could hear the snarl of a bear intent on getting an easy meal and the frightened whinnying of a newborn foal.

Taking in the scene as he approached, Curly could see a frightened mare standing between her foal and the same grizzly bear that Curly had run out of his camp. His stallion began to shy, and Curly was dumped onto the ground unhurt but afoot. The bear rose up on its hind legs to intimidate the mare, but she would not abandon her offspring. Just as the bear dropped back to all fours and started forward, a flash of color burst through the brush. Strawberry charged, unfazed by the bear.

Sensing the stallion's approach, the bear whirled toward his attacker. He was not about to be driven from the meal he was anticipating. The stallion avoided the blow that was aimed at his head and clamped his teeth into the bear's flank. Then, he spun and kicked at the bear with his powerful hind legs. The bear gave a "whoof" and managed to rake his claws down the side of the powerful horse, opening several gashes. The stud was game but no match for the large predator.

When he saw the battle, Curly knew the grizzly would kill the valiant stallion if he did not take a hand. Even if he did intervene, the bear still might kill the roan. Swinging his carbine to his shoulder, he began to fire into the ferocious beast. The bullets seemed to have no effect, and the bear continued to inflict further injury onto the protector of the mare and the foal.

The bear knocked the stallion to the ground and started forward to deliver the fatal blow when Curly's last bullet hit something vital. *Ursus Arctos Horribilis* crumpled in death near his severely injured victim. Curly walked cautiously towards the two fallen combatants. He wasn't sure if the stallion was dead, but he reloaded just in case the bear wasn't and decided Curly would make a good meal. Standing as far as he could from the crumpled form of the bear, Curly poked with the barrel of his rifle. When there was no response, he jabbed it again to be sure.

Curly breathed a sigh of relief and looked at the downed stallion. "Sorry I didn't get here a little quicker, Strawberry. You sure did your best, but even you weren't no match for a big griz." He took the few steps to the stallion's head and saw the horse's eyes widen. "He didn't do you in!" Curly's voice rose. He dropped beside the stallion whose instinct, even now, was to fight anything he saw as a threat to his herd. Curly had to jump back to avoid being kicked as the injured animal stuck out weakly with his forefeet.

"There big fella. You just lie easy now. We'll see if we can patch you up. It's for sure you're buzzard meat if I don't do something." The newborn foal squealed as it tried to find its feet. The mare stood trembling nearby. "Looks like your lady friend stayed here with you. That's a fine-looking foal she's got there too. I can't do too much without some bandages, but if you'll try to keep from kicking some sense into me, I'll see what I can do for you."

Curly's quiet voice seemed to calm the big horse, or maybe it was the loss of blood. Either way, he allowed Curly to do what he could to staunch the flow of blood. After doing what he could on the spot, Curly headed back to his camp. His own mount had already run back to the relative safety it offered. All he could do was head back that way on foot.

"I never seen the like before. Most wild horses would've run, but that feller sure did put up a fight for those under his rule. It'd be a pure shame if'n he died as a result." Curly continued to talk to himself as he walked back to his camp.

He gathered up some supplies, saddled his gelding, and rode back to the scene of the battle. The gelding fought against going near the dead bear and the injured stallion. The smell of blood and bear was too much for him. Curly didn't try to force the gelding forward but made sure to tie him fast to avoid having to walk back to camp a second time.

Several days of patient tending saw the stallion regain his feet, but he would never be strong enough to lead the wild herd again. He was game, but the fight with the bear had left muscles scarred and slowed his movements. The mare and foal stayed close by and watched as Curly nursed the injured stallion. When the stallion was able to move about, Curly led him to the holding pen where the mares and other stallion were becoming accustomed to Curly's movements. The roan limped to the pen willingly but laid his ears back and whinnied a challenge to the appaloosa stallion already there. The smell of the other horse awakened his fighting spirit even though he was in no condition for a battle. The appaloosa answered and rushed toward the fence as Curly struggled to calm the two previous enemies. The mare and foal had followed her mate to the pen.

Knowing that putting both stallions into the pen together would end with the roan being killed, Curly decided to picket him a short way from the rest of the horses.

The next few days, Curly worked with his captured herd and did his best to get the two wild stallions accustomed to each other.

Working against their instincts proved difficult, but Curly managed to get them to tolerate each other, once they realized they were not a threat to one another. It helped that the roan was still weak. By bringing him closer to the holding pen each day, the two began to accept one another being in close proximity. The mare and young filly stayed close and began to follow Curly everywhere he went with the roan stallion.

With a herd of forty-five mares, foals and the two stallions, Curly decided it was time for him to figure out how to move them back to the Lazy H. "I figured on driving 'em back," he said to himself. "I just never figured I'd have me a stud all stove up to haul along. I best ponder this a bit." He was riding his own ungelded horse this morning as he moved through the holding pen. The appaloosa stallion had begun to ignore this other stallion. Only the roan seemed to provoke any hostility to him. This gave Curly an idea.

Early the next morning, Curly put his plan into action. He dabbed a loop around the neck of Strawberry and tied him a distance from the holding pen in the direction he planned to drive the rest of the herd. The mare and filly continued to follow their old herd stallion and stayed near him while Curly began hazing his newly acquired wealth toward the northeast and home. By doing so, he could concentrate on pushing the herd away from their familiar range toward their new home. He worked his own horse to a lather to keep the bunch quitters from returning to the fields from which they were taken.

Once the herd was moving well, he switched his saddles to his gelding and returned for the roan. Strawberry followed compliantly. Still too weak for a real battle, he was now trusting this man-thing that had saved his life. "Well Strawberry. I figure you won't ever be broke to the saddle, but you'll sure throw some good foals. We'll take it easy so's you can keep up."

Each time one of the wild bunch tried to break back to where they had come from, Curly would drop the lead rope and herd them back into the group. Each time, the roan stallion stood and awaited his return. That first night Curly strung a rope corral around the horses to keep them bunched tight. His horses and the injured stallion were picketed outside of the makeshift pen.

Each day was a repeat of the previous, and each night saw them closer to the Lazy H. By the third day, the horses had become accustomed to traveling. Even with the injured stud, they made about twenty miles per day. At that rate, it would be just over a week until Curly would see Raven Wing again with his promised twenty horses. He smiled at the thought.

CHAPTER 26

Riding onto the Lazy H from an unfamiliar route, Curly was shocked to see a ramshackle collection of huts and tents on what he was sure was Lazy H range. He'd never ventured onto this section before, but there was no doubt where he was.

He drove his herd through the midst of the newly sprung up "town". "Hey friend," he hollered to a passerby. "What's going on here?"

"Gold" was the one-word answer before a shabbily dressed drunk staggered away.

"Gold?" Curly said out loud to himself. "I reckon Jim and Tom need to hear about this."

"Yee-ha," he bellowed at his herd, driving them at top speed through the collection of hovels. Strawberry struggled against the lead rope but managed to keep pace with the mare and filly following on his heels.

Once they were through the new settlement, he slowed the horses. He'd made it this far without losing a single head. He had no desire to lose or injure any on the final leg of their journey. Gold held an allure for many, but Curly wasn't one of them. He loved the open range and a good horse far more than riches. What he saw let him know that gold fever was rampant, and those who had it held no regard for whose property the gold was located on nor the injury they were inflicting on the range.

As the herd scattered onto the rich graze near the ranch yard, Curly rode to the house with Strawberry in tow. He swung from the saddle. His mind was on what he had seen just a short time before.

Suddenly, the door burst open and a black-haired woman ran into Curly's arms, nearly toppling him to the ground. Raven Wing flung her arms unashamedly around his neck, causing dust to billow from his shirt into the fresh afternoon air.

"You have returned!" she exclaimed. "I see one stallion and a mare following behind. He is a handsome one. And the mare, she is beautiful. Are these the ones you brought for me?"

Curly lifted her from the ground in an embrace and kissed her soundly. "These three are just a sample. The rest are out on the range feeding right now." His smile turned grim. "I need to see Tom and Jim right away. Are they here?"

"Jim and Preacher have not returned yet but should be back any day now. They left shortly after you did."

"Left? Where to?" Curly replied.

Quickly, Raven Wing explained Jim and Preacher's departure. "It should not be much longer, and Tom will be back before nightfall. Can your news wait that long?"

Curly's grin spread across his dusty face. "I reckon it'll hafta wait until Tom gets back. It's urgent, but he ain't here so, how about you tell me what you been up to?"

"I have been waiting and praying for you. I have also become a big sister." Raven Wing laughed at Curly's look of consternation.

"No, my father has not returned from the grave to give my mother another child. Sarah needed a big sister to tell her secrets to, so I am now her big sister, and she is my little sister to whom I tell my secrets."

"Oh, that makes sense." Curly scratched his bald head, and his face betrayed the fact that it did not make sense to him.

Raven Wing continued to smile. "Now, my wild horse hunter, tell me what you have been up to. You said you have more horses than I have seen, and that stallion looks like he is limping. How was he injured?"

"Well, that there stud sure was a wild one, but…" Curly started to tell the story and stopped himself short. "Do you figure we might take a ride while I tell you all about my boring trip? Not that there's much to tell, but you did ask."

Dinah had come out onto the porch while they were talking. "Welcome back Curly. That's a fine pair of horses you have there. That little filly looks like she'll grow into a fine animal in time too. I heard you mention needing to talk to Tom and Jim. Tom will be back for supper. Why don't you two get reacquainted? I can handle things for a bit. Sarah'll want to know you're back too. She's around somewhere. Just watch for that dog of hers and you'll find her. Now you two go on."

"Hello, Miss Dinah. I'm looking forward to some of your cooking," Curly said. Then he looked at Raven Wing and continued. "But, I reckon I can wait for that until I have a chance to get cleaned up and talk to Raven Wing. Not meaning to insult your cooking, but I have some other things on my mind just now."

"Alright. You know where the wash basin is, and I figure you two have enough sense to be here when supper is served."

"I'll have her home at a proper hour," Curly quipped back. "Now, let's go get that mare of yours saddled up, and I'll tell you about my adventure."

The two strolled hand in hand to the barn where Splash was stabled. Curly threw Raven Wing's light-weight saddle onto her horse's back and tightened the cinch after slipping the bridle over her head. He sniffed himself during the process. "Whew! I think I best wash up before we go for that ride. I'll be right back."

He slipped behind the barn to a rain barrel, stripped off his shirt, and quickly scrubbed dust, dirt and sweat from his torso. He dunked his shirt a few times to remove some of the grime it contained. Donning his shirt again, he walked back through the barn to where his belle awaited him, dripping water with every step.

"Well, I sure hope I smell better than a skunk what's been dead for a week now."

"You smelled like a man to me, Curly. A man who had his mind set on a task and did not quit until he had finished it. Now you still smell like a man, but one who has washed. I think I like this smell better." Raven Wing took his arm in hers and they walked to the horses where he helped her to mount before swinging astride his own weary mount.

"Shall we go see your wedding presents?" he asked. He swung his horse and lead the way back along the trail he had taken into the ranch yard.

Raven Wing trotted Splash up beside Curly. "Wedding presents? I should very much like to see that, and I should like to hear your tale." They rode toward where the remainder of the horses Curly had gathered were grazing.

"Well," Curly began as they rode side by side. "Like I said, there ain't much to tell. I spent a bit of time watching a few herds before picking the ones I wanted for us. Then, I just talked them all into following me back here."

"Curly, you are such a fibber. You are a charmer when it comes to horses, but even you could not talk wild horses into following you home like a puppy."

Curly chuckled. "I reckon I left a few things out, but the fact is, I brung some fine critters back with me." His face clouded slightly as he thought of the ride through the shanty town he had driven the herd through. Then he smiled again. "Truth be told, it took a bit of calculating to outsmart the stallions in those wild bunches. They don't stay free by being foolish. And they sure have plenty of spirit.

"You take that roan stud I brought in. He wanted to do me in when he figured out he was trapped. And you and I know no horse can fight a grizzly and come out on top, but he charged into a fight with one to protect that mare and filly that follow him around. He got hisself lamed up pretty bad, but he never thought he could lose. He charged in with teeth bared and hooves a flying. That griz never knew what was coming his way." Curly's face shined when he recounted how Strawberry fought to defend part of his harem. "He'll carry them scars for the rest of his days, but we finished off that ole bear. I surely couldn't leave him to the buzzards, so I doctored him up as best I could. He's game and he'll sure throw some fine offspring even as crippled up as he is."

"He fought a grizzly bear? And you said *we* finished off the bear. Do you mean that you too fought the bear?"

"Naw Raven Wing. Strawberry fought it. I just shot it up a bit. I was a bit busy trying to keep that stubborn stud from getting killed, so I shot the bear until it decided to die. I never did skin it out proper for a rug. Dabbed a rope around one of its legs and hauled it a bit away from Strawberry whilst I tended to him. That mare and her filly are who he was fighting for. I reckon that's why she follows him around so close."

The two started to come onto the rest of Curly's captured hors-es. "What a beautiful appaloosa stallion," she said. Raven Wing pointed to the second herd stallion Curly had brought in with him.

"He don't have a name as yet, but he's one fine critter. I figure if I left him and Strawberry together, they'd fight it out. Straw-berry'd be no match for him now, all stove up like he is. Before he tangled with that grizzly, that appaloosa's best chance would have been to outrun that big roan. They're both some prime horseflesh though."

How many did you bring with you?" Raven Wing asked.

"Forty-five, counting those three up near the house. I said I'd bring twenty. I reckon I got carried away a bit. I figure we can get a decent start with a herd that size. Tom said something about swapping for some breeding stock. What do you think?"

Raven Wing stared uncomprehendingly at Curly after he an-nounced how many horses he had captured. "Forty-five?" she re-peated. "But how did you capture so many so swiftly? You must be the best horse hunter in the territory. Never have I heard of anyone capturing so many and driving them all alone from the wilds."

"Well, I did have a bit of a reason for doing so." He looked at her and smiled. They continued to ride through the skittish herd as

Curly pointed to them and recounted each of their attributes. "A couple of those mares are going to be dropping foals soon too," he announced.

CHAPTER 27

Denver was teaming with prospectors, gamblers, merchants and every other possible profession west of the Mississippi River. Larimer Street was home to many of the mining interests, and it was there that Jim and Preacher found themselves seeking information.

"Do you reckon we should just start knocking on doors of those who claim to be mining engineers, or should we ask around a bit first?" Jim asked Preacher.

"I figure, either way we'll get the same results. Probably less likely to stir up problems if we do our own looking though. The fewer ears to hear our questions, the fewer trying to find out why we're asking them," Preacher responded. "Less likely to get our throats slit that way."

For the next few days, the two men carefully inquired at several of the "reputable" mining and engineering companies. They finally found a man named Arthek who claimed to have a way of extracting gold, in certain circumstances, without destroying the land. It was more costly than strip mining, but it was supposed to leave the land pretty much as it was found. The Cornish, he said, had been mining this way for centuries. Careful inquiry told the two all they needed to know. Most miners and mining companies passed him by because they were less worried about destroying the land than they were in making as large a profit as possible. Those few who had employed him were very satisfied with the results.

Arthek met the two men in his office on their fourth day in town. He quickly grasped what they wanted and offered his services.

"We know how to extract minerals without ruining the whole country, but too many want to take the shortcuts without regard to the results, other than profits," he stated. "If you're just wanting the gold out, there's plenty of cheaper ways to go about it. If you don't want your land to become a barren wasteland it'll cost ya, but it can be done. I have the know-how to do it, too."

"If all we wanted was to get the gold out, we wouldn't need someone like you," Jim countered. "How do we go about extracting the gold and keeping the streams and creeks clear? I've seen diggings where the water wasn't fit for man nor beast, and you couldn't grow anything but rocks for years. We don't want that."

Preacher spoke up. "Like Jim said, we don't need no mining engineer to wreck the countryside. We can do that easy enough on our own. What we need is someone who knows how to *not* do that. It sounds like you might be that person."

"To be honest, gentlemen, I am that person. I do appreciate your drawings, but I would need to see the location to do things right. Would you allow me to travel with you to your claim?"

"I think we could do that," Jim replied. "When would you be ready to leave? We can book passage on the rails tomorrow if that is acceptable to you."

"Tomorrow will do nicely. Not many here are worried about what they leave behind when there's gold involved, so business has been slow. I would enjoy the venture."

The men worked out the details, and then Jim and Preacher made the travel arrangements. They would meet at the train depot the next day and travel by horseback from Helena to the Lazy H. It looked as though things would work out without too much of a hitch.

The sun rose with brilliant crimsons the next morning, indicating a storm was brewing. The weather was something the men could anticipate. The storm they would find upon returning to the *Lazy H* was not.

"I got the horses loaded," Preacher said. "I think I'll ride with them for a bit. I'm still not too keen on watching the landscape pass by at the speed this here contraption moves. Kinda makes my stomach churn."

"Suit yourself," Jim replied. "I think I'll see what there is to see once the horses are settled in. The seats look a bit more comfortable than the stock car."

"I'll ride here with Jim," Arthek stated.

Preacher headed back to ride with the horses as a young woman boarded alone. She carried a parasol and was clearly new to the West. Her eyes darted around the crowded car looking for a seat. Just as she started past Jim, the train lurched into motion. It threw her off balance and landed her on Jim's lap.

"Pardon me," she yelped. She tried to rise but the shaking of the train toppled her back onto Jim's lap a second time.

Jim smiled. "No harm done ma'am," he replied. "If I'd known that riding in the passenger cars would be this interesting, I would have ridden in them to Denver instead of riding in the stock car with the horses."

Not quite sure how to respond, the young woman shoved herself back up in a huff. "I'm glad you find my plight amusing, but I would appreciate you keeping your coarse comments to yourself." She scowled at Jim.

"I'm James Harding, ma'am. I'm sorry for your plight, but it isn't everyday a beautiful woman just falls into my lap." He smiled at her. "I don't reckon there are a lot of empty seats, but you can have mine, and I'll sit next to Mister Arthek." Jim moved to sit next to the mining engineer. There were no other seats nearby, so the young lady cautiously took the offered seat.

"Are you new to the West?" Jim asked.

"Why, yes. How did you know?"

"You still have that look about you," was Jim's simple reply. "A bit uncertain but determined."

"Do you offer all of the ladies who are new to the West your seat on the train?" she asked.

"Well, seeing as how this is only my second trip on the rails, and last time I rode with my horse in the stock car, I reckon so. I mean, I've only had the opportunity once, so not sure in the future, but there's a good chance I might, especially if they're as pretty as you."

Arthek chuckled. "What my young acquaintance is trying to say is, so far, he has always offered his seat when given the opportunity, but of course, he has only had this single opportunity. My name is Arthek." He rose cautiously, extended his hand and shook hers gently. "This rather unrefined young man is James. And who do we have the pleasure of sharing this journey with?"

"I'm Emily. Emily Tate. My friends call me Em, but you," she stared straight at Jim, "may call me Miss Tate."

"Well Miss Tate, it is a pleasure making your acquaintance. I hope the remainder of the journey is a little less bumpy," Arthek replied.

"Where are you heading?" Jim asked.

"I'm going to meet my fiancé in a town called Broken Bow. He says it's beautiful there, and there is plenty of land for a farm and to build a home. He came west to find a place for us." She had made sure to emphasize the word "fiancé" when she spoke.

"What a coincidence. We're heading that way too. That's where I'm from. Well, a bit outside of town, but maybe I know him. What's his name?" James asked.

"His name is Beauregard Leonidas Templeton. I doubt you would know him. He usually does not consort with ruffians like yourself," she replied.

"Beauregard Leonidas Templeton? You're right as rain, I sure don't recall anyone with that moniker, and I do believe I would remember that name. It sounds rather grandiose for backwards little old Montana," James quipped.

"He's a gentleman!"

"I'd quit before I dug a deeper hole Jim," Arthek interjected.

"I reckon you're right. My apologies Miss Tate. I figure we all have a long ride ahead of us. I'm going to try to get some shut eye." James tipped his hat down over his eyes and leaned back in the seat.

The sway of the train soon rocked him and most of the other passengers to sleep. Emily tried to get comfortable and soon slept as well. The train chugged along the tracks and slowed as it struggled to climb one of the grades along the route. Just as it crested the hill, there was a loud thud on the roof of the car. The train ground to a halt as the sound of more thuds awakened those riding in the passenger car.

"What's all that noise?" Emily asked groggily. "Are we there already?"

James sat up and tipped his hat back. "I don't think so," he replied. He began to rise as the doors sprang open and masked gunmen sprang through the opening.

"I'd just sit right back down there mister, unless you'd like a dose of lead poisoning," growled one of the gunmen.

Jim gritted his teeth, sat back down, and scowled at the bandit. He could feel the impotent rage welling up in him, but he was in no position to resist. There were too many bystanders, and Emily would be in the line of fire. He seethed at finding himself in this position, but there was nothing to be done about it.

"Ya'll just sit back whilst the boys help to lighten your load. Pass your funds to the aisle and we'll take up a collection for those less fortunate, meaning us, of course. Don't be holding back. You know the Good Book says 'God loves a cheerful giver,' so smile while you're giving."

Arthek looked as if he were ready to make a fight of it. Jim looked at him and shook his head, and Arthek slowly relaxed. Jim's experiences had taught him that there was a time to stand down and a time to fight. This was one of the former times. "We'd just get some folks hurt or killed," Jim whispered.

"Listen to him," the leader of the outlaws stated. "He's showing good sense."

"You'll receive justice," Jim said to the bandit. "Maybe not now, nor even in this lifetime, but it will come." A calm demeanor hid his inner fury. His smile was discomforting to the masked gunman. James calmly dropped the few dollars he had in his pocket into the gunman's gunny sack.

"Maybe," replied the gunman. "But it won't be today."

"What about you missy? I don't see you making a donation."

"I… I only have enough for my room when I get to Helena and the stagecoach to Broken Bow. Please," she pleaded.

"Aww, in that case, you'll just have to find some other way to get where you're going. Now hand over what you got!"

"Don't you think you've got enough already from everyone else? She's fresh from the East. Let her be," Jim interjected. "Or maybe you think it's nice making a lady beg to keep what little she has?" His voice grew gruff.

"You think maybe I oughta let her keep her meager funds, huh cowboy? Maybe you think I carry this here popgun just for show?"

"You really don't want to know what I think," Jim growled as he slowly rose to his feet.

"Maybe I do, if you got the grit to tell me to my face."

Jim smiled sardonically. "If you must know, you are a coward who hides behind a mask and a gun to make people think you're hard. You're too lazy to work for what others have so you steal it, thinking it will satisfy you, but it never will. You think threatening women and unarmed citizens is somehow virtuous. It's not. I can go on if you want."

The bandit squinted his eyes and his face turned purple with rage. "I oughta kill you for…"

Just then, a shot rang out toward the rear of the train followed by a quick volley. A scream of pain could be heard above the gunfire. "Let's get out of here," shouted the leader. The bandits scuttled out of the passenger car and mounted the horses that had been held in a nearby copse of trees.

"Baker bought it," came a cry from one of the bandits who had been on another part of the train. "Some wild man yelling something about, '*Thou shalt not steal*,' come out of the stock car and let him have it."

The door swung open again and in stepped Preacher with his gun still in hand. He glanced around before holstering his weapon. "Them fellers was trying to steal the horses. I figured they maybe never heard the eighth commandment. Course, they didn't want to listen, so's I had to teach 'em the hard way. Unfortunately, one of them won't get the chance to mend his ways."

"Should have known you'd be involved in their 'instruction'," Jim replied. "I heard several shots. Were you hit?"

"Me? Why them fellers couldn't hit a bull in the butt with a bass fiddle. Just glad the horses weren't hit by stray bullets." Preacher noticed the young lady beside Jim. "You do beat all. I leave you alone for just a bit and you find yourself some pretty female company." He turned to Emily. "I'm right pleased to meet you miss. I'm Preacher. I hope this young rapscallion hasn't been too bothersome. He's usually pretty good, if'n I'm around to keep an eye on him."

Emily stared at Preacher for a moment. "Did you say you're a preacher?" she asked. "I never heard of a preacher carrying a gun about so openly."

Preacher laughed. "Shucks. No ma'am. I'm not a preacher. I am Preacher. Least-wise, that's what folks call me. As for carrying a weapon openly, sometimes you need to defend yourself or others. Jesus even told his disciples that if they had two cloaks to sell one and buy a sword for their journeys. I like my old hogleg a bit better than a sword. I don't think the Savior would mind too much me using it instead of an extra-long pig sticker. Now, who might you be?"

Emily stared at this strange man before her. For a few seconds, she could not answer. Finally, Jim answered for her. "Preacher, this young lady is Miss Emily Tate, recently from the East. She's headed to Broken Bow to meet her fiancé, Beauregard Leonidas Templeton. Can't say as I have heard of him, but we're all headed the same direction, so we figured to keep each other company."

Emily found her voice again. "I heard one to the outlaws yell something about 'Baker bought it'. What did he mean?"

"Never knew his name, but out here, that means he bought the farm. He's no longer amongst the living." Preacher shook his head solemnly. "Crime don't pay except in lead, hanging, or a short life of always looking over your shoulder. Too bad most won't learn that until it's too late for them. God gives them ample chance, but they tend to make the wrong choice more often than not."

"You mean, you shot him?" Emily gasped.

"Well, seein' as how he was trying to shoot me, it seemed like the thing to do," Preacher replied. "We don't cotton to getting' shot up out here too much nor to getting robbed. There ain't a lawman around every corner to call on like back east so we mostly discourage killing and thieving ourselves."

"But you didn't discourage him, you killed him," Emily said. Her eyes widened as she stared uncomprehendingly at Preacher.

"I'd say he's pretty much completely and permanently discouraged now," Preacher replied with a grin. "I reckon I'll just head back to the stock car and make sure the horses are settled down before this smoke belching beast gets moving too fast. A couple of those boys might be packing some lead, so I got some new folks to be praying for now, too." He turned on his heel and strolled back out the door of the passenger car as the train slowly gained speed. He could be heard grousing about noisy, newfangled contraptions as he disappeared into the night.

"Where did he come from?" Emily asked. "Do you know him?"

Jim replied. "That's Preacher. He's no man to tangle with, but he'll give you the shirt off his back even after you tried to do him hurt." Jim's eyes seemed to stare into the past as he remembered his first meeting with Preacher.

"But he killed a man," Emily countered.

Jim stared at the young woman for a few seconds before responding. "I've seen him spare lives far more often than he takes them. Like he said, out here a man has to stand up for justice himself. There isn't a constable around every corner, and sometimes force must be met with force. He's mostly peaceable, but he has a strong sense of right and wrong. I don't figure you'll understand it, being fresh from the East, but it takes tough men to make it out here and to make the West hospitable for decent folks who will come later. When they come, men like Preacher will settle down and become model citizens. Until then, men like him will be about the business of making this wilderness fit for civilization."

Arthek looked at Jim. "You should be making speeches. That was as good of one as I ever heard those politicians make, and a lot more honest."

Jim shook his head. "Thank you, but no thank you. I think I'll stick to the business we are heading back to Broken Bow for. I have no taste for politicking."

CHAPTER 28

The rest of the journey to Helena was uneventful. During the final stretch of the trip, Jim, Arthek, and Emily engaged in small talk, and Emily began to feel more relaxed with both men. When the train pulled into the station, the engineer quickly sought the sheriff to report the robbery while the passengers disembarked and went their separate ways.

"So, Miss Tate, are you staying here for a few days or are you going to take the next stage to Broken Bow?" Arthek asked.

"I would really like to get there as soon as possible. I really don't have much in the way of funds. How often does the stage run?"

"There isn't a real schedule," Jim replied. "They run once a week or so, unless there are enough passengers to make it worthwhile to make another run. We can walk you to the stage depot and find out when they are expecting to make the next run," he offered.

"What about my luggage?" Emily asked. A confused look crossed her face.

Preacher walked toward the small group. "I'll keep my eyes peeled for it and keep guard over it whilst you're checking the stage schedule. Nobody'll bother it none," he said, smiling. "I sure am glad to be out of that there train and back outdoors where a body can feel the ground under his feet 'stead of having it swaying and rocking. I was born for open skies, a horse to ride, and solid ground under my feet."

Emily looked at Jim and Arthek. "He will keep watch, and it should not take us long to make our inquiry," Arthek reassured her.

"Well, I suppose it would be prudent to check," Emily replied.

The three of them started toward the center of town, and then Arthek turned back to the train. "It would not be right to leave Preacher to watch for the bags and unload the horses by himself. I'll stay and lend him a hand."

Jim nodded. He and Emily continued toward the center of town. "He's a strange man," Emily stated.

"Arthek? He seems alright to me," Jim replied. "A bit formal at times, but nothing strange about that, even out here."

"No. Preacher," Emily gave Jim a quizzical look. "He seems so rough and yet to hear him speak of praying for those whom he shot and who tried to shoot him... it just seems strange."

"I suppose maybe it does. The first time I met him, he sure showed me the straight and narrow." Jim smiled at the memory. "He never starts a fight, but he sure isn't one to back away if the cause is just. I was spoiling for a fight when we met, and he took the starch right out of me. Then he introduced me to his best friend. Things haven't been the same since then."

"The way you two interact, I thought you were his best friend." Emily turned slightly toward Jim which stopped them both.

"We've been close friends since that day, but 'there is a friend that sticks closer than a brother'. That's who he introduced me to that day. I was hunting a man to kill him for leading a raid on my home and killing my family. Preacher convinced me to leave it to his friend to take care of. It wasn't easy, but I turned that man's fate, and mine, over to Jesus that day. I have no idea if Jacobs is alive or not, but I do know I'm not the same man I was when I met Preacher and Jesus. Preacher doesn't preach in a church, at least not often, but he preaches with his life."

They walked the rest of the way in silence as Emily contemplated what she had just heard.

Entering the stage office, they walked to the counter where the agent was dozing. Jim tapped lightly on the counter. There was no movement, so he tapped a little louder. When he still received no response, he cleared his throat and gave a hard slap to the countertop jarring the agent from his slumber. "What's the meaning of all the noise? Can't you see I'm busy?" The agent stared at the two young people before him. "Well, what do you want?"

Jim winked at Emily. "I'd love a few thousand dollars, but I guess we would settle for seeing when the next stage to Broken Bow is running. Besides, the 'love of money is the root of all kinds of evil'. I can do without evil right now."

"Smart aleck youngster," The agent grumbled as he pointed at the schedule nailed to the wall. "If you'd just look yonder, you'd see the schedule and wouldn't have to bother me with your silly questions."

"Thank you, sir," Emily responded. "We are sorry to disturb your repose."

"Re... what? Are you making fun of me?" The agent stared at Emily.

"Repose, sir. Your rest." Emily smiled sweetly.

The agent's demeanor changed. "Sorry to be so gruff, ma'am. You see, I ain't been getting much sleep of late and sometimes I doze off in the heat of the day. When I get woke sudden-like, I tend to be a bit rough."

"We'll take a look at the schedule, and let you get back to your busy day," Jim said, glancing at the schedule. "Are there any specials running in the next few days?" He asked.

"Nobody is heading out into Cheyenne territory too often. They sure ain't fond of us white folk moving in on their land. There's been some trouble brewing."

"I suppose they wouldn't be too happy about that," Jim replied. He smiled as he looked over the schedule. "Is this right? No runs for three weeks?"

"If'n that's what it says, that's what it means," the agent retorted.

"Three weeks?" Emily cried in despair. "But I don't know if I have enough for that many days lodging and stage fare. I did not anticipate such a delay." She sat wearily on a bench in the office. Her face contorted as tears began to flow.

"That blubbering won't change nothin' miss," the station agent growled.

"Neither will your attitude mister," Jim growled angrily.

After a moment, the agent looked at Emily and grinned slightly. "I reckon I was a bit harsh miss. I surely am sorry you're in such a fix, but I just don't know what I can do to make it better."

"That's quite okay, sir. I'm certain no harm was intended," Emily graciously accepted the apology. "I do so wish there was some way to get to Broken Bow sooner though."

"You could maybe hire a rig, but that would cost you more than stage fare. If'n you wouldn't mind cleaning the office, I could maybe get the bosses to pay you a few dollars so you could wait until the next stage runs. I can't make no guarantee, but I can ask," the stage agent offered.

Emily stammered a bit. Just as she seemed ready to make a decision, Preacher and Arthek meandered through the door. "Well, we got the horses unloaded and we brung Miss Emily's bags. We might need to pick up a few things before we head out," Preacher stated. "Arthek reckons we may need some special supplies. We'll probably have to hire us a wagon and team or maybe buy one if we can get a good price to haul it."

"Did you learn when the next stage is?" Arthek asked.

"That we did. It's not for three weeks. Kinda left Miss Emily in a pinch. We were just discussing some options with the agent here when you two walked in."

Preacher whistled. "Three weeks. Miss Emily, you got the funds to stay that long here? And is there a fit place for a decent lady to stay that long in this town?" He swiveled his gaze from Emily to the agent.

"There's a couple of widow women that run a nice clean boarding house up the street," the agent offered. "They'd be happy for some extra boarders. Of course, I don't know what they'd charge you."

"But I really don't want to wait three weeks for the stage," Emily replied. "I don't know if I have enough, and what if the stage is delayed? I don't know anyone here."

"I wish I knew how to help missy, but I'm just the agent. I just sell the tickets. I don't make the schedule."

Jim turned to Preacher. "If we pick up a wagon, she could ride along with us. We're headed that way anyway. She'd get to Broken Bow quicker, and it would allow her to save her funds."

"I don't know," Emily responded. "It doesn't seem proper to travel without a chaperon."

"Well now, Miss Emily. We are a bit less formal out here, but you do have a point." Preacher looked at the station agent. "Are there any other ladies going west that are waiting for the stage? Perhaps they might want to go a little sooner too?"

The agent scratched his chin. "I ain't supposed to let on that we got passengers waiting, but I figure if the main office can't get the stage to run a decent schedule, who am I to keep people waiting. There's a couple with their daughter wanting to go that way. They might take you up on an offer to accompany you. Not sure where they'll be staying, but about this time of day, plenty of travelers go to the Blue Bonnet to eat. You might look there. The man's a medium built feller with a round face. His wife is nigh as tall as him. She looks to be a few months along. Their gal's maybe eight or nine. Typical freckle-faced kid with braids. Go by the name of Davidson, I think. They been here about a week so far. They keep checking back every day to see if there's a special. I'm thinking their funds are getting tight, and they'd be anxious to get on the trail."

"Thanks," Preacher replied. "I'm feeling a bit hungry myself. Which way did you say it was to the Blue Bonnet?"

"Mind if we leave our belongings here?" Jim asked.

"They'll be safe enough if you bring 'em in," replied the agent. "Can't say for sure if you leave them outside."

They brought in Emily's trunk along with their duffle. The agent gave them directions, and the four of them headed to the diner.

"If we find that family, perhaps we could all travel together," Arthek stated. "It would seem like the prudent thing to do."

"That may be just the ticket," Preacher exclaimed. "But first things first. My belly button is becoming close friends with my backbone. Let's find that diner the agent told us about and wrap ourselves around a good meal? That railroad grub leaves something to be desired, namely taste."

They walked the rest of the way in silence, each one with their own private thoughts. The blue bonnet flowers painted on the doors, and the lady's blue bonnet painted on the windows made the sign unnecessary. If you couldn't figure out the name of the establishment from those, you probably wouldn't be able to read the words anyway.

Preacher held the door open for Emily. "After you," he said graciously. The four of them trooped in and found seats. Just as the agent had said, the diner slowly filled with travelers seeking a good meal. Their ears were met by a combination of laughter and levity mixed with quiet murmurs from weary travelers. Soft blue cloth covered the tables, adding to the homey feel.

As they sat, a basket of warm bread was placed on the table before them. The smell of fresh baking filled the restaurant, which made everyone's mouth water. A dish containing fresh butter was placed on the table next to the bread. "I'll be back in two shakes," said a smiling woman. "I hope you're hungry, because the boss's stew is sure to fill you up. And she don't skimp on portions neither."

A few minutes later, the four had huge bowls of fragrant stew placed before them. A pot of coffee with four mugs followed. "We got tea, too, if the lady likes." Emily shook her head no. "You all just give a holler if you need a refill. Doesn't happen often, but it sure makes Missus Hobson smile when it does. Says it shows someone appreciates her cooking besides her husband." She snickered. "And by looking at him you can tell he surely does enjoy her cooking."

Preacher bowed to pray. "Lord, this here meal surely does smell wonderful, and we surely thank you for it. We ask that you shower yer blessings on them that prepared and served it. Amen." He looked up and cut off a slab of the bread on the table, dipped his spoon into the butter, and spread a big dollop on the still warm bread. "Can't ask for better than fresh baked bread and fresh churned butter to start a meal with."

CHAPTER 29

While they were enjoying their meal, a family entered. The man looked around and then spoke quietly to his wife. The little girl gazed around in anticipation of a meal. Tears could be seen in the woman's eyes as her husband gave her some of their meager funds. "You and Abby go on and have a good meal. I'll be just fine. I'm not really hungry."

"But... ," his bride started.

The man just smiled and gave her a hug. "No buts about it. You and Abby get yourselves a good meal. I'll make do."

"There's enough for all of us," his bride began to protest.

"Don't you fret. Go on now and get yourselves a decent meal. When the stage pulls out, they'll set us up with food along the way. Once we get to Broken Bow, things will look up. Just wait and see. For now, you two just enjoy your meal. I have some things I need to check on."

Slowly, the mother and daughter found a seat while the husband walked back out into the growing dusk. "What's wrong mommy? Isn't daddy hungry too?" the little girl asked.

"He has a lot on his mind," the woman replied. She tried to smile. What were they to do if the stage did not pull out soon. All of their cash was tied up in a small homestead near a place called Broken Bow. "Don't worry Abby. God always provides."

Preacher overheard her. "That, He surely does ma'am. Might you be the Davidson family?"

"We're the Donaldsons," she replied cautiously. "Who might you be?"

"Well, I might be Saint Nicholas hisself," Preacher replied winking at the little girl. "But most folks just call me Preacher. I wasn't meaning to listen in, but I couldn't help overhearing that you folks are heading toward Broken Bow. It just so happens, we're heading that way ourselves and have found ourselves in a quandary. You see, Miss Emily wants to get out there right quick, but the stage ain't running for a good bit. Us three ain't planning to wait on a stage, so we was going to get us a wagon and some supplies and head out right smartly. The trouble is, Miss Emily don't have herself a chaperon. If you folks wouldn't mind the company, we'd be pleased to have you ride along with us. Why don't you go grab your man and have him come back in so's we can talk?"

Missus Donaldson looked questioningly at Preacher.

"You might as well do as he says ma'am," Jim said. "He's right sure of himself, and he can be a might stubborn once he's set his mind to something. From what we gathered at the stage office, they have no idea when the next stage will be going that way. This may work out for all of us. Kind of like God ordained it."

"I don't know what to say!" Missus Donaldson exclaimed.

"I'd say, don't say anything and go get Mister Donaldson," piped in Arthek. "It may be that Preacher has an answer to all of our dilemmas. Go fetch your husband and join us here."

Missus Donaldson looked at Abby. "You stay here while I go get your father," she said. Then she looked at the assortment of strangers seated at the table. "Can she sit with you until I return?"

"Why, of course she can," Emily replied. "It will be a pleasure having some female company for a change." She smiled. "You go get your husband."

"Are you sure she won't be a bother?"

"You go on now," Preacher replied. "We'll be right here when you get back."

Missus Donaldson dashed out the door into the growing darkness. When she returned a few moments later with her husband, Emily and Abby were in an animated conversation. Abby's eyes were wide as she gestured with her hands.

Mister and Missus Donaldson arrived to catch a little of the conversation. "You mean Preacher chased all of the train robbers away?" Abby asked.

"Twern't me," Preacher interjected. "It was their own guilty conscience that made 'em skedaddle. I just reminded them that thieving is a bad thing to be doing."

The Donaldsons arrived as the story ended. "Mommy, Daddy," she began. "Preacher chased away the train robbers and saved everyone on the train. He's like Billy the Kid, but a lot nicer, and he's not a robber."

"I'm far from Mister Bonney. I don't associate with criminals nor seek out trouble. There's a definite difference between seeking trouble and being ready for it. But I think you meant that in a nice way, so I do thank you."

"I'm sorry, Mister Preacher. I only meant you weren't scared of nothing."

"I know that Abby. Now don't you give it another thought. And you can call me Preacher, not Mister Preacher."

"Whatever have you been telling my daughter?" Mister Donaldson asked.

Emily looked at the homesteader. "I was just telling her about our train trip here. I suppose I may have gone a little overboard. I'm Emily."

"I'm Elijah," said Mister Donaldson. "And this here's my wife, Maggie. It looks like you already met Abby. It's a pleasure to meet you." Introductions were made and the Donaldsons sat down.

"I hope you don't mind, but I ordered some fried chicken with all the fixins for you folks," Preacher stated. "Abby said she hadn't had any since ya'll left Indiana. That's a fair piece to go without fried chicken, and it sounded like it'd be a treat for you folks. This stew is plenty for us, but I've a feeling you'll appreciate the chicken."

"I thank you Preacher, but we don't have the funds for such a meal," responded Mister Donaldson. "I reckon we'll make due with some soup."

"Nonsense," said Jim. "We have the funds, and we invited you, so it's our lookout for the cost. Don't give it another thought."

"We don't take charity," Donaldson retorted.

"Charity? Who said anything about charity? We asked you to join us for a meal and to talk to you about some travel arrangements," piped in Emily. "You see, we have a bit of a dilemma we were hoping you could help us with. Since you are our guests, it would be rude for us to expect you to pay anything."

"She has you there Elijah," said Missus Donaldson. "Why don't we hear them out? Besides, fried chicken does sound good."

Her husband squirmed slightly. He had skipped more than a few meals so his wife and child could eat, and the meal offered sounded delicious. "Okay Maggie, we'll hear them out. And we thank you for your hospitality," he said to Preacher.

Preacher chuckled. "Don't thank me. The youngster's paying." He looked meaningfully at Jim who shrugged his shoulders.

"You invite them, and I'll pay the freight," he replied with a smile. "We are glad you could join us, Mister Donaldson."

Before anything else could be said, a huge platter of chicken arrived along with mashed potatoes, a gravy boat, some carrots, biscuits, and a plate with butter on it.

The Donaldsons looked hungrily at the feast. "I hope you don't mind if I give thanks," Elijah said. "I figure we might have a few things to be thankful for before this night is over."

"We wouldn't mind that at all," Jim replied. "In fact, it would be a nice change of pace to have someone else say grace. We'd be honored."

Everyone bowed their heads. The Donaldsons held hands as the patriarch prayed. "Lord, we thank you for this meal, and for our new friends. We ask for your blessing on them and those who made this meal. I'm not real sure of the why of this yet, but you are, and I ask you to give wisdom to us tonight and always. In the name of Jesus Christ, our Lord and Savior, Amen."

Preacher looked at his companions thoughtfully. Whatever it was he was thinking, he kept it to himself as he passed the platter of chicken to Maggie.

Taking a small piece, she passed the platter to her husband who took a wing before placing a leg onto Abby's plate.

"Please take more than that," Arthek said. "Why, that is barely enough to feed a ground squirrel. Don't insult the cook."

Maggie and Elijah looked sheepishly at Arthek. "Well, go on man," Arthek continued. "Put some food on those plates. What we have to talk to you about will require more strength than that little bit will give you. Besides, there is plenty for all."

Maggie looked longingly at the heaping platter before taking a second piece of chicken. Then she skewered a large breast and placed it on her husband's plate. "Please," she implored him.

His smile told her all she needed to know. "Thank you," he replied. There was no more resistance to the offered hospitality.

"Well folks," Jim started when the meal was done. "Why don't we have some berry cobler and coffee while we talk? The waitress said they have the best cobbler this side of anywhere."

Abby beamed and nodded her approval to the cobbler. What-ever the grownups wanted to talk about was fine with her as long as she could have some cobbler.

Elijah looked at his family's benefactors. "I suppose you didn't invite us here just for our company. And you sure didn't invite us to rob us. If that's the case, you made a mighty poor choice."

Emily laughed. "In a sense, we did invite you for your company. You see, we understand that you are traveling in the same direction that we are and are awaiting the stage." She didn't wait for a response before pressing on. "Since it appears that nobody knows when that stage may run next, and I have a strong desire to get to my destination as early as possible, we wanted to ask if you may want to travel together with us? As I am unmarried, I need a chaperon to travel with men who are not my family members. Well, there appears to be nobody else going the same direction, and we thought you may want to get to your destination with as little delay as possible as well. Traveling together might fulfill both of those needs and desires."

"We don't have money for a rig." Elijah looked dejected as he spoke. "Otherwise, we would have started out on our own already."

Preacher nearly jumped out of his chair. "By gum, that works out just right. We need someone to drive an extra rig, and since Jim and me prefer riding to driving a wagon, we could maybe use you to drive for us, and Miss Emily could come along without no worries."

"Could we Daddy?" Abby implored her father.

"It won't be easy going," Jim reminded them. "But I don't think it would be any worse than riding a stage for that long, and we can get started as soon as tomorrow sometime."

"Well, I don't know. What do you think Maggie? It would mean sleeping out in the wild, but we could get underway sooner."

Before Maggie could respond, Abby piped in. "Sleeping out in the wild? What fun!" she exclaimed. "We could have campfires and sing songs and listen to the crickets and count the stars. Can we, please?" Her exuberant response caused the adults to laugh.

"There's a bit more to it than a camping trip," Jim said, when he stopped laughing. "But you could do those things too."

Maggie bit her lip. "It would get us underway sooner, and I don't suppose it would be any harder sleeping on the ground or in a wagon than it would on a hard bench at a stage stop." She looked toward her husband.

"I reckon I'm outvoted, even if I did want to wait for the stage, which I don't." He turned to their hosts. "What would we need to bring with us?"

"We need to make sure we can secure an outfit and a few supplies that Arthek here says we'll need, but as long as there are no issues with that, all you'll need to bring is yourselves and whatever baggage you are taking with you. We'll be checking on those things at first light. What say we meet here tomorrow morning, say seven o'clock, and have a hearty breakfast before we set out?" Jim asked.

"That sounds fine to me," Elijah said. "I'm sure my girls will like the breakfast before we go. I'll make do with some coffee though. Need to save what we can for when we get to our new home." He tried to smile.

"I forgot to tell you that if you're going to be driving one of our wagons, we couldn't ask you to do that for free. We can't pay a lot, but how does two dollars a day and food sound? You can drive, and your missus can help with the cooking and such. I figure it will take at least two weeks to make the trek. Let's call it fifteen days. I pay in advance," Jim concluded.

"I don't know what to say," Elijah replied. "We were just looking for a way to get out to our new home. I wasn't thinking about hiring on to drive a wagon." He extended his hand. "Thank you. My Maggie is a right good cook, and I'll be happy to play mule skinner." He took Jim's hand in a powerful grip and pumped it vigorously. "You hired yourself a driver."

They proceeded to discuss arrangements before going their own way. Preacher walked Emily to the boarding house that the stage agent had recommended. "I'll be back tomorrow morning bright and early," he said before heading back to meet with Jim and Arthek near the livery.

***

"Well, we may or may not be able to get an outfit here," Jim began. "It seems that the owner is out for the evening, and his hired man isn't in a position to make that decision. I suppose we'll have to wait for morning and see. He said that they have some horses broke to harness, but he doesn't know if the boss will sell them or not."

"Nothing for us to do but to wait and see then," the older man replied. "You got our horses bedded down, don't you?"

"They are quite comfortable," Arthek interjected. "Now, for us, I'm not quite so sure. It appears that there are a limited number of sleeping accommodations available in this town, and it sounds as though many are quite disreputable."

"We could always sleep here if the hostler doesn't mind," Jim stated.

"Well, let's ask him. We've definitely slept in worse places," Preacher drawled.

The hostler had no objections, but he told them, "There's a family sleeping in one of the empty stalls, so you'll have to sleep in the loft. Nice folks. Just a bit low on funds."

"No need to think about who that might be," Arthek whispered. "At least it's warm and dry. I took a liking to that sprout of theirs. This may just be an interesting trip."

The three men returned to the stage office to gather their belongings before bedding down for the night. They could hear the

Donaldsons talking softly when they returned but left them to their personal thoughts. Morning would come soon enough.

CHAPTER 30

Curly told Tom about the shanty town, but they decided to hold off until Jim and Preacher returned. "It won't do to charge up there without a plan," Tom told him. "I know cattle and horses. Those two know men. It'd be best if we wait for them to get back. I'm thinking they know how to handle something like this better than you or I do." The next several days saw Curly dividing his time between breaking horses, scouting the ramshackle borough that seemed to spring up overnight, and riding into Broken Bow inquiring about Jim and Preacher's return.

"I saw Boise up there," he confided to Tom one evening. "I don't reckon he saw me, but he was there, bold as brass. Next time he and I meet, I'm not too sure it'll be just fists that settle things. I can't abide a thief and a Judas. It looks like he might be both."

"Don't go off halfcocked Curly. I know you don't care much for him. Neither do I as far as that goes, but we can't just shoot him on sight. Why don't you ride into town tomorrow morning and see if Jim and Preacher are back yet?"

"I reckon I'll do just that. I sure hope they get back here pronto. I got a bad feeling about that crew up there in those hills."

Early the next morning, Curly headed into Broken Bow. His mission was simple. See if Jim and Preacher had returned. If they had, he was to fill them in on the recent developments. If not, he was to return to the ranch and see if he could saddle break some of his wild horses. Two of them had dropped foals recently, so now he had extra work to keep him busy and away from the new burg in the hills. That storm would keep until Jim and Preacher returned.

CHAPTER 31

Arthek stretched and yawned. He assumed he was the first of the travelers to rise. To his surprise, Jim and Preacher were both in conversation with someone who could only be the livery owner. He climbed from the loft and joined Jim and Preacher. In a back stall, the Donaldson family began to stir.

"Well, good morning Arthek. We wasn't sure if you'd died in your sleep since you didn't move when we climbed out of the loft." Preacher indicated the man to whom they were speaking. "This here's Mister Carlson. He owns this here place. We were just discussing a wagon or two and some horses or maybe some mules. He says he might be able to fix us up."

"It is my pleasure to meet you sir," Arthek said. "Please, don't let me interrupt, but is there an outhouse here?"

"It's round back," said Carlson.

Arthek took his leave, and the three men continued their conversation. As they were haggling, Elijah approached. "I do appreciate you allowing us to use your barn to sleep in. If you make a deal with these gentlemen, we'll be leaving with them. I sure do hope you can come to terms."

"I don't mind you folks sleeping here. Your little one needed somewhere warm to sleep, but we'll come to an agreement. I'm sure of that. What I'm not sure of is who'll get the best end of the deal. These two have traded a few horses in their time. Now let us get back to dickering."

Twenty minutes later, the deal was sealed with a handshake. Money changed hands and a wagon with four sturdy horses was brought to the front of the livery. "You take good care of them horses," Carlson said. "They'll do all you ask of them if you do. Treat them wrong, and they'll balk every chance they get."

"That we shall remember," Arthek promised. "Now, we should get to the diner and then pick up our supplies."

Abby arrived, still groggy and with straw in her hair. "Do they have names?" she asked. "They should have names."

"Well now Abby, we ain't named them yet so maybe you could give them names, if they don't have one yet." Preacher looked at the livery owner who chuckled.

"I've sold and traded a lot of horses in my time, but I've only named one and he died on me, so I quit naming them. Generally, I just call them 'horse'."

"Horse isn't a good name. I think I'll call this one George, that one Henry, that one Samson, and the last one Brownie. I think all horses should have names. How else could you tell them apart?"

"I generally just say 'that sorrel over there with three white stockings,' or 'that paint mare,' or whatever color they happen to be. 'Course now, if you want to give them proper names, you just go ahead," the livery owner said as he shook his head.

By this time, Maggie had arrived. "Why don't you folks head over to The Blue Bonnet and we'll be along directly," Jim said to the Donaldsons. "Since you're going to be driving the wagon, why don't you throw your belongings in and drive it to the diner? We'll gather our horses and gear and meet you there."

The Donaldsons quickly gathered their meager belongings and placed them in the wagon while Jim and Arthek collected the mounts and settled the stable bill. Preacher strolled to the boarding house to escort Emily to The Blue Bonnet. Her baggage was still at the stage office, and they would pick that up before heading out of town.

"We should have Arthek secure the supplies we'll need when we get back to the Lazy H. Are they still at the train depot?" Arthek nodded in the affirmative. "The ladies can find what we'll need as far as food stuffs over at the general store, I would think," Jim said. "Preacher and I will see if we can find some tarps to cover the wagon and to use for cover when it rains. Does anyone need a bedroll or some blankets?"

"I hadn't thought of that when I came west," Emily confessed. She looked down at her feet.

"Don't you fret about that," Maggie said while she comforted the young woman. "We've got plenty to share."

"We'll get some extras in case there are some cold nights. Preacher and I are used to this kind of travel, but it can get cold at night, and it never hurts to have an extra blanket or two. Just have the bill ready when we get there, and I'll take care of it. Elijah, you bring the wagon and come with Preacher and me, and we can all get started." Each party set off to their assigned destinations.

"This is going to be fun mommy!" exclaimed Abby. "Just like a camping trip. I hope we see lots of animals and maybe some Indians." She skipped alongside the two grown women.

"I'm afraid I have never been camping before," said Emily. "Are there really Indians where we are going? The stage agent made it sound like they were everywhere and very dangerous."

"I'm sure they are around, but I don't think we should be worried. God's protected us this far. He won't let us down now." Maggie's face was serene. "Besides, Preacher and Jim seem quite competent. Speaking of Jim, is he your beau?"

Emily laughed. "My, no. We met on the train. I'm heading to Broken Bow to meet my fiancé, Beauregard Templeton. This just seemed to be the fastest way to get there."

"Oh. I hadn't heard. I just thought. Oh, never mind what I thought."

The trio entered the general store. Beans, bacon, flour, salt, coffee, sugar, and other staples were ordered. "I heard Jim tell Elijah it would be about two weeks. I hope we have enough to make the trip. The men can supply us with fresh meat if need be, but we need to make sure we have enough of the basics. I wonder if any of those men thought to get a skillet or a Dutch oven? I reckon we might as well get both and extra of everything. Better to have extra and not need it than to not have enough," Maggie remarked.

Jim stepped through the door as Maggie was asking about the cookware. "I plumb forgot about those," he admitted. "Don't forget potatoes and some carrots if they have them. We already got the grain for the horses. We'll get blankets and ground cloths while we're here. Arthek should be ready with the other supplies once we get finished up here."

As predicted, Arthek was standing in front of a pile of odd equipment and supplies when Elijah pulled the wagon up near the depot. "What in the wide world is all of this stuff?" Elijah asked.

"Just a few items we'll need for our task once we reach Jim's ranch. Some are pretty delicate, but most are just heavy. That's why we needed a wagon," was Arthek's reply. The "few" items weighed as much as all of the other supplies combined, but no further questions were asked. Arthek mounted his horse and the small caravan proceeded from town.

Jim took the lead with Preacher bringing up the rear. Arthek rode beside the wagon. The peaceful start of the trek belied what was to come at the end of the journey.

The first night out of Helena, Preacher pulled Jim to the side as Elijah got a fire going. The women broke out some of the provisions and began to prepare the evening meal.

"Anybody following us?" Jim asked.

"Looks like we're all alone out here. I don't think anyone paid us any attention."

"That's good. I was hoping we didn't arouse any curiosity with Arthek's contraptions. I'm guessing most folks were too busy with their own worries to worry about some strangers buying a wagon. Truth be told, I was more worried about someone following us hoping to rob us if they saw us spending so much and then pulling out. Not to worry, I guess. Not too many would want to follow us where we're going when the pickings would be easier in town. Let's get some shut eye."

"I'll tend first watch. I'll wake Arthek and he can wake Elijah. He can wake you for last watch," Preacher suggested.

"Sounds fine as frog hair to me," Jim replied.

The crickets began chirping and some lightning bugs began to blink after the meal. Abby ran around trying to catch some of the lightning bugs near the rim of firelight. The men discussed the day's journey and night watch while the ladies cleaned up after the meal.

Elijah pulled a guitar from their belongings and began to strum a few cords of a familiar song. Everyone gathered and listened as he played and sang quietly.

"We'd best get some rest. We'll be pulling out early tomorrow," Jim said when the song was finished.

CHAPTER 32

As night fell on the tenth day of their journey, Emily and Abby were gathering wood for the evening cook fire when everyone heard a blood curdling scream coming from their direction. Guns drawn, Jim and Preacher arrived first, followed closely by Arthek and Elijah bearing rifles. Three young Cheyenne braves raced their ponies toward Emily and Abby, laughing exuberantly. A larger group of Cheyenne could be seen in the distance. Recognizing it as a hunting party rather than a raiding or war party, Jim shouted in their tongue, drawing their attention from the two females they had been hurtling toward, to the four armed men heading their direction.

Spinning their mounts in a show of superb horsemanship, they retreated toward their kinsmen, grins still on their faces. The four men approached the sobbing Emily and wide-eyed Abby who kept watch on the band of Cheyenne on the not too distant plain. "What do you think boy?" Preacher asked Jim. "I don't reckon they were too unfriendly, but there was only three in that batch."

"They have women and children with them, from what I can see. My guess is, they're following game. The young fellers were probably out scouting for meat, saw these two, and figured to have some fun. I figure I might take a ride out and do some palavering. We have some extra flour and sugar, don't we?"

Abby finally found her tongue. "Those were real live Indians weren't they? I never saw one before." Her face was still pale from fright.

"Those were Cheyenne," Jim replied. "Finer friends you'll never find, and worse enemies you'll never have."

Emily had stopped sobbing and leaned against Arthek. "They looked so fierce. I was sure we were going to be killed and scalped."

Jim chuckled. "Not likely. They might have dragged you off and married you off to some warrior, but I don't think they would have scalped you. If it had been a war party, that might be different. Just the same, I think I should go out and make some talk with them. Make sure of what they're thinking. You think you can get these ladies back to the wagon while I take some of our extra food for their young?" he asked Arthek and Preacher.

Elijah scooped Abby up into his arms. "Are you sure they won't cause trouble?"

"That's what I intend to find out," Jim replied. "A little bit of food for their youngsters can't hurt but don't ever give it out of fear. They despise cowards but appreciate generosity toward their children. If it was just braves, I'd handle things different." He gathered some flour and sugar, then noticed an extra bag of beans and some bacon. "I don't think we'll miss this little bit. Go ahead and get to fixing dinner but make some extra. We may have guests," he said as he mounted and rode toward the column of Cheyenne. He looked back over his shoulder. "One thing. If I come a fogging it back here, we could be in for trouble."

Jim rode purposefully toward the slowly moving band of Indians. He made no attempt at stealth but rode at a leisurely pace toward them. "I sure hope they know Two Bears," he mumbled to himself. When he was about fifty yards from the Cheyenne, two men rode toward him. He halted and raised his hand in greeting. "I am Can't Die. Are these the people of my friend, Two Bears?" he asked in Cheyenne.

"No," was the single word response. "You come with us," the brave continued.

"That was my intent," Jim said confidently. "Please lead on."

Jim scanned the throng that began to gather around him. They were not the friendly people he knew so well. "Why so many sad faces?" he asked. "Does the hunt not go well?"

"You ask much. You can ask Black Hawk. He will decide what to tell you and what not to."

"Black Hawk? I know of him. He is a great leader but is usually far south from here." Jim looked around again. He fell silent as his escort led him to a man who was nearly fifty but still strong.

"This one comes to us saying he is Can't Die and knows Two Bears. White men deceive. I think he lies. He is here to spy for the blue coats."

"I speak the truth," Jim retorted. "If you dare to say I lie again, you will have to defend your lies. I, Can't Die, friend of Two Bears, will not be disrespected." To allow the insult to go unanswered would be a shame in the eye of the Cheyenne.

"You dare to..."

The brave's response was cut short by a motion from Black Hawk. "So, you are Can't die?" the leader said to Jim. "You do not look as fierce as the stories told of you. Perhaps Standing Elk is right. Any white man can say he is Can't Die."

"But what white man would ride into your camp and announce such a thing in Cheyenne? Most white men do not know your tongue, and of those who do, very few know of the name given to me by Two Bears. If you doubt, look." Jim peeled off his shirt revealing a torso crisscrossed with scars. "Gray Cloud's medicine healed me and made me strong for what I had to do."

"Ha!" shouted the older warrior. "So, you are who is spoken of among the tribes. Standing Elk, be glad you did not insult him further. He is a guest."

"He could not know," Jim replied. "Come, I have a little for your pots. Beans, flour, sugar, bacon, and coffee. There is not much, but we are happy to share. How is the hunting?"

Standing Elk scowled but said no more as talk welled up.

"Black Hawk, would you and Standing Elk do us the honor of joining us to eat tonight? I told the women to make extra for guests. You can tell us of your journey and why you are so far north."

Before Standing Elk could reply, Black Hawk answered. "We will be your guests this night, but tomorrow, we must move on. Game has become scarce because of white hunters who kill for hides and leave the meat to rot. It is not good."

Jim nodded in response. So, it was true what he had heard about the buffalo hunters taking hides by the thousands and leaving the carcasses for the scavengers. "No, it is not good. Two Bears has not told me of this, but I have heard such stories."

He handed the meager provisions to Standing Elk who handed them to one of the women standing nearby. Black Hawk shouted to one of the nearby warriors to distribute the food to the children and elderly first. Whatever was left would be shared with the rest of the band. Then the three men rode toward the white man's camp.

***

"Hello there Jimmy boy," shouted Preacher. "Who's your friends? It don't look like Two Bears to me." The other two men stood nervously beside the wagon.

"This is Standing Elk and Black Hawk of the Southern Cheyenne. They've come north looking for game. Seems like the hide hunters killed off too many buffalo. There isn't much left for them to the south."

Preacher grunted. "It's sad. A way of life dying because of greed and ignorance." Then he said in Cheyenne, "You're welcome at our fire." He looked at Jim and smiled. "A bit rusty, but I can still say a few things."

Standing Elk laughed. "You talk pretty good, but we understand your tongue. Although, it is good to hear a white man at least try to speak in our language."

Abby had sneaked from behind the wagon and stared at the two Cheyenne.

Standing Elk scowled, but Black Hawk stared back at her. "Have you never seen a human being before?" he asked.

"Why, yes sir, but I've never seen an Indian before."

"We are the Tsistsistas. That means *beautiful people*. We call ourselves human beings. We are great and proud warriors too. And what are you, little girl?"

She looked at him dumbfounded. "I'm a little girl, and I'm a human being too. Haven't you seen a little girl before?" She scrunched her brow.

"I do not know. Do they all look like you?" The three mounted men began to chuckle at Abby's consternation.

The rest of the camp had begun to relax with the possible exception of Emily, who was still upset from her earlier shock.

Elijah broke the silence. "Why don't you climb on down? The women just about have supper ready, and there's coffee on the fire."

The three dismounted and Maggie poured coffee for the men. Jim sipped his as the two Cheyenne took a sip before asking for sugar. They added a healthy dose and sipped again. They then smiled as they enjoyed their coffee.

As dinner was being ladled onto plates, Jim asked again about the hunting.

"It has been very bad. The buffalo to the south have been slaughtered and left to rot. We have followed what is left of the herds north. We have tried not to invade others' hunting grounds, but that is not always easy. There used to be enough for all. Now, there is very little. Even rabbits and prairie dogs hide from us." It was Standing Elk who spoke.

Preacher listened in. "It's a sad thing to see the buffalo gone. God gave us those critters for food, not to waste." He shook his head sorrowfully. "I've seen how many just one would provide for, and they're leaving hundreds for the scavengers."

Black Hawk scowled. "The white men do not respect the land. The Great Spirit gave plenty for all, but the white man, he wants it all."

"Why are they just killing them?" Elijah asked. "It doesn't seem right."

"Right or not, that's what's happening," said Jim as he shook his head. "I wish folks would see it's causing people to starve and making enemies where there's no need to."

"We should drive all the whites from our lands," Standing Elk stated emphatically.

Preacher had been listening in. "I figured it'd be better if we were all just good stewards of what God gives us. I figure, there'd be a heap less fighting over what we can't take with us when we pass on. You Cheyenne have the right idea. Take what you need and leave some for those who follow."

Standing Elk grunted a begrudging agreement, and Black Hawk nodded. "It would be better, but too many are not willing to live that way. There is too much distrust and fear."

"I pray that there can be trust and friendship between us. You are welcome at our fire any time. We are happy to share what is in our pots with you." Jim looked steadily at their two guests.

Standing Elk looked at Emily and chuckled as he noticed her nervousness. "Your squaw has not the iron of her man," he said to Jim.

Jim realized the implication and laughed. "She's not mine," he replied. "She's promised to one with a name as long as the sky. We're just escorting her to him. After that, she's his lookout, not mine."

Emily skulked off, but Abbey came closer. "That's not nice to pick on Emily," she said. She looked sternly at Jim and Standing Elk who were both caught off guard.

"Little Girl might be a human being after all," laughed Black Hawk. "She certainly has the spirit of one." Then he turned to Abby. "It is good to be brave little girl. I think I will call you, Little Human. It is a good name."

Abby looked askance at Jim, but it was her father who spoke. "It is indeed a good name," he said to Abby. He smiled at Black Hawk. "Perhaps one day you can visit Little Human at our home. You will always be welcome."

***

With the meal finished, the Cheyenne returned to their camp and the men sat around talking for a little while. Abby climbed under the wagon and stared wide-eyed at the fires in the Indian camp until she fell asleep. Emily and Maggie sipped coffee and listened in on the men's conversation.

"You don't figure they'll sneak into camp or attack us do you?" Elijah asked. "The station agent seemed pretty sure they were on the rampage."

"If they wanted to attack us, we'd already be dead," Preacher replied. "Besides, we have one of their legends riding with us. Young Jim here is known among the Cheyenne. Now if they was Blackfoot or Crow, we might have a problem, but not so with the Cheyenne. They set store by Jim for some reason or another. We're safe enough."

"We're a lot safer with them nearby than others I've met," Jim stated. "They're good folks. Just pushed to the point that they're deciding if they're ready to fight back or not."

"Do you think the little bit of food we gave them bought us some good will?" Elijah asked. "It seemed like so little for so many."

"It didn't buy us anything," Jim said. "It was a show of respect and friendship. Like I said, if they thought we were trying to 'buy' their goodwill, they would have rejected it completely and considered us cowards. They have no use for cowards. They respect even their enemies as long as they show courage. That's why I offered to share from what we had extra."

Emily spoke up. "What about the ones who were attacking Abby and me earlier? Might they come back tonight?"

"That was far from an attack. It was just some young braves having some fun. No different than some cowhands on a Saturday night. They meant no harm. Just having some fun at your expense. Why don't we all turn in and get some sleep? We should be at our destination in just a couple of days."

The next morning, there was a venison quarter hanging from a limb on the edge of the camp, and several rifle shots were heard in the distance. "It looks and sounds like hunting has improved," observed Preacher. Sounds like they found at least a few buffalo, and that deer haunch is sure fresh. I sure pray they find good hunting the rest of their journey."

As they were preparing to pull out, Standing Elk trotted his horse into their midst. "Black Hawk said to give this to Little Human. When other Human Beings see it, they will know she is one too." He tossed a necklace made from buffalo teeth to Jim.

"I will make sure she gets it. And thank you for the venison. It sounded as though the hunting has improved."

Standing Elk smiled. "Black Hawk says it is Little Human's medicine. I think the buffalo just got tired of running." He whirled his horse and cantered back toward the Cheyenne camp.

The next few days were uneventful, and the small group rolled into Broken Bow in high spirits. All in all, it had been a pleasant trip.

CHAPTER 33

"Elijah, why don't you get the team watered while we check to see what's been happening in our absence?" Jim said. "I'll check in with some folks we know to let them know we're back."

"Not that they'd miss you too much," Preacher said to Jim. "Now, someone like me, that's a different story. I'll figure they'd sleep a whole heap better knowing I've arrived safely back here after taking a journey with you."

Jim just grinned and shook his head. Before he had ridden fifty yards, he saw Curly riding into town. They saw each other at the same time and rode toward one another.

"Curly, I figured you'd still be out catching horses. What are you doing in town?"

"Is Preacher here too?" Curly asked.

"Of course he is. What's going on?"

"I'm sure pleased you two are back. We got some talking to do. It seems like some squatters moved in on that area where we don't run no cows. I don't know most of them, but Boise is there. They were talking about gold."

"That's what we were trying to avoid." Jim scowled. "Let's go tell the others." He turned his horse and the two rode back to where

Preacher and Arthek still sat on their horses. "Preacher, Arthek, it sounds like we have trouble waiting for us. Curly says there's squatters on our claim. It'll spell trouble for sure."

"Let's get off the street to somewhere that we can talk," Preacher suggested. "Someplace not so open nor crowded."

"Let's see if Arthur Bollinger's around. It wouldn't hurt to have some legal input," Jim suggested. "I hope Miss Tate's settled in and looking in the right direction for Mister Beauregard Leonidas Templeton. She's likely to get him shot if she calls him by his full name."

"Beauregard Leonidas Templeton? That's a mouthful alright." Curly smiled as he drawled the name. "Could be someone would have some fun at his expense if'n she used his whole moniker. Can't say as I've heard that one."

The men rode off in the direction of Arthur Bollinger's office. Finding him alone in his office, they entered. "Hi, Mister Bollinger. We have a question for you." Jim began to explain what he knew with Curly filling in the gaps. "So, you see, we kinda need to know where we stand and how to deal with this, hopefully without guns blazing."

Arthur Bollinger stroked his goatee. "Legally, you have full title to that land. That being said, it could take some time and legal wrangling to throw the claim jumpers off. During that time, they could rob you blind and destroy the whole Lazy H. It could be that some don't know they're on private land. They might not be so hard to move along, but there is gold involved, so no telling what their reaction might be. Those that know it's private property might be a lot harder to evict. I'll draw up some legal papers for you to post, but I can't say how effective that will be. Give me a few hours, and I'll have them ready for you."

"That's the place to start then. If they don't go, though, I reckon we'll have to move them," Jim replied.

The men walked back through town to where Elijah was caring for the horses. "Elijah, where exactly did you say your homestead was? Jim asked. "I don't recall any new places nearby."

"It's out a bit northwest of town. I'm not surprised you haven't seen it. The cabin is rather small, but we'll add to it as we need. I've kinda kept to myself while staking it and setting up the house. Plenty of game, and some of the richest dirt I've seen west of the Mississippi. Could be we're going to be neighbors."

"We'd like that fine. I'm betting Tom and Dinah would love some friendly neighbors, and their little girl would sure like having another little girl around to play with," Jim said. "Do you figure to have a crop farm? Corn, taters, tomatoes and so on?"

"Well, I don't figure we've enough land for cattle, other than a milch cow or two, but I've been known to grow some fair vegetables, and maybe we'll put in a small orchard to go with it."

"That sounds fine to me," Preacher replied. "By the by, does anyone know if Emily has found her man with the two-dollar name?"

Maggie came from the general store and heard the last question. "No, she hasn't yet, and most people she has asked had never heard such a name. Someone said there might be a Bo Temple but no Beauregard Templeton."

"Could be he shortened his name a mite when he arrived. He wouldn't be the first to do it neither," Preacher observed. "A man can shorten his handle, but he can't change his looks too much. Did this Bo Temple match her man's description?"

"It was a pretty vague description that could have been any man. Mayhap, she can stay with us while she searches for him. We can put the word out that she's here. If he's any kind of man, he'll come find her." Maggie looked at her husband, who nodded his assent.

"She could keep Maggie and Abbey company while I get some things done that need doing," said Elijah.

Emily came down the street. She searched some of the other businesses to no avail. "He just isn't here," she stated dejectedly. "Nobody even seems to have heard of him. I almost expected him to have set up shop by now. He's a lawyer, and there seems like there might be plenty of clients for him."

"If we would have known he was an attorney, we could have asked Mister Bollinger about him. He should know if anyone new hung out their shingle," Jim replied. "In the meantime, Maggie mentioned, you might be able to stay with them while you look for Beauregard. I'll ask Arthur next time I get a chance. Could be he's heard about him."

"You would do that for me?" Emily asked. "That would ease my mind if you would."

"Sure thing. We'll be picking up some legal papers before we head out of town anyway. I'll ask him then." Jim turned to Elijah. "If you wouldn't mind following us with the wagon out to the Lazy H so we can unload, we'd be obliged and we'd be happy to help you get settled into your new home. A good bit of what's in it is your belongings."

"I was wondering about getting the wagon to your place. We'd be happy to follow you there. It'll be good to meet your partner and his wife. If they're anything like you, it will be a pleasure to meet them."

"They ain't nothing like Jim," Preacher interjected. "They're good Christian folk. Not heathens like my young friend here."

"Heathen? You're one to talk. Trouble seems to follow you everywhere you go."

"We was talking about Tom and Dinah now, and they are good Christian folk ain't they? And I never said nothin' about me. God fearing gentle soul that I am."

Jim started to reply but decided to surrender rather than talk himself into an even deeper hole. "I reckon they are that," he responded.

"Then it's settled," Maggie stated. "We'll follow you to your ranch and help unload. Then, you can come over and see our new home." She turned to her husband. "It is fit for folks to see, isn't it?"

"Maggie, you fret too much. The roof was still on it, and it was still standing when I came back to get you and Abbey. All we need to know is that it is our home now, and these folks are sure enough welcome any time. I'm certain they've seen a bit of dust before." He smiled at his bride.

Jim pulled Elijah aside. "We may have some trouble when we get back to the Lazy H. It appears some squatters have moved onto a part of the range and are making a mess of things. We are going to have to remove them. I wanted to give you some warning in case they come your way on their way out. I don't think they'll be too happy with us when we move them out."

"Why'd they be upset about getting moved off land they don't own? There's plenty out here for everyone."

"It's more than just land," Jim explained. "We discovered gold on the back section of the ranch and that's what they're after. Like I said, they won't be too happy when we tell them to go."

"Gold?" responded Elijah in a whisper. "Is that what all the stuff Arthek brought along is for? I just figured you were doing some surveying."

"We are doing some of that, but there is some equipment that's for more than just surveying. I'm not quite sure how any of it works, but he does. We don't want to destroy the land when we go after the gold. He says he knows how to do that, so we brought him along."

Maggie strolled over. "Can a lady butt in? I need to make sure my husband hasn't forgotten anything we'll need when we get to the house. Like maybe a broom or some kerosene for the lamps. Mind if I borrow him back?"

"You go right ahead, Maggie. Elijah, you mind what I told you."

The two walked off together discussing the immediate needs of their new home. What little they had brought out was already secured in the wagon, and there was enough room in it for anything else they might need.

"Arthek, why don't you and Emily see if there is anything she might like at the general store. Preacher, Curly, and I have a bit of talking to do. We'll meet you at the Silver Nugget when you get done. Let the Donaldsons know if you see them. The Nugget's a decent place where ladies and children are allowed. Can't say the same for some of the other places." The groups each went their own direction.

***

When they reached the Silver Nugget, Jim, Preacher, and Curly found a quiet table away from other patrons. "Okay Curly, give us all the information you have," Jim said. "How many are there? How bad do things look? Is the water downstream already fouled?"

"Well," Curly began. "There's a passel of tents, but only one building that looks like it would withstand a decent breeze. Looks like someone stacked some flat rocks up for walls. I'd guess about forty or more folks there. None too wholesome, if you catch my meaning. I did see Boise, like I said, and a couple of fellers in the stone house seemed to be the ones running the show. The crick's getting muddied up some, but the stock still has plenty of places for fresh water. At least until a dry spell hits. Why don't we just take the whole crew in there and run 'em out?"

"We may have to do that in the end, but I'd prefer not having to shoot anybody if we can avoid it," replied Jim. "You said two men seem to be running the whole shebang?" He looked at Preacher. "Maybe the ones from Rosebud?"

Preacher scratched his chin. "That'd be a good guess. Their kind don't worry none about the legalities of things. That shopkeeper sure showed an extra amount of interest when I paid him with gold."

The comment about the shopkeeper drew Curly's interest. "Would he be the one who mistreated Raven Wing? I might have something to say to him."

Preacher looked knowingly at the bald puncher. "You may want to thank him. If he'd treated her right and been honest with her, you'd have never met her. I'd let that lay. Besides, we got bigger fish to fry."

"Preacher's right Curly," Jim said. "For now, let's figure out the problem at hand."

Curly fretted. He was anxious to get back to the ranch. "I still say we should just gather the boys and drive them out. They didn't look all that salty, and they sure never asked if they could move in."

"Like I said already Curly, we'll try some more gentle persuasion first. Just keep your hat on until we see the lay of the land," Jim replied. "If need be, we can always do it your way later."

The men fell silent as a waitress brought coffee. Once she was out of earshot, they resumed their conversation. "How long do you figure they've been there?" Jim asked.

"From the looks of things, I don't reckon they could have been there more than a few weeks. That being said, none of them look much like they plan on making any permanent homesteads. Some tents and a lean-to or two. Except for that stone building, nothing looks solid."

"Time could be on our side then," said Preacher. "They ain't set for the long haul. As long as they aren't gettin' rich, they might be convinced it ain't worth the effort to stay once they get served with the facts."

Elijah, Maggie and Abby walked in, and Preacher waved them over.

"Arthek told us to meet you here," stated Elijah.

"We figured this place is respectable and you being fairly new here, it just made good sense," replied Preacher. "Abby, I hear tell this place has sarsaparilla sody pop. You ever had it?"

"What's sody pop?" she asked, crinkling her nose. "What do you do with it?"

"Well, it's a kind of drink, like water or milk exceptin' it tastes a bit different. It sure sounds like you never had none, so with your folks permission, of course, I reckon it's time you had some. If it's alright with you, Elijah and Maggie."

"I heard of it. You sure it's okay for her to drink?" Maggie asked.

"Well, the medicinal uses are questionable, but it won't do her any harm, Maggie," Preacher replied. "I drink it from time to time my own self. It's sody pop. I reckon the makers of it figured that they's some who prefer to have their wits about them while drinking something."

"Well, if you're sure," Maggie said with a touch of concern.

Jim laughed. "I drink it myself when I can get some. It's sweet tasting and harmless. Some say it settles your stomach. All I know is, it doesn't muddle your mind nor judgment."

Arthek and Emily arrived, and the group placed their order. When their order arrived and everyone started eating, Abby looked dubiously at the bottle of sarsaparilla before her. She took a sniff before taking a tentative sip. A smile split her face as she took a longer pull at the bottle. "This is good. Thank you, Preacher."

"You are most welcome. Now we need to finish our meal and get some rest if we're going to get to the Lazy H tomorrow." He turned to Emily. "Did you find your man? This town ain't that big that an easterner could hide out for very long, especially with a moniker like his. Could be he is that Bo Temple feller and just shortened his name, but you can never be sure. You planning to stay here in town until you locate him?"

"I hadn't thought about it much, but I think that would be best. At least he will know where to look for me. I can continue to make inquiries too."

Jim spoke up. "It might be at that, but this isn't the East and folks aren't quite as civilized. Just use your head. Do you have enough funds? It's not as expensive as Denver, so they will stretch a bit further. Still…"

"I think I have enough for a few days. After that, I will just have to find work. I'm sure I will find Beauregard before then."

"The offer still stands to stay with us," Maggie offered. "It'd be nice to have the company. On top of that, you can save what little you have left for an emergency."

"Thank you. I will give it some thought. I just don't want to miss Beauregard."

"We'll ask again before we leave in the morning, and leave word where he can contact you," Jim said. "If you decide to stay with the Donaldsons." He turned to Arthek. "Will you be ready to leave in the morning?"

"Without a doubt. I have everything packed away in the wagon. All I need to know is the time."

"I think Bollinger opens shop early. Why not have breakfast here? We can call on Bollinger right after that, ask about Emily's beau, and head out to the Lazy H."

Everyone agreed and went their separate ways after supper. Emily chose to go with the Donaldsons.

CHAPTER 34

Bollinger was in his office the next morning when Jim and Preacher arrived. "You said this Templeton is an attorney? Can't say I've heard that name, but there was a lawyer who arrived and headed out to Rosebud a few weeks ago. Could be him. I feel sorry for Emily if he's mixed up with that crowd. That kind is always trying to find a way around the law or outright break it if it suits them." Then he changed the subject. "Here's those papers you'll be wanting. I sure hope they do the trick."

"So do we," Jim replied.

Emily decided to travel with them when they left town since she didn't know anyone else. Abby was ecstatic to have someone besides her mom to talk to.

"Our place is off to the south just a bit in a small canyon," Elijah said when they were about three miles out of town. "Got a small spring and enough ground to put in enough crops for us to live on and maybe some to sell or trade. Anyone hereabouts raise any corn, or beans, or melons? I'm sure most of the ranches put some oats in for their stock."

"Not many put anything in, including oats. Mostly hay, and the hands cut and stack it against the winter. It kinda grows on its own. It might be nice to have something different for a change."

"You haven't told them about the apples you hope to plant, have you?" Maggie asked. "There's something to be said for fresh apples in the fall and fresh squeezed cider." She licked her lips, closed her eyes, and smiled dreamily.

"That sure does sound good," said Preacher. "I never saw any trees in your wagon, though."

"We brought plenty of seeds so even if not all of them take, we'll have plenty that will. It'll be a few years before we have a crop, but it will be worth it. There were even a few wild apple trees in the canyon. I'll have to really prune 'em to get 'em to produce anything worthwhile."

Conversation continued during the leisurely trip to the Lazy H. Dinah came from the house when the wagons pulled up in the yard. She shaded her eyes and recognized Jim, Preacher, and Curly. "Well, welcome home you three," she said. "It looks like you managed to find some friends along the way. Tom'll be pleased to see you. The boy's noon wherever they're working, but they should all be here for supper. Climb on down." Little Tom, now almost two, hid behind his mother until he was sure it was safe.

Sarah raced from the barn with Rufus bounding after her, barking all the while. The wagon horses snorted and stamped until Sarah caught Rufus by the collar and calmed him down. "Hi Jim. Hi Curly. Hi Preacher," she shouted before noticing anyone else.

"Well, hello Sarah," Curly hollered in reply. "How's my second-best gal doing?"

"Second best? Oh, that's right. Raven Wing is your best, best girl. I'm doing good. Raven Wing took the milk cow down to the creek, but she sure will be happy you're back. Who are all of these people?" she then asked.

Abby, who had been dozing in the back of the wagon, sat up. Sarah's eyes lit up with the thought of another girl about her own age to play with. "Hi, I'm Sarah. I live here. Who are you?"

Abby looked a bit befuddled. "I'm Abby. Where is here?"

"Here is my house. Well, mine and my mommy and daddy's and Little Tom's. Do you want to meet Rufus? He's my dog."

"Can I Mommy?" Abby asked. It had been a long time since she had someone her own age to play with.

"Of course, honey. Just don't go too far. We have to go to our own home as soon as we get everything unloaded here."

Abby climbed down from the wagon, and the two girls ran off to play while the adults introduced themselves. "Why don't you all stay for supper?" Dinah asked. "We have plenty, and I'm sure Tom and the crew would love to meet you."

"We would love to Dinah, but Abby and I have never seen our new home, and we're anxious to. Perhaps another time?"

"What about you, Mister Arthek? You're more than welcome," Dinah insisted.

"I'd be happy to accept your hospitality Missus Dalton. Just let us unload my equipment and say farewell to the Donaldsons. I'm sure we shall see them again soon, and Miss Tate also. All the best to you, Emily, in finding your man."

Just then, a cow bell could be heard approaching from the creek. Curly turned to look in that direction as the milk cow came into view. He swatted the dust from his clothing and swung his horse toward the approaching cow. Raven Wing recognized him and started in his direction. Before she had gone more than a few feet, she found herself being scooped from the ground by an exuberant

Curly. Emily looked on with disgust as Curly swung Raven Wing onto his horse with him and kissed her.

Emily turned to Preacher. "Isn't she an Indian? I thought Curly was a white man," she said.

"Miss Tate, out here, we judge folks based on who they are, not what color their skin is. Miss Raven Wing is every bit a lady, Indian or not, and Curly intends to marry her. We have a few Lakota hands on the ranch, and the Cheyenne visit from time to time. I'd not be maligning her."

"I'm sorry. I just thought, with Curly being white and her being..."

"An Indian?" Jim finished for her. "Like Preacher said, we judge folks by who they are, not their skin color. To be honest, I don't think Curly could find a finer woman than Raven Wing. Let's let it drop."

Emily was dubious but said no more.

Curly rode up and set Raven Wing gently on the ground before alighting himself. "Miss Emily, Mister and Missus Donaldson, I'd like you to meet my intended, Raven Wing." While a bit surprised, Elijah and Maggie recovered and extended their hands. Emily was a bit slower, but she, too, shook hands.

Raven Wing noticed Emily's hesitation. "You not worry," she said, keeping a straight face. "I not scalp anyone in many moons. Maybe burn at stake, but no scalps." She said it monotone, as if she struggled with English. When Emily recoiled, Curly interjected.

"Raven Wing, why you funning this gal? She's fresh from the East and you're like to scare her half to death." He shook his head. "Miss Emily, she's just funning you. She never scalped anyone in all her born days, nor has she ever burned anyone at the stake."

Raven Wing smiled. "Forgive me. I should not have acted the way I did. It is truly a pleasure to meet you. Do you prefer Miss Tate, or is Emily appropriate?"

Emily recovered quickly and replied, "Emily is fine. It appears that things are far less formal out here."

"You're right as rain Emily," chimed in Dinah. "So, what brings you out here from the East? And how did you meet up with Jim and Preacher?"

The men started unloading the wagon as the women talked. "I came west to meet my fiancé, Beauregard Leonidas Templeton, but nobody seems to have heard of him. He was supposed to meet me here in Broken Bow. I met Jim and Preacher on the train from Denver. I must tell you of our ordeal when we have time."

Little Tom had made his way to Preacher's side, where he tugged on Preacher's pant leg. "Up, up," he pleaded until Preacher picked the youngster up and set him on the wagon seat.

"You sit tight whilst we get this stuff unloaded. Then we can see what kind of mischief you and I can get into." Little Tom giggled but sat patiently while the wagon was unloaded.

"Do you still think there is time to get to your place before dark Elijah?" Jim asked. "Like Dinah said, we have plenty, and Tom'll sure be upset at not meeting our new neighbors."

"I'm not sure if we will make it before dark. Let me ask Maggie what she thinks. It might be best to arrive in the early morning instead of at dark and still needing to prepare a meal. It'd be nice to meet this Tom too."

Elijah then shouted, "Hey Maggie, we've been asked to supper. I'm not too sure we'll get to our place before dark. What do you say?"

Dinah looked at Maggie. "We'd be happy to have you. The girls are getting along. I'm sure they would love the extra time. Sarah doesn't have anyone her own age to play with. You can bunk here and start out at first light. We can even ride along to give you a hand."

"If you're sure it would be no trouble," Maggie replied.

"It would be our pleasure. We don't get a lot of company other than Two Bears and his people. I'm sure Tom would like to meet you folks as well."

Maggie relented. "Elijah, we're staying for supper."

"Well Jim, that answers that," Elijah said with a smile.

CHAPTER 35

J im and Tom had some of the hands help the Donaldsons get moved into their new home just a couple of miles from the ranch headquarters. When asked, none of the hands had heard of Beauregard Templeton. Jim hadn't expected them to have, but he knew there was a chance.

"We'll keep asking around," Jim told her a few days later while visiting the Donaldsons. "It's a big country, but a man doesn't usually just disappear without someone hearing something."

A few days later, Jim, Preacher, Tom and Curly were looking over the horses that Curly had captured. "They sure aren't the regular broomtails you normally see," Tom stated. "Do you reckon they'll give you and Raven Wing a start?"

Curly smiled. "I figure so. That is, if'n you and Jim'll swap me a few of 'em for some cattle. I saw some pretty country not too far from here that looks likely to make a good home for us."

Jim looked longingly at the horses. "I figure we can swap a couple of culls for some of those nags."

Curly glared at him. "Nags? Why, any one of them is better than a lot of those swayback crowbaits you ride now. Just look at that mare and foal over there. Sleek and strong of limb. I'd say her and her foal's worth a few head of breeding stock by their lonesome."

Tom smiled. "Not to worry Curly. We'll make you a fair deal. Right now though, I think we have some other things to discuss." He turned to Jim. "What are we going to do about the squatters?" He asked. "I know you've been thinking on it since you got back."

"I think Preacher and I will ride up and post some of those legal papers that Bollinger did up. We can get a better lay of the land that way too. Hopefully, some of them will pull out once they get notice."

"How come you rope me into all your confrontational situations? If I didn't know better, I'd think you was always trying to get me into a scrap. Me with all my gentle ways, and you hunting trouble." Preacher smiled. "What are we waiting for? No sense putting off until tomorrow what should prove fun and interesting today."

"You and your *gentle* nature? I'd say you're looking forward to this little venture," Tom said. "You two want any company?"

"Not this trip," Jim stated. "We may need a show of force later, but for now, we'll try to do it peaceably. In the meantime why don't you and Curly work out some of the details on that stock swap? We could use some decent mounts. We'll be back before nightfall."

Jim and Preacher swung aboard their mounts and trotted off in the direction of the gold claim.

***

The two men were greeted by a hodgepodge of makeshift shelters. Like Curly had said, many looked like a strong breeze would blow them away. The area was littered with hunks of broken rock mixed with broken bottles and refuse.

"This can't stand," Jim growled to Preacher. "They will leave or be buried here."

"Take it easy Jim. We need to get the lay of the land before you pop a cork. I do agree with you, though. We can't let this stand."

They continued down the littered trail until they reached what looked like the center of the collection of shacks. Preacher glanced around. "You gonna just post that up somewhere, or you gonna announce it so's everyone knows."

"I reckon to announce it loud and clear. We don't want any confusion." Jim shouted for attention only to be ignored. Failing in his endeavor, he drew a weapon from his saddle scabbard and pointed it at the sky. The thunderous boom of the ten-gauge shotgun drew all eyes to him.

"Now that I have your attention, I have an announcement to make. For those of you who may not understand the legal terms on this paper I'm going to post, you're all trespassing on Lazy H land. You'll have forty-eight hours to pack up and get out. I'm James Harding, and I own this spread. You've fouled one of the streams our cattle use for drinking during the dry season and moved onto land that isn't yours. Take what you brought and get out." He swung down from the saddle and tacked one of the notices to a small tree that had somehow managed to not be destroyed. "You've had your notice."

As Jim started to swing back astride, one of the crowd ripped the paper from the tree and threw it to the ground. "I think you're the one who's gonna get out," he shouted. "I don't see no notice."

Jim slowly turned to the man. "What's your name?" he asked.

"Nunya," was the reply. "Nunya Business." He laughed at his poor joke.

"Well Nunya," Jim replied. "You're going to post the next notice yourself. Then you'll pack up and get out now, not in two days."

"And if I don't?"

Jim wasted no time. He struck instantly. The contentious man had his nose broken and his ribs bruised before he knew he was in a fight. By the time he realized it, he lay unconscious in the dust. Jim took a bucket of water and doused his opponent, who shook his head, flailing water from his hair.

"I hope that answered your question. Now here's the new notice. Tack it up where the old one was. Then get out and stay out."

Jim started to turn away when the man threw the new notice to the ground and reached for his gun. Preacher's old Dragoon Colt bellowed, and the man tumbled to the ground never to rise again. Jim spun back around drawing his right-hand Colt. "I reckon his soul left this world, but his body will still be here. A couple of you fellers bury him deep, and one of you best post that notice."

As the crowd moved cautiously to obey, a man came from the stone structure that Curly had mentioned. "What is the meaning of all of this? What happened to Jeffers?"

"If that was that feller's name, I guess he got himself shot trying to back shoot someone: me. I figure he inherited a place here on the Lazy H the hard way."

"And who might you be?" the new arrival asked.

"Well, I might be Paul Bunyan or General Crook, but I'm not. I'm James Harding, and I own the Lazy H Ranch including everything you see here. Now, who might you be?"

"I'm Bo Temple, Attorney at Law, and you are trespassing."

"Bo Temple? That wouldn't be short for Beauregard Leonidas Templeton, now would it?" Preacher asked.

"How would you know that?" Bo demanded.

"There's a gal that came out here who's been looking for you since she arrived. She's staying with some nice folks a few miles from Lazy H headquarters," Preacher responded. "Now you, being one of those lawyer types, I figure you can read what Jim had pinned up on that tree. I hope we don't see this rabble here again."

"You can't throw men off their claims," Templeton fumed, but it was to the backs of the two men as they rode away.

Beauregard picked up the notice that was still lying on the ground where Jeffers had thrown it. The second one was obediently tacked back to the scrubby tree where the original had been tacked. He walked back into the stone building. Two sets of eyes watched from the shadow of the stone building.

"What was all the ruckus about," asked one of the two when Bo returned. It was Simmons who asked. "And who were those two?"

"It was someone named James Harding. He said he owns this land and posted this notice outside," was the response. "I haven't had time to read it yet, but I am sure we can fight it in court. Even if his claim is legitimate, I can file several motions and tie it up for a good long time, Mister Simmons."

McCabe glared at the young attorney. "That's what we pay you to do, ain't it?"

"Mister McCabe, I assure you, I will have no problem dealing with these yokels in a court of law. You have nothing to fear."

Simmons interrupted. "I'm confident Mister Temple will help us hold this claim. He's proven quite competent so far."

CHAPTER 36

"Do you reckon we ought to tell Miss Emily we saw her intended?" Preacher asked as they rode away from the noise and congestion. "Her man has hisself mixed up with a bad lot."

"She has a right to know, but I'm not sure we should be in a rush to get that information to her. I'm sure she'll be pleased he's here. I'm just not too sure how she'll take it with him taking up with outlaws and apparently fitting right in," Jim replied. "Let's give it a day or two before we rain on her parade."

"I suppose you're right about that. I pray he breaks loose from them before he winds up with a noose around his neck."

"I hope he does too," Jim replied.

The two rode the rest of the way to the ranch in relative silence.

They arrived at the ranch just before dusk. Tom and Curly came from the house to greet them. "I see you're all in one piece. So, how'd they take it?" Tom asked.

"Well, one of them won't be leaving," Jim responded. "I just hope the rest take the notice to heart and pull up stakes. I sure don't want to start a graveyard up there."

"I have my doubts though." Preacher shook his head, and the two men swung from their saddles. "I'm pretty sure we didn't see the big augers, but you can bet your boots they saw us and know who we are."

"I'd have to agree with you, Preacher. They are the type to know what's going on in their operation. They didn't know us in Rosebud, but they found out we were there fast enough. I don't think it will be any different here."

Jim turned to the other two men. "Let us take care of these horses, and we'll come in and give you the rundown. They sure are making a mess up there though." He and Preacher unsaddled their mounts and rubbed them down before turning them loose in the corral.

The coal oil lamps were burning, and Dinah had reheated supper for the two men by the time they walked in the door. Dinah and Raven Wing brought the meal and coffee. "I made a few changes while you and Preacher were gone. Curly, why don't you go grab Josh and have him join us," Tom suggested. "If he thinks he can be foreman, he can start learning what the job entails. Don't you forget to come back too."

A few minutes later, Curly returned with a wiry puncher with a slight bit of gray at the temple. "This here is Joshua," Tom announced. "He says he's worked cattle from here to Mexico but wants a chance to ramrod an outfit rather than just ride for one. The last couple of weeks, he's been doing a right good job keeping everyone working, and he seems to know the business. We're growing and can use a foreman now."

"Howdy Josh," greeted both Jim and Preacher as he shook hands with both men.

The men discussed the situation near the gold find. Curly provided information from his observation while Jim and Preacher each added their own perspective. "It sounds like we got our work cut out for us," stated Joshua. "If there's gold, they won't be likely to give up too easily."

"There's gold, and I am afraid you're right about that Josh," Tom replied. "Jim and Preacher have been gone a bit to see if there's some way to extract it without destroying the range. That's what that Arthek feller is here for."

"What we saw up there confirms what Curly told us," Jim stated. "Unfortunately, there's one who won't be leaving. He tried to draw down on me when my back was turned. They'll be planting him by now. Let's pray there aren't more that follow his example. We gave them two days to clear out."

"Speaking about praying, it might be a good idea to do a bit of that now, before we make our plans." It was Preacher who spoke. The men nodded in agreement and doffed their hats. "Lord, we ain't nearly smart enough to know how we ought to handle this here situation. We don't want more killing, but we can't let them that are stealing and tearing up your creation to keep doing so. Guide us and show us what we need to do. Amen"

Amens were muttered and the men put their hats back on before the talk resumed. "Let's hear what you two have to say," Tom said. "We ought to be able to think of something if we have the lay of the land. There's five of us."

"Don't you forget there's a couple of womenfolk here that might have some insight," Dinah interrupted. "We might not like the idea of our menfolk getting shot up because they stormed the castle instead of thinking things through. And believe it or not, we are more than just a couple of pretty faces."

Tom looked embarrassed. "Well, you're free to listen in. If the shooting starts though, we want you gals far from it."

Jim chuckled as he thought about his first meeting with Dinah a few years before. "I don't know Tom. If I remember right, Dinah's a pretty fair shot. She dang near shot my toes off when we first met." Now it was Dinah's turn to be embarrassed.[1]

Tom laughed as he thought back to that day. "Fair shot or not, I don't want my sweetheart anywhere near a gunfight if it comes to that."

Preacher was much more somber. "It will," he stated. "They got the fever, and most won't want to give it up. They think they'll be rich as King Solomon. Let's hope they see reason."

The group talked for several hours. Dinah and Raven Wing turned in while the men continued to discuss the options.

"I still say we bring all the boys in and just drive 'em out," Curly snarled. "They's thieves and got no claim to that ground."

"There was a time that I would have agreed with you Curly," Jim responded. "But that will get a lot of folks killed. It may still come to that, but even if a few take the hint and pull up stakes, that would sway the odds in our favor."

Curly looked dubious.

"Mind if I say something?" Josh asked. He had sat quietly for most of the conversation. "If we go up there in full force, they'll balk. Will kinda get their backs up, if you know what I mean. It might not hurt to go up with a smaller, well-armed, group at the

---

1. **You can read about their first encounter in *Vengeance Is Mine.***

end of their two days. Let 'em know we're serious and ready for a fight but not looking for one."

"That sounds sensible," Tom said. "Maybe we ought to turn in for the night and start fresh in the morning. I for one, think Josh is onto something."

The men all agreed and turned in for the night, deciding to resume their discussion after breakfast.

CHAPTER 37

Once the hands had been given their tasks for the day, Jim, Preacher, Joshua, Tom, Arthek, and Curly sat down to talk again. Dinah joined them.

"Hey Jim," Curly started. "Let me ask you something. Are you gonna need men to work the claim? I mean, most of us hands aren't too fond of the blister end of a shovel. Maybe a couple of those fellers would rather work for wages than be run off or fight."

Tom looked at Jim. "He could have a point. It might win us some goodwill. How many men would it take to run a claim the way you're thinking Arthek?"

"A couple dozen or so. If the claim is rich enough to support it," Arthek responded.

"It sounds like we might have the beginnings of a plan. We can offer those who want to stay on a job. Take it or leave it. Those who choose to fight it out can have all the fighting they can handle plus," Jim replied. They all nodded in agreement.

Tom continued the conversation. "Tomorrow, we need about six of our boys, armed with shotguns, to make the final appeal to them to clear out or join up. I think I might just enjoy the ride."

"Oh no you don't, Thomas!" Dinah interjected. "I heard what you got planned for tomorrow and you, my dear husband, are not going up there."

"Now Dinah, my dear, there's no need for worry. Besides, I need to back their play," Tom smiled but Dinah's face was drawn. She walked away.

"Dinah's right," said Joshua. "We're just going up to give final warning. No need to tip our hand yet. We got some salty fellers there, and I think a half dozen with shotguns can reason with them without you having to take a risk."

Tom scowled at the rest of the men but relented. "Okay. But if it comes to shooting, you're not leaving me behind. This is Dinah's and my home too."

"We'll pray it don't come to a shooting war," said Preacher. "Now, who you got in mind for this excursion?' Preacher directed his question towards Joshua.

"I hadn't thought much on that. You know the crew better than me. Who would you suggest?"

Curly spoke up. "Sandy's pretty salty. We rode together quite a while, and he's steady. And you can sure enough count me in."

"Bob's been around a while too," Tom stated. "Never knew him to go off half-cocked nor to back down."

"That's five. How about it, Joshua? You want to round it up to a half dozen?" Jim asked.

"I don't figure I'd be much of a ramrod if I left this stuff to others. Count me in."

"If you have room for one more, I'd like to ride along. At least I can get a clearer picture of the formation to see what we might need to do once this is all settled. And before you ask, yes I do know how to handle myself in a scrap," Arthek spoke up.

"I never thought about you riding into a hornet's nest," Preacher said. "But, if you're of a mind to, who are we to say no?"

***

With the beginnings of a plan in place, the men set about preparing for the trip. Joshua talked to the hands when they returned for the evening meal. Bob nodded soberly when he was advised what they would be doing the next day. Sandy, on the other hand, met the potential confrontation with a grin. "You mean we get to kick those rock muckers out. Yeehaw!"

"Simmer down there, Sandy. We ain't going in looking for a fight," Preacher admonished. "If it comes to it, we'll be ready, but our hope is for a peaceful resolution."

"You... peaceful? Preacher? I heard tell you can outwrestle a grizzly and ain't above slapping its nose with a willow switch, just to start things off," Sandy said laughing.

"Why Sandy, I'm a right peaceful man. I prefer not to wrestle grizzlies. Of course, if it can't be helped, I fight to win," Preacher responded.

"Preacher's right," Tom said. "If a fight has to happen, let's make sure we know what we're up against. This trip is just to encourage them folks to vamoose."

Sandy looked dejected for a minute. "Well, at least I won't have to drag any steers out of the brush tomorrow. There is that."

***

That night, the ranch had visitors. The Donaldsons and Emily arrived late in the afternoon. "Hello the house," Elijah shouted before jumping from the wagon box and helping the women to the ground. Abby had already jumped to the ground and found Sarah. The two scampered off to play.

"I must say, we weren't expecting company today," said Tom as he extended his hand to Elijah. "But you are certainly welcome. What brings you by today?"

"It was me," confessed Emily, before anyone else could speak. "I wanted to know if anyone had any news about my Beauregard. I know it's only been a few days, but I hoped for news. The area around Broken Bow isn't that well-populated so I thought anyone new might be talked about. At least I hoped you might have heard something."

Everyone fell momentarily silent. While discussing the gang up near the gold claim, Beauregard's name had been mentioned. Nobody wanted to be the bearer of the news.

Emily noticed the change. "What's wrong? Has something happened to Beauregard? Is he all right? Where is he?" Her eyes darted from face to face. Nobody spoke.

Preacher took her by the arm. "Why don't you come with me Miss Emily. I'm afraid the news we got might not be what you are hoping for. No, he ain't dead, but it ain't good." Emily, now ashen-faced, followed Preacher meekly.

Once they were out of earshot of everyone else, Preacher gently explained the situation. "Ya see, he's shortened his name some to Bo Temple. That happens sometimes out here. A fancy moniker don't mean much, but a man's character and company do. Your man got himself tied up with a rough crowd. He's lawyering, just for the wrong folks. Like I said, he ain't dead, but it ain't good. If he sticks with them, he might wind up dangling from a rope."

Emily brightened slightly. "You mean he's here and alive? Can I go see him?" Then her face clouded. "What do you mean, 'dangling from a rope'?"

"Well, I don't reckon we're planning no social call when we visit tomorrow. How about we ask him to come see you instead. It'll be safer that way," Preacher replied. "Don't worry about that rope. We'll keep his neck out of one this time, but if he keeps company with the wicked, like he's doing now, he will come to trouble."

"I don't understand. What kind of trouble? And why would he be in trouble of any kind if he is practicing the law?"

"Well," drawled Preacher. "There's a saying, 'lie down with dogs wake up with fleas'. He done laid down with some mighty mangy curs. If he don't break free of them, and quick, he'll just be one of the pack. I hate to be the one to tell you, but those he's took up with are trying to take over land that rightly belongs to someone else. We call it claim jumpin' or squatting, It makes no never mind. It's thieving, plain and simple. Any man out here knows that. If they join up with such, then they ain't no better themselves."

"Are you saying that Beauregard is a thief?" Emily's temper flared.

"I never said such. I just said he best get shut of them he's with, or he'll be branded as such. If he stays there knowing the truth, then I reckon he is a thief. I hate to tell you that girl, but that's the truth."

Emily shivered and her face turned pale. "Do you really think they might hang him?"

"Naw. Jim'll see he don't hang, but he might run him outta the country. When we go tomorrow, we'll encourage him to come see you." Preacher walked back to the rest of the group.

***

By the time Preacher returned, Jim had explained about finding Beauregard with the claim jumpers. It was a more somber group than when the Donaldsons first arrived.

Raven Wing broke the tension. "Tomorrow is another day. Today, we have friends visiting. Let us enjoy their company."

The two girls came skipping from near the corral. "Mother, Sarah showed me Miss Raven Wing's horse, Splash. Did you know that horses can look like they have paint splashed all over their rumps? She said it's an app...appa something or other. She's really pretty and nice."

"It's appaloosa, Honey," replied her mom. "I have seen very few, and yes, they are beautiful."

"Curly caught some wild ones," Sarah told Maggie. "He even healed a big stallion that fought a grizzly bear."

Maggie, Emily and Abby all looked at Curly who squirmed under their scrutiny. "Aw, twern't nothing much. He's strong and a fighter. Course, he's stove up now, but he'll throw some fine foals. Fact being, there's a few of his out in the pasture with their mamas. Be careful if you go look at 'em though. They're still a bit wild, and if that appaloosa stud's out there, he can get right mean if he don't know ya."

The rest of the evening was spent in friendly conversation. Refreshments were served. While the men talked about the upcoming confrontation, the women and girls talked about home and dreams. The girls ran off to chase fireflies as the sun set.

"Do you think they will fight over that land that the men were talking about?" Emily asked. "It's just land, and there is plenty out here."

"It is more than just land Emily. There's the gold, of course, but there's more than that," replied Dinah. "If they are allowed to stay, then it invites others to come and take what Jim and my Tom worked for. Those men are taking what belongs to someone else. If they refuse to leave, yes, there will be a fight. Men may die. I don't like it, but sometimes, men must do what is right even if us women don't like it. To be honest, I don't think they like it either."

"Preacher said that Beauregard is mixed up in it somehow. They might kill him too," Emily stated.

"Only if he takes up arms against them," Raven Wing replied. "I have only known Jim, Tom and Preacher for a short time, but I have seen both strength and mercy in all of them."

"Preacher said they will encourage Beauregard to come see me. I pray that he will listen to me and not fight them."

Elijah's voice broke through the evening air. "Maggie, it's getting late. I figure we ought to get ourselves home. Where's Abby at? Abby, it's time to go," he called.

Abby and Sarah appeared out of the shadows. She had her hands cupped together, holding something. "Look Daddy," she said as she slowly opened her hands. A beetle crept onto her fingers before taking flight. It lit up as it flew back toward the darkness. "Sarah taught me how to catch them. You move real quiet and slow. Then they don't know you're trying to catch them until you did."

"Well, I reckon it worked. You just be careful of things that sneak up on you slow and quiet."

"You be careful on the way home tonight," Dinah hollered as she waved goodbye.

CHAPTER 38

The next morning broke with a foreboding overcast sky. The storm clouds blotted out the sun as the six men mounted for their mission. Tom stood beside them as they mounted. "Maybe them clouds are a harbinger of things to come. I certainly hope not."

"You do some prayin' that we do what's right up there," Preacher said. "We'll do a bit while we're riding too. We don't want nobody to get themselves hurt or killed today."

"If Emily comes by today, tell her we'll do our best to bring Mister Templeton to talk to her, even if we have to tie him to his saddle." Everyone chuckled nervously at Jim's comment.

A slight rain began as the small group rode from the ranch yard. Apart from the occasional click of hoof on stone, the men rode in relative silence until they were within a half mile of the ramshackle burg that had sprung up. A grim mood settled on them.

"Okay everyone," Jim began. "The way I see it, we ride right into the heart of those shacks. Keep your eyes peeled and your shotguns handy. We ride with them in plain view so they know we mean business, and nobody gets any stupid ideas. Like Josh said, this is just their final warning. We aren't looking for a fight, this time, but we'll be ready just the same. I'll do the talking. Curly, you had a good idea too. We will need men to work the mine. Maybe a few that didn't know any better would rather work and make something than lose everything. It's worth a try."

The small cavalcade rode silently into the huddle of shacks. The shotguns rested menacingly across the pommels of their saddles. Water slashed on their horses' hocks as puddles began to form. Due to the result of their last entrance, several curious onlookers began to gather. The small group fanned out, facing outward.

"Hello," Jim bellowed. When the crowd quieted, he continued. "We gave you forty-eight hours to clear out when we were here last. It looks like one or two left, but the rest of you didn't understand what we posted. Your time is up. Next time we come here it will be to throw whoever is left off. You'll either leave or be buried here with one possible option."

"You got no call to run us off. We bought these claims fair and square," a prospector shouted. "We got legal claim. We spent good money on 'em."

"I don't know who sold you the claims, but they weren't theirs to sell. All of this land is owned by the Lazy H Ranch. Anyone who told you otherwise is a liar," Jim growled in return. "I said there is an option for those of you who are willing to do some honest work for honest pay. Right now, this," he waived his shotgun around the camp, "is more than an eyesore. It's polluting our cattle's drinking water and fouling our creeks down below. For those interested in an honest job, we'll hire you ourselves, but you'll extract the gold the way we say for wages. If you aren't interested, leave."

Beauregard came from the stone building into the intensifying rain. "Just who do you think you are sir? You come here and say this belongs to the Lazy H. Where is your proof? We will take this to court and see who is the liar."

"Mister Templeton, there are two reasons I don't either kill you or stomp you for what you just said. First, you are new to the West, so you may not understand the ramifications of calling a man a liar. Second, and this is the more important reason, there is a young lady waiting to see you and I promised her I would encourage you to come see her. I can't do that if you can't ride. I recommend you saddle a horse and mount up. The rest of you heard what I said. You got a choice to make. We will be back for your decision."

One of the prospectors stepped forward. "You say the Lazy H owns this here land? Why're you giving us a choice of leave, fight or hire on? If'n we really are jumping your claim, why offer us a job?" he asked.

"I'll shoot straight," Jim responded. "We'll need men to work the claim the right way. We brought in an engineer so we won't rip out the gold, leave a hideous scar, and foul the land. I'd rather hire you than run you off with nothing to show for your efforts or bury you. What's your name mister? And do you want a job?"

"I'm Ed, Ed Samson," the burly man said. "I been a hard rock miner before. My supposed claim ain't produced more than a few dollars worth of dust, but it cost me a pretty penny. If you're serious about taking some of us on, I reckon I'll take a job once the dust settles." He extended his hand and took Jim's in a firm grip. "There may be a couple others who'll take you up on that offer. I'll talk to 'em."

"Just stay out of the scrap if it comes to one, and the job's yours." Jim lifted his voice. "Any of you that want to take me up on my offer of a job, talk to Ed. As for the rest of you, next time we come back will be to throw you off the Lazy H. Mister Templeton, have you saddled a horse yet?"

Just then, McCabe and Simmons stepped from the stone building. Two shotguns swiveled to cover the newcomers. "Mister Harding, I believe it is," Simmons began. "I believe you are trespassing. If you insist on taking Mister Temple with you, you can add kidnapping to your crimes."

Sandy laughed. "Mister, I don't give two hoots what you believe, If Jim says he owns this land, he owns it. Stick around and maybe he'll give you a three-foot by six-foot parcel for you to rest permanent-like under."

McCabe started forward only to stop when Jim eared back the hammers on his shotgun. "You had your fun and your warning. McCabe, I know who you are and what you are. Save yourself some grief and get off my spread."

Jim turned his attention back to Beauregard. "Saddle up now, or I'll tie you across a horse bareback. You got two minutes."

A very rattled Beauregard Templeton left and returned with a saddled horse. "Once you talk to Miss Emily, you'll be free to go wherever you want. Until you talk to her, you are our guest," Preacher said. "After that, you're a grown man. Pick your side carefully."

The men turned their horses and began to retreat slowly. Sandy kept his horse facing the crowd until the rest were safely on their way. Swinging his mount in a tight circle he gave a piercing yell and fired his shotgun into the air before galloping after the others. The squatters froze for a few seconds. That gave Sandy all the time he needed to reach the rest of the Lazy H crew.

"You sure are one loco hombre," Josh said, shaking his head.

"Well, I didn't want them thinking we weren't ready for a party if they started it," Sandy laughed. "Besides, they seemed kinda sleepy, so I figured to wake 'em all up."

"I only pray that some of them do wake up to the truth and move on or take our offer before we return." Jim's face clouded as he spoke.

"Preacher," Jim said quietly to his friend. "It's the same gold that got my family killed. I'm not sure anymore what's the right of it. Letting it be stolen sure isn't but..." He shook his head sadly.

"We'll do some praying and talking when we get back to the ranch. I reckon He knows the answer even before we ask the question."

Jim smiled slightly at his friend's admonishment. "We'll sure need clarity before we go up there again."

***

Beauregard spoke up when they were a couple of miles along the trail. "You know we will tie you up in court for perhaps years if you decide to go forward with your ridiculous claim. McCabe and Simmons said they have title to all of that property. I just haven't had the chance to file it for them yet. Once I do, you won't be so pompous."

"Shut your pie hole," Curly barked. "You might be new to the West, but even a tenderfoot like you should be able to see you hoodwinked them men up there. Them two you're working for got no claim to that land. Once them miners know the truth, maybe we'll let 'em lynch ya."

"Sounds like the right thing to do," Sandy added with a smile. "I got a feeling, once them fellers up there realize they've been taken, they'll be looking for their pound of flesh. Not that you amount to much more than a few ounces."

Templeton blanched. "But they have legal title to that land."

"No, they don't," Bob retorted. "An' I figure you already know that. Yer just trying to hide behind some legal wrangling that ya know's a lie."

***

The rest of the ride was in silence. Beauregard rode in the middle of the armed men as if he were a prisoner, alternately glaring at the men around him and looking around as if seeking an escape.

Arriving at the ranch, the men dismounted. Tom came from the house to greet them. "Tom, this is Beauregard Leonidas Templeton. Mister Templeton, you go on inside," Jim ordered. "Sandy, why don't you ride over and see about fetching Emily from the Donaldsons. Bob, you ride on into town and bring Bollinger out here. We'll see if this Bo Temple has any sense, or if he's just as crooked as those he's working with."

Jim and Tom followed Beauregard into the house as Bob and Sandy set off on their assigned tasks. Dinah and Raven Wing came out as the men entered. "You'd best take Sarah and see if there's been any foxes in the hen house," Tom told Dinah. "And I'm certain sure Curly'll want to see you, Raven Wing," Tom told the women. "He surely will."

The ladies exited the house. Raven Wing easily found Curly checking on the roan stallion.

Once inside, they confronted Templeton. Jim spoke first. "We all know full well, whatever claims you helped them sell up there are fakes. We're giving you a chance to break away clean only because of Emily. If it wasn't for her, you'd be up in that little stone building waiting to be dragged out."

"You have no call to drag me here and threaten me," He responded. "I shall have you brought up on kidnapping charges. Those men told me they have clear title. Now you are making the same claim. Who is to believe who? It sounds like a matter for the courts, and we shall see what they have to say."

Tom spoke softly. "I have a feeling you have little concern for the right and wrong of things, but only what you can make from it. A year or so back, and everyone of those up there would already be dead." Preacher then walked in. "Preacher here slowed him down a bit. That being said, don't take him showing mercy as weakness. If you cross a certain line, mercy is no longer given. It sounds like you're really close to that line."

"He kidnapped me and I need to be careful," snapped Beauregard.

"You just hold your horses," Preacher snapped. "You ain't been kidnapped, just encouraged to visit. Sandy went to get your gal. We just plan to entertain you until she arrives. Maybe we'll educate you a little bit on the way things work out here."

"I've told you. Those men hold title to that land. It will take you months in the courts to contest their claims. In the meantime, you will be squandering your money on frivolous court filings."

Jim's lips drew to a fine line and his eyes burned like blue flames. "You and I both know," he drawled. "They don't hold anything resembling legal rights to that land. My family was butchered because of that gold and I have no intention of allowing thieves and the like to steal it. There may be a fight over who owns the claim, but it won't be in a courtroom wasting time. You and they will vacate that land by force if necessary, but you will vacate."

The mood grew more tense until the men heard buggy wheels creaking outside. They could hear Sandy's voice. "Hello, everyone. I done got to ride with one of the prettiest gals in these parts all the way from Maggie and Elijah's. She don't talk much except about her 'Beauregard'. Still, I got to escort her through all that dangerous territory betwixt the Donaldsons and here."

Tom laughed. "The only thing dangerous to her in this territory is you, Sandy."

Emily hopped from the buggy. "Sandy said Beauregard is here. Where is he? Is he alright? Can I see him?"

Jim stepped onto the porch. "He's inside, and yes you can see him. That's why he's here. Talk some sense into him if you can. If not, he can take his medicine with the rest of them grifters. We'll treat him no different. He'll have had more warning than I give to most."

Emily dashed into the house as Preacher came out, leaving her and Beauregard alone to talk. Her excited voice could be heard outside, but the words were unintelligible.

The men walked to the buggy and stood near Sandy. "She sure is a pretty thing," he said. "But she ain't got a lick of sense where it comes to that Bo feller. I tried to explain to her that he was no good. Would she listen? No. According to her, he is single-handedly going to bring law and order to the lawless West. Never mind that he's in cahoots with the biggest crooks this side of the Missouri or any other river."

"Beauty don't mean brains," Preacher said.

Inside the house, Emily flung herself into Beauregard's arms. "Are you alright? Did they hurt you?" she asked.

"I'm just fine," he replied. "They dragged me here against my will and threatened me with harm if I resisted. I shall have them charged with kidnapping and jailed for their insolence. What of you, Em? How did you get here and when?"

"I only arrived a few days ago. I traveled by train to Helena, where I met Jim and Preacher. After that, we came by wagon. Beauregard, it was so frightening and exhilarating at the same time! Preacher stopped a train robbery, and we ate supper with some wild Indians"

"But why are you here?" Beauregard asked. "I'm working on a land deal that should be very lucrative, but I wasn't quite ready for you to be here yet."

Emily stepped back. "Aren't you glad to see me? I came to be with you."

"Of course I am," was his response. "I just wasn't expecting you quite so soon. I just need to tie this deal up, and we'll be set for years. I landed a deal over mining with some men a few miles from here. I'm not sure how solid their claim is, but they are making money and needed an attorney to do their legal papers. So far, they have sold a dozen small claims and are building a stone house next to the richest vein. We'll be rich." He stepped towards Emily, who backed away.

A shadow crossed her face. "You don't know how solid their claim is, but they are making money? Getting rich makes dishonesty and theft okay? That gold you are talking about belongs to

Jim and Tom. You have to know those men are not the legitimate owners. Please tell me you will walk away from them."

His eyes narrowed and the greed was plain to read. "How do you know this Jim and Tom own that mine? How do you know they aren't trying to jump the claim themselves? Either way, I can tie things up in court for a long time, giving Simmons and McCabe a chance to pull more gold out and pay me a bigger fee. Every man deserves the best representation he can get."

"Either way?" Emily's voice rose. "What do you mean, either way? Aren't you supposed to uphold the law? Doesn't integrity mean anything to you? I know Jim and Tom rightfully own that claim. Otherwise, why would they have hired a mining engineer to keep from fouling the streams? Why travel all the way to Denver to do that?"

"Maybe to throw people off," he retorted. His lips drew back in a sneer. "Oh, I see now. You're sweet on Jim. That makes him right and me wrong."

She clenched her teeth. Her face turned crimson, and she slapped his face. "I came all the way out here to see you, and you say that to me?" She turned and stalked from the house.

"Emily, wait," Beauregard shouted. "I was doing it for you."

"I don't want to hear it. Sandy, will you take me back to the Donaldsons, please?"

"Sure thing, Miss Emily," Sandy drawled. "I'd be honored to escort you to wherever you want to go."

"But Emily," Beauregard protested.

"Templeton, shut your pie hole. The lady doesn't want to talk to you," Sandy interrupted. He walked Emily to the buggy and helped her aboard. When he saw her lips quivering, he turned back to Beauregard. "You done this little lady wrong. I recommend you clear out before I get back. All she did on the way here was talk about how great a man you are. You ain't great, and to my way of thinking, you come up short on the man end of things too." He tied his horse to the back of the buggy and jumped aboard. Turning the buggy, he drove from the yard with Emily leaning against his shoulder.

"Well, you heard what Emily had to say. What's your decision?" Preacher asked. "You can ride back to that row of shacks, you can ride into Broken Bow and head back east, or you can mount up and ride to anywhere you want."

Templeton looked down at the ground. Then he tilted back his head and laughed. "You turned her against me. Now you want to turn me against my friends. Oh no. You're not running me off. We'll be waiting for you next time you come into our little settlement."

Tom slowly shook his head. "I'm right sorry you feel that way. We sure never turned Emily against you. As for your friends, they will abandon you as soon as you are no longer useful to them. I guess you better get on out of here if that's what you think. It's your last chance to change your mind."

"My mind is made up," Templeton bellowed. He mounted and spurred his mount out of the yard.

They all watched sadly as he rode away. "'Be not deceived: evil communications corrupt good manners,'" Preacher mumbled.

Curly and Raven Wing approached from where they had been talking, and Dinah came from the flower garden with Little Tom in tow. Tom put his arm around Dinah, and she leaned against him.

"It looks like we got a fight on our hands my beautiful bride. Templeton made things clear as to what the intentions are of the leaders up there, and he won't break from them even for Miss Emily."

She looked up at her husband. "Isn't there any other way?"

Jim spoke before Tom could reply. "I'm sorry Dinah. I don't see any other way. If we wait for the courts, it could take a year or more. By then, they will have destroyed that whole section. I'm not the man I was when we first met, so I won't just charge in without a thought or plan. That being said, we can't let them stay. If you appease a thief, it just makes them want more."

"You will be going too, Curly?" Raven Wing asked.

"I don't reckon I can do anything else." He winked at her. "I know we'll be starting our own place soon, but I owe Jim and Tom. They been good to both of us." He kissed her gently.

Joshua, who had been standing nearby, spoke. "You figure I ought to send some runners and round up the boys? I don't figure you're planning on going back with just a half dozen, are you?"

"Pull 'em all in," Jim breathed out. "If they ask, let them know what's going on. Our men need to know what they're up against and why."

"Don't fret none, Miss Dinah. We may just be able to learn 'em a lesson on right and wrong, without having to do more than bend their ear a bit." Preacher smiled at Dinah as he spoke.

A few minutes later, Bob arrived with Bollinger in tow. "Arthur," Jim greeted him. "Swing on down and come on in. We just got done talking to the opposing legal counsel. He didn't seem too interested in facts."

"Hi Jim. I had a feeling they wouldn't take kindly to being told the truth. I figure you already gave them a couple of notices?"

"Yessir, we surely did do that," Preacher responded. "I figure they ain't too well versed in the Seventh Commandment nor the Tenth. Might be they need a bit of Bible learning."

Bollinger laughed. "I heard a bit about your method of teaching. You aren't what one would call delicate. Of course, the lesson does get learned."

"Are you going to ride up with us on our next trip, or do you have some other legal papers for us to take along?" Tom inquired.

"Well, it so happens that I do have your writ for immediate eviction from all properties belonging to the Lazy H Ranch, including the section where the gold claim is located. Judge Harper signed off on it yesterday afternoon. This is the first chance I have had to get it to you. Bob came at just the right time."

The hands began to drift in. Once everyone was gathered, Joshua directed them to take care of their mounts and gather in the bunkhouse. Dinah and Raven Wing could be heard preparing supper. It was still early, but they never questioned what was happening until Sandy returned from his errand. He smiled broadly.

"Well, if you don't look like the cat what swallowed the canary," Toby quipped. "You must have some idea 'bout what's going on. C'mon, spill the beans."

"All I know is I got to ride shotgun for one pretty young lady while you all had to go chouse cows all day. I reckon we'll know soon enough though."

Jim, Tom and Preacher entered the bunkhouse followed by Curly. "I'd imagine you are all wondering why we called you in early today. You've probably noticed a few of our creeks getting muddied up without a lot of rain to explain it, and from what we saw when we did some scouting, you may have noticed a few steers are missing too," Jim began. "Truth be told, we have a nest of rats living on our range that need to be moved out or eradicated."

"Rats?" Toby asked.

"The two-legged kind," Curly interjected. "A whole heap uglier and meaner than the four-legged variety."

"Like Curly said, these are two legged rats. A den of thieves and swindlers. Some may just be looking to strike it rich, but they've been warned like the rest. Bollinger brought out the last of the legal papers we need to put them off the property. I don't expect them to go quietly, but they will go."

"Some of you men have been here since before I came to my senses and came back home. I won't ask any one of you to ride with us when we head up to that snake den if you aren't of a mind for a fight. No hard feelings and no questions asked." He paused.

It was Sandy who spoke first. "Heck boss, I ain't had a good scrap in quite a while. When do we start?" Several others quickly agreed.

"Whoa now youngster," Preacher said. "This won't be no Saturday night brawl. Those fellers mean business and I mean from the barrel of a gun type of business."

"I ride for the brand," said Bob. "I'm too set in my ways to change." The rest of the hands quickly followed Bob's lead including Arthek.

Curly stepped forward as well. "Count me in boss."

"But you and Raven Wing are getting married soon. There's no need for you to go with us," Tom cautioned.

"I reckon I'll just go along for the ride. I don't like the looks of them fellers up there. Besides, I done told Raven Wing I was going.

She knows I can't back out on you now. She'd be mad as a wet hen if I didn't stick with you."

"As long as she don't blame us if you get hurt."

"We'll take a day or so to plan and prepare. I prefer no shooting, but I don't want anything left standing in that camp," Jim said solemnly. "There may be some men up there who aren't with the claim jumpers. They're just some men looking to make a living. We don't want a fight with them if we can avoid it."

***

For the next couple of days Jim, Tom and Preacher worked on strategies to reclaim the gold mine. During that time, the hands practiced with their pistols and prepared for the upcoming fight. Sandy sneaked off each evening to call on Emily, who was upset and confused about how Beauregard could get mixed up in such a scheme.

The day before the raid was planned, the Donaldsons paid a call on the Lazy H. Emily rode with them. Her eyes were downcast, red and puffy.

"Emily," Sandy whooped as he rushed to help her from the wagon. Seeing her face, he continued. "What's the matter gal? You look like you're heading to a wake."

"Hi Sandy," was her mumbled reply. "In a way, I guess you could call it that. I'm heading back east in a few days."

Sandy looked down at his boots, then smiled. "A few days? That means I get to see you for at least that much longer."

"I'm so sorry, Sandy. I'm just not cut out for life out here." She dabbed her eyes.

"Shucks, Emily. You got no reason to apologize. We had some fun and I can tell all my compadres that I once walked in the moonlight with the prettiest gal to ever grace Montana."

She smiled in response. "You are such a tease. I need to tell Jim and Preacher and the Daltons. Everyone has been so kind, you included." She gave him a peck on the cheek before heading into the house.

After the Donaldsons left that evening, Jim, Tom, and Preacher joined the men in the bunkhouse. "Now's your last chance to change your mind," Tom stated. "We'll be heading up tonight and move in on them from the east as the sun rises. Any questions?"

"What do we do if they start shootin'?" Toby asked.

"You shoot back," was the simple reply. "Don't rely on those hoglegs of yours. You'll be carrying shotguns and extra shells. They may not seem so elegant, but they sure are more effective. A man might face a six-gun. A ten-gauge loaded with buckshot? Not nearly as likely."

"I told you about some of the miners who might not fight," Jim said after Tom's instructions. "Leave them be. Any other questions?" Hearing none, he told the men to turn in for a few hours.

CHAPTER 39

At two o'clock in the morning, Jim rousted the men out of their beds. There were a few grumbles which quickly ended as coffee with biscuits and gravy were dished up. The men quickly ate and got ready to ride. They muffled their horsed hooves and secured anything that might rattle during the ride.

"Fellers," Preacher called out. "We're riding into a potential hornet's nest. I figure we oughta ask for the Lord's protection before we ride. Just 'cause we're in the right, don't mean we're immune to danger and bullets. Take off your hats."

The men obediently doffed their hats and bowed. "Lord," Preacher started. "You know full well what we're riding into. We'd ask for you to keep us safe and to change the hearts of them that are seeking to steal what ain't theirs. Give us wisdom to do what's right in your eyes. Amen"

Muttered amens followed. Dinah held Tom's hand as the men began to ride from the ranch yard. "Thomas Bartholomew Dalton, don't you take any chances. You come back to me in one piece. I love you."

He pulled her close in an embrace. "I love you too my beautiful bride. Don't you worry none. There's nothing this side of Heaven that'll keep me from coming home to you." He kissed her gently and then swung aboard and followed the rest of the crew into the chilly morning air.

The cavalcade halted on the outskirts of the encampment an hour before dawn. A few small cook fires could be seen. Otherwise, the camp was silent. Joshua, and Tom passed through the cowhands. "Check your loads," they whispered. "It won't be long now." A nervous anticipation ran through the group.

Just as they were preparing to mount up, a group of men approached out of the gloom. Shotguns swiveled to cover the advancing band. "Jim? It's me. Ed Samson. Are you out here?" came a whisper from the night.

"I'm here Ed," Jim replied in hushed tones. "What are you doing out here?"

"Can I come in?"

"Sure. Just you, though. My boys are a bit nervous. Take it easy men, I know this feller."

Ed Samson walked quickly to where Jim was. "I told you I'd spread the word. Had to do it quiet-like so the big augers didn't catch wind. A few people have disappeared who spoke against them. Can't prove nothing, but we have our suspicions. Those job offers still stand?"

"Of course they do. Just stay out of the way, and when this is all over, we'll put you on the payroll."

"No can do," Ed responded quietly. "We figure we signed on to work for you, so we're in. On your side, of course. There's eight of us, counting me. Mind if I call 'em in?"

"Sure."

Samson's group quietly joined the ranch crew. Introductions were quietly made and Jim laid out their plan. "How do we know who's who?" Jim asked.

"We're all wearing a sort of yellow scarf. It's been kinda hard sneaking out of the camp the last couple of nights to see if you was out here. I figured you'd be coming soon, so we came out to keep a watch so we could join you."

"We're here now and it's almost dawn. Time to start moving. Joshua, pass the word. Mount up and be ready to ride. These men will follow on our heels."

The men rode quietly to within a hundred feet of the disorderly collection of tents and lean-tos. On signal, Preacher drew his pistol and fired it into the air before returning it to the holster. Shouts rose from the throats of the raiders as they spurred their horses into the camp. Men sprang from their beds only to be barreled over by charging horses. Two of the cowhands tossed ropes over some of the uprights of the makeshift shelters and dragged them to the ground. Men dodged the onslaught only to be struck from another angle by a different attacker.

Within a few minutes, most of the shelters were destroyed, sluice boxes were pulled to the ground and many of the squatters were corralled without much resistance. Most, but not all.

A few miners decided to make a fight after retrieving some weapons from the wreckage. Tom and two cowhands tumbled from their saddles, wounded. Shotguns bellowed in response and four of the defenders inherited a six-foot by three-foot patch of ground. Arthek jumped from his mount to help the injured attackers. As quickly as it started, it was over. Four of the claim jumpers had been killed and a few others injured, including Boise.

The rest were docile prisoners. The only resistance still to overcome was the stone structure close to the main source of gold.

"How's Tom?" Jim shouted.

"Just a scratch," Tom replied. "I think I may have bruised some ribs falling off the horse to go along with the gunshot. I'll live. I think our boys will be fine as well. You get rid of the last few rats in the nest."

"Hello McCabe and Simmons," Jim bellowed. "You can come out now, or we can drag you out. Either way, you are coming out of there and leaving this country."

A rifle shot answered Jim's ultimatum. "We don't plan to leave. You can all mount up and ride off. If you try to come and dig us out, just remember: these stone walls were built for defense. Bullets won't penetrate these walls, but they will sure perforate human hides."

Keeping their prisoners under guard, Jim pulled back. "Any ideas?" he asked. "Whoever it was doing the talking is right. We can't shoot our way into that place without someone getting killed. We already have Tom and a few others hurt. I don't want to see anyone else get hurt or killed if I can help it."

"I might have an idea," Arthek said after a moment's thought. "I wasn't sure what we would be up against, so I brought up some blasting powder. It never hurts to be prepared, my father always said."

"That sounds good, but how do we get it close enough to that building to do any good?" Preacher asked.

"I've been giving that some thought too. Have you ever heard of a catapult? They used them centuries ago to hurl rocks and such at fortifications. We don't need a very big one for what I have in mind.

We may even be able to make a sling shot of some type using a pair of trees. We have some rope, and I'm sure we can scavenge some leather to hold a powder cask in. We can bend the trees back and hurl the cask onto the house."

"I'm not sure I follow you, but let's give it a try," Tom said. "Whatever Arthek says he needs, get it for him," he ordered the Lazy H hands.

Arthek swiftly gave instructions. Out of sight of the stone house, several ropes were strung between two trees. A canvas hammock, of sorts, was strung between two sets of ropes making a basket into which their projectile would be placed. "Get a couple of horses and bend those trees back. We'll try a couple of big stones first to get our aim and range before we waste any powder.

The hands jumped to do the engineer's bidding. They considered this some new kind of game.

"This I gotta see," Sandy whooped. "I've seen folks use saplings for snares, but never a full-grown tree." He laughed as he wrapped the rope around his saddle horn. Curly had the other rope dallied around his saddle horn. Both men backed their horses away from the trees and their intended target. The trees bent toward the ground, and Arthek placed a ten-pound boulder into the canvas hammock.

"Now, when I say so, you two turn loose of those ropes. We'll see if this contraption works or not. One, two, three... NOW!" he shouted.

When the ropes were released, the stone sailed through the air and missed its intended target by several yards. Again and again, Curly and Sandy bent the trees which allowed Arthek to load another stone. On the fifth try, the stone slammed into the side of the stone house. "I think we have it now. Mark where you were when you released the ropes. We'll use that as our guide."

"Hello stone house," Arthek called out. "I am quite sure you heard and possibly felt the results of our stone throwing experiment. I would suggest you come out now. Our next projectile will not be a stone but rather some blasting powder in sufficient quantity to break down the walls of your building."

"You're bluffing," hollered McCabe. "Go ahead and throw some more rocks at us. We still ain't coming out."

"Well, he was given a chance. Now we shall see if I have done my calculations correctly or not," Arthek mused.

This time, when the trees were bent a cask of powder was substituted for the stone. The fuse was cut to length and lit. "Let her fly boys," Arthek commanded. The powder arched gracefully toward the building with its fuse sending sparks into the air. The concussion of the explosion sent a large section of the wall crumbling to the ground.

"I think we scored a direct hit!" Arthek exclaimed.

Three men stumbled from the wreckage and smoke.

"McCabe, Simmons," shouted Jim. "You two will stand trial for several crimes. Beauregard Leonidas Templeton, you are to leave this territory and never return. Emily is heading back east, but I don't think she really cares for you to contact her again."

"You ain't taking me in," McCabe challenged. "You won't shoot an unarmed man, and you ain't man enough to take me any other way."

"McCabe you're a thief, a liar, a coward and a bully. I don't think I like you," Jim replied softly. He walked toward McCabe and slapped him across the mouth. "You talk tough, but are you?" Jim's eyes glinted.

McCabe was strong, but he was not a skilled fighter. He swung a haymaker that Jim easily ducked. Jim then threw a counter punch to McCabe's ribs followed by a punch to the back of his opponent's neck dropping him like a pole-axed steer.

Seeing McCabe crumple to the ground, Simmons reached for a hideout gun. As he brought it from his sleeve, Jim reacted with lighting speed. His draw was a blur. Simmons never knew what hit him as he folded to the dust, another guest of flames, darkness, and gnashing of teeth.

Groggily, McCabe began to rise. Some of the men who followed Samson started forward. One of them carried a rope. "We'll take care of those two high-binders," one of them purred, indicating Beauregard and McCabe.

Looking at the carnage, Jim stepped between them. "I think there's been enough killing for one day. Simmons is dead and McCabe is nothing without his leadership. As for this easterner, if he's fool enough to hang around after this, he's dumber than I thought."

Once the injured were attended to, the prisoners were herded to the edge of the stream. "Drag the dead over to the other side of that creek a good long ways and plant them deep. Joshua, see that they do it proper. We don't want the bodies dug up by scavengers. Let me know when they're done," Jim ordered.

An hour later, Joshua strode over to where Jim was checking on Tom. "All done, boss. What do we do with them?" Joshua said as he indicated the prisoners.

"Preacher, do you have some words of wisdom for these men?" Tom inquired.

Preacher's voice boomed out. "Ya'll better listen up good. The Bible tells us that stealing and coveting, that's wanting what others have, are sinful behaviors. It also says that the wage of sin is death. Some here already received their wages. For the rest of you, like Jesus said, go and sin no more. Ya'll better go now, repent for your sins, and don't come back."

"What about our gear?"

"Consider it forfeit," Tom responded. "Now get out of the territory."

"McCabe and Templeton, you stay put." Jim's words took them by surprise as the rest of the miners began to flee the area.

"Josh, grab a couple of swaybacks and bring them here. No saddles and a couple of lengths of rope. Nothing worthwhile as far as horses go," Jim continued.

McCabe glared at Jim. Beauregard whimpered. "You said you weren't going to hang us," he whined.

Jim grinned. "Oh, you won't hang, at least not today. I have an idea. You won't like this a whole heap more, but at least you'll still be alive.

Joshua arrived. He lead two scrawny horses with backbones that looked like a jagged ridge line. Preacher caught on as did Bob, who was standing nearby. Preacher and Bob grabbed McCabe and bound his hands behind his back. Dropping the lead ropes, Joshua spun Templeton around. Together, he and Jim tied his hands behind his back.

"Okay boys," Jim yelled to the men who backed him. "Hoist them onto their horses, backwards."

The order was cheerfully carried out. The prisoner's feet were tied under the horses' bellies.

"I don't care to see either one of you again. Once you're free, just keep on going. Don't try to come back. Yeeaah!" Jim slapped the horses on the rump to start them on their way. Shouts of derision followed the pair from the camp.

"It looks like they're all cleared out," Arthek yelled.

"Yep. The question now is, will they be back, or will others follow them and try to move in?" Preacher responded. "Gold has that effect on folks. Turns 'em from rational thinking folks into plain ole fools. Brings out the evil in many. *The love of money is the root of all kinds of evil.*"

"You're right Preacher," Jim replied. "I sometimes wish pa had never found the gold here. If he'd just had the ranch and not the gold, Jacobs wouldn't have come back and Pa, and Ma and Rachael would still be alive." Jim hung his head. "All for some shiny metal that's too soft to make tools out of, but people still kill each other for it," Jim said dejectedly.[1]

"But you're rich, my man," chimed in Arthek. "Rich, and there's no reason to think we have to destroy your ranch to extract the gold. That's why you brought me along, isn't it?"

Tom, with his arm in a sling, spoke up. "I can see Jim's point, but you can't unfind the gold. I reckon we're stuck with it. There are worse things than being rich," he said with a grin.

---

1. **To learn more about what happened to Jim's family, read *Vengeance Is Mine*.**

Jim walked off and stared up at the rock face from which the gold was to be mined. "Lord," he started. "Now that we have it, I'm not sure what to do with it. Like Tom said, we can't unfind it, but I don't know if I want to be rich, nor if this gold would be the way to do it if I did. It's all yours anyway. Your gold, your hill, your creek. Anyhow, Lord, you know what you're doing. Thanks for listening."

Preacher walked up as Jim finished his prayer. "Didn't mean to eavesdrop. You thinkin' this here is some kind of curse rather than a blessing?"

"Something like that. Some of our boys got hurt, Tom got shot up some, and some of the squatters were buried right here where they had hoped to make their fortune, even if it was by stealing from someone else. I just don't know, Preacher. Too bad I can't just give it back to God and forget the whole mess. I used it to fund my hunt for revenge, and it nearly destroyed me too."

"Not sure I know how to help you with that, boy. You gotta square it betwixt you and God, and all of those around you," Preacher replied.

Jim took a closer look at the escarpment. "Arthek, Arthek come here!" Jim shouted. He moved excitedly toward the rock face where the gold deposits were. Arthek came on the run.

"What is it, Jim? You look like you've had an epiphany," Arthek replied.

"I think I know what to do with this whole mess. I'm going to give it back to God. How much of that blasting powder do we have left?" Jim asked.

"We still have a goodly bit. I didn't use much. Why? What are you thinking?"

"I'm thinking we give this gold back to God. Do you figure we have enough to bring that whole face down and bury everything good and deep?" Jim's voice rose in excitement.

"I suppose, but why would anyone want to do that?" Arthek asked.

"To remove temptation. A lot of men have made fools of themselves over it. Plenty have died, my family included. I'm not sure it's worth the misery it causes. If we bury it deep enough, maybe it won't be a snare for anyone else."

Arthek looked dubiously at Jim. "I'd say you're the one being a fool, but it's not my gold. Your partner might disagree with you about this, though."

Tom approached the group. "I caught a bit of what you said, Jim. I can't say I agree totally, but I understand, and you do still have a fifty-one percent share in the ranch, so it's your call. Mind if I take a couple of nuggets so I can make Dinah some earrings or a pendant before you bury it?"

"Take all you want Tom. I think Dinah would appreciate you thinking of her," Jim replied.

Tom collected a few pieces of quartz encased gold. "These ought to do," he said as he shoved them into his pocket. "Maybe she won't be quite so mad at you for letting me get shot up when she sees these," he said, chuckling.

Jim had the men haul all that they could up near the base of the rock face. He let them take what they wanted from the piles of ore before telling everyone to move back.

"Okay Arthek, let's bury this before I change my mind."

"As you wish, my friend. I must say that this was one of the richest deposits I have ever seen. Something to tell my grandchildren about." He whistled as he began to plant the charges. "This is your last chance to change your mind, Jim."

Jim shook his head and Arthek lit the fuses. "Fire in the hole!" he shouted and everyone ducked for cover. A few seconds later, the ground shook violently beneath them. The horses panicked and broke free, racing as far away from the blast as they could.

At first, the rock face clung to the mesa behind it, like a drowning man clutching at a straw. Then, it slowly released its grip and crashed to the valley floor. Dust filled the air, making it impossible to see for several minutes.

The men, choking on the dust, began shouting to one another. "Is everyone alright?" Tom yelled. One by one, the men replied.

When the dust finally settled, Preacher laughed uncontrollably and pointed to the rocky cliff. Everyone looked at him as he stared up at the fresh face of the cliff.

"What's so funny," Jim shouted. "Have you lost your mind?"

"Well boy, I'll tell you. Take a lookie up yonder. It appears that some young fool didn't bury anything. It looks more like the young fool got himself more gold instead. I reckon I'd say it's a fool's gold if you was to ask me. You being the fool, of course."

Sure enough, the blast had uncovered an even richer vein of gold rather than burying it under tons of rock and debris. Jim stared. "But it was supposed to bury it. I don't want it." His voice quavered.

Tom spoke up. "Maybe not, but you got it anyway. You gave it back to God, and He returned it to you. What did Preacher call it? A fool's gold? Might be a nice name for the mine. 'Fool's Gold Mine.'"

The men all laughed. When the horses had settled down and those that had pulled loose were recovered, they all headed back to the ranch house laughing about what had transpired. "Arthek, Ed, the rest of you miners," Jim called out. "It looks like you still have a job." The Fool's Gold Mining Company was born.

It's not money that is the root of all evil, but the love of it. "But they that will be rich fall into temptation and a snare, and into many foolish and hurtful lusts which drown men in destruction and perdition. For the love of money is the root of all evil: which while some coveted after, they have erred from the faith and pierced themselves through with many sorrows. But thou, O man of God, flee these things and follow after righteousness, godliness, faith, love, patience, meekness.
1 Timothy 6:9-11 KJV

About the Author

The son of a World War II-era veteran and father of a soldier, Phillip is a decorated military veteran and former drill instructor himself. Phillip Hardy served his country with honor for thirteen years. He was also the owner, editor, and chief writer for a monthly newspaper dedicated to delivering news in a fun format. He is a member of several writing groups and is dedicated to making his stories the best available in their genre. Now, Phillip shares his experience and ideas with other aspiring authors while learning from the members in each of those groups. Married to his beautiful bride Ruth, Phillip is a devoted husband and father.

For more information on Mr. Hardy or upcoming books, visit https://www.authorphilhardy.comor email him at phil@loneoak productions.net.

www.ingramcontent.com/pod-product-compliance
Lightning Source LLC
Chambersburg PA
CBHW020744310726
48969CB00002B/406